Dance With Me ; bk. 2

W9-BRB-990

TAKE THE LEAD

TAKE THE LEAD

SHELLEY SHEPARD GRAY

THORNDIKE PRESS
A part of Gale, a Cengage Company

Henderson County Public Library

Copyright © 2020 by Shelley Shepard Gray.
The Dance with Me Series.
Thorndike Press, a part of Gale, a Cengage Company.

ALL RIGHTS RESERVED
The characters and events in this book are fictitious. Any similarity to
real persons, living or dead, is coincidental and not intended by the
author.
Thorndike Press® Large Print Romance.
The text of this Large Print edition is unabridged.
Other aspects of the book may vary from the original edition.
Set in 16 pt. Plantin.

**LIBRARY OF CONGRESS CIP DATA ON FILE.
CATALOGUING IN PUBLICATION FOR THIS BOOK
IS AVAILABLE FROM THE LIBRARY OF CONGRESS.**

ISBN-13: 978-1-4328-8489-5 (hardcover alk. paper)

Published in 2021 by arrangement with Blackstone Publishing.

Printed in Mexico
Print Number: 01   Print Year: 2021

For my editor, Ember. Thank you for loving Shannon, Traci, and Kimber as much as I do. Every author should be blessed to have so much support.

"If you've got nothing to dance about,
find a reason to sing."

Melody Carstairs

"Let us read, and let us dance;
these two amusements will never do
any harm to the world."

Voltaire

LETTER TO READERS

In the middle of writing this book, it happened again. Instead of worrying about hitting my page count for the day, I found myself worrying about all the characters in my book — just like they were real people. When I was walking the dog, I'd wonder if Gwen was going to be okay. I'd stop in the middle of washing dishes and smile about Traci and Matt learning to waltz. Then there were Shannon and Dylan and Jennifer and Kimber! Each one of them had found a little place in my heart as well.

By now, after watching me write for so many years, my husband seems to have a sixth sense about this switch. He'll start asking me how my people are instead of how the book is going. That's usually all I need to launch into some story about what's happening to them. My sweet husband doesn't even remind me anymore that everyone is made up.

I hope you, too, connected with some of the characters in the series. The trilogy will end with *Save the Last Dance,* which is Kimber's story. In it, Kimber steps away from modeling, meets a mechanic named Gunnar, and even gets talked into learning the cha-cha from Shannon — all during the month of December. LOL, I guess all the characters in Kimber's book have become "real" to me too.

Thank you for giving *Take the Lead* a try, it truly means a lot.

With my best, Shelley

CHAPTER 1

Thursday, April 11

"I need some help, here!" Officer Traci Lucky announced, one arm wrapped around Gwen, her barely coherent burden. Gwen Camp was a dangerously skinny woman — who was probably in her twenties but who already looked closer to forty — with blue eyes, long dishwater-blond hair, and pasty skin. And she was pregnant.

Traci had found Gwen curled in a ball on the floor in the back of a house that she and her partner, Dylan, had just raided on suspicion of being a meth lab. That tip turned out to be wrong — there was no meth lab — but they'd found enough drug paraphernalia for Dylan to call in reinforcements.

Unfortunately, as Traci had gotten on her phone to call for an ambulance, Gwen had surged to her feet and started freaking out. Even hopped up, it seemed that Gwen

11

didn't want to incur the expense of an ambulance. After a couple minutes of arguing, she and Traci had come to a compromise. Gwen agreed to go to the hospital if Traci would take her in her police cruiser.

That was how Traci ended up here now, walking into Bridgeport Hospital's emergency room with one of her hands wrapped around Gwen's upper arm so she wouldn't either collapse on her feet or change her mind and run back out into the street. The poor girl really did need some help.

Unfortunately, Traci's urgent call for assistance was being ignored.

That hadn't happened before.

Bridgeport's usually sleepy emergency room was currently a hotbed of action. Easily thirty people filled the waiting area. Over in the reception area, nurses, attendants, and support staff were running around like they'd been transported to the middle of downtown Cincinnati.

Instead of the usual security guard, Emerson, one of Traci's coworkers in the Bridgeport Police Department, was standing off to the side talking on his phone.

What the devil was going on?

Gwen pulled on her arm, bringing Traci right back to the job at hand. "I wanna go now."

"No way. You're getting checked by the doctors."

Gwen frowned as she tugged on her arm again. "Can I at least sit down? I'm so tired."

It was nearly two in the morning. Though Traci felt sorry for the girl, she was feeling tired, too. It had been a really long shift. "Are you ready to listen and sit where I tell you, Miss Camp?"

Gwen's already disgruntled expression darkened. "Yeah, but I told you I don't need to be here."

"And I told you that you need to be examined. *Your baby* needs to get checked out." Yes, her voice was wicked sharp and her tone brooked no argument. But this girl was beginning to get on her last nerve.

It took a second, but Traci's words eventually settled in. "Oh," Gwen said. A little bit after, Gwen got that vacant look on her face that Traci knew too well. This momma-to-be was either high as a kite or coming off something and was about to crash.

Traci gritted her teeth. She loved being a cop. *Loved it.* Few things — the hours, the craziness, or even the paperwork — got to her anymore. However, out of everything she saw in her line of work — and in all the years in Cleveland, she'd seen a lot — pregnant mothers who also happened to be drug addicts was her kryptonite. She hated it. Hated it.

Though she knew the reason why — her mother had taken in her fair share of alcohol and drugs while pregnant with Traci. Because of that, Traci had been born an addict and had spent most of her life trying to overcome that stigma.

She was an adult now, of course, and she had a good job and a good life. But sometimes those old wounds hit hard. All she saw when she came in contact with a pregnant woman on drugs was a lifetime spent making up for nine months of a mother's neglect.

When she noticed Gwen curve a hand around her belly, Traci knew she couldn't wait any longer. Still afraid to deposit Gwen in a chair — especially since there wasn't an empty seat to be seen — Traci approached the crowded reception desk with Gwen in tow.

"Excuse me."

The harried receptionist, who had been scanning something on her computer screen, took in Traci's uniform and Gwen's condition, and froze. "Yes?"

Traci pushed her way through. "We need some assistance please. This woman needs an obstetrician."

The woman looked over Gwen curiously. "Is she in labor?"

"No," said Gwen.

"What's the emergency, then?" Sharon asked.

Well aware of the number of people listening, and that Gwen's relatively calm state was nearing its end, she said, "Do we really need to discuss this here?"

"I'm sorry, but —"

Putting a bit more force into her voice, Traci continued. "Look, we need to see someone as soon as possible. "Where can I go? You got an empty room back there?" She gestured to the partitioned triage area.

"Well, I'm not sure," the receptionist said, just as if they were talking about the chances of rain. "As you can see, we are very busy now . . ."

"She can't just come in here and take a spot. We've been waiting for an hour," a man standing to Traci's right interrupted.

In another life, Traci might have agreed with him. She knew she was absolutely using her uniform to get her way. But she knew that if she didn't push this, Gwen would disappear back into the woodwork of the town and this baby would be born without a lick of care. And, well, if that happened? Traci didn't know if she would be

15

able to handle that.

"She needs to be seen stat. I have to get back to work."

The man folded his arms over his chest. "Well, I do too."

There was no way she was going to get into an argument with folks in line. "Sharon, where can we go?"

Looking as if she knew she was fighting a battle she couldn't win, Sharon gestured to a nearby orderly. "Chris, take this woman to five," she said to an orderly. "I think it just opened up."

"Thanks," Traci said.

"Hey, wait!" the man grumbled. "That's not fair. I've been waiting —"

Traci ignored him as she shuttled Gwen through the electronic gate and to a set of double doors. The doors swung open, revealing a beehive of well-organized activity.

Gwen got quieter with each step, and almost seemed to grow younger as well. Her eyes widened as she took everything in. Within seconds, two nurses took charge of Gwen. After getting her weight, they escorted Gwen to a curtained room.

Traci stood outside the curtain, half listening to the nurses' questions and Gwen's mumbled half-coherent replies. Everything she heard made her cringe and ache to leave. Why had she gotten saddled with this girl, anyway? It felt too personal and too hard.

"Who are you here for?"

Traci looked up and blinked. There, standing right in front of her, was a movie-star handsome man in light-blue scrubs and a white lab coat. A stethoscope hung around his neck.

Getting to her feet, Traci pointed to the closed curtain. "I escorted that woman."

He pulled down the chart. "Gwen Camp?"

"Yep. She's obviously pregnant."

"How far along is she?"

"I don't know. I found her on the floor in a house we just raided. I'm guessing she's on a number of drugs."

He was writing notes. "Any idea what she took?"

"No. My guess is meth, but it could be opioids."

"Okay."

"Um, she looks malnourished too. She's really skinny." When he looked up again, she held out her hand. "Sorry. I should have done this at the beginning. I'm Traci Lucky."

"Good to meet you, Officer," he replied as they shook hands. "Matt Rossi."

"Good to meet you too." She lowered her

voice. "Just to let you know, Gwen isn't exactly here willingly. She's a flight risk."

Worry instead of disdain filled the doctor's eyes, which made Traci feel even worse. She should have more compassion for the girl. And, she was a girl. Definitely younger than she'd initially thought, probably not yet twenty-one.

Her feelings of guilt ratcheted up. Honestly, where was her compassion? Obviously something awful had happened to put Gwen in this situation.

"Officer, are you going to be here for a while?"

She nodded. "I'm staying until you give me an idea of what I should do with her. I'm pretty certain if I walked out now she'd run." Plus, she'd promised Gwen that she wouldn't leave her.

"Okay, then." He turned and walked through the curtain, greeting Gwen as he did.

Not wanting to hear any more, Traci took a few steps to the right, finally ending up leaning against the closed door of a supply closet. And as the orderlies, doctors, and nurses passed by, she reminded herself that Gwen's life was not her mother's. Gwen's baby was not going to be Traci.

Every child born in such a heartbreaking

18

situation didn't end up growing up in a succession of mediocre foster families before eventually ending up in a group home. Some, no doubt, did just fine.

And then, because she was alone and no one could see, she closed her eyes and said a little prayer for that baby.

Almost forty minutes later, the doctor came out.

Traci strode forward. "How is she?"

"Struggling." He sighed. "You were right, she is badly malnourished and on something. Her blood pressure is elevated and she complained of some light cramping. After we got some blood, we did an ultrasound."

"Yes?"

"I thought she might be around four months pregnant. Based on the size of the baby, I'd say she's at least five months. Maybe closer to six."

"That far along?" The girl was such a little thing.

"My main concern is the low amount of amniotic fluid and that elevated blood pressure. She needs to be admitted."

"All right." Honestly, that was for the best. If Dr. Rossi had released her, Traci didn't know where she'd place the girl.

The doctor continued. "As I said, we took

19

some blood and ran a couple of tests. Her baby's heartbeat seems strong but I'd still like to know what's in her system before we go any further." He ran a hand through his hair, making the short dark strands stand up on end. "I'm going to recommend she get some more tests. We need to see some of those results before we decide anything else."

"So, it's likely she'll need to be here at least twenty-four hours."

He nodded. "I'm going to recommend she remain hospitalized at least until Saturday. But, like I said, we need some more answers until you can get her someplace better."

Until she found someplace better for Gwen.

Though a part of Traci had known this was the likely outcome, the responsibility hit her hard. For the near future, she was in charge of Gwen Camp.

It seemed no good deed ever *did* go unpunished.

But instead of reacting, she kept up her professional demeanor. "Thank you for seeing her so quickly, Dr. Rossi."

"It's what I'm here for." His gaze was warm as he suddenly smiled. "Hey, good job on getting her here."

Maybe it was because he was so nice. Or

he cared so much and was making her want to be better, too. But whatever the reason, she found herself smiling back. And, feeling a little bit better about the world.

"I've got to go. I'll say goodbye but be back tomorrow."

He looked surprised. "Really? Do you make follow up visits for everyone you bring in?"

"No, but I'm committed now. Plus, I've got some personal reasons for getting so involved."

"Maybe I'll see you tomorrow then."

"I hope so," she replied before she caught herself. After all, this wasn't some meet-cute. She was doing her job and so was he. They were working.

"Dr. Rossi, we need you," a nurse called out.

"I've got to go. See you, Officer Lucky." He smiled again before walking down the hall.

Traci stayed where she was and watched him disappear. But as she turned to walk back to Gwen, she realized that the future didn't feel as bleak as it had just an hour ago.

Huh.

CHAPTER 2

WALTZ: *This is the most commonly thought of dance when someone mentions ballroom dancing. It is twenty-eight bars per minute, done in a 3–4 time, and can be fairly romantic.*

Monday

"Officer Lucky's down the hall, Dr. Rossi," Marissa, the head nurse on duty announced as Matt arrived on the obstetrics floor.

"Has she been there long?" Matt asked.

"Over an hour."

"And our patient? Miss Camp?"

Marissa scanned through her computer screen. "She's been stable. Her baby is hanging in there, too." She read out loud the latest results from the blood tests.

Matt sighed in relief. The numbers were almost normal. "Thanks for letting me know."

"Anytime, doc," she said before turning to

a nurse who'd just approached the station.

Though Matt usually would have been only thinking about his patient, as he walked down the hall, he could only seem to think about Officer Lucky. He'd barely met her, but she'd left a huge impression. She could be described as about five-six, a hundred fifteen pounds, with brown hair and brown eyes. But those characteristics did little to accurately describe the way Traci *was*. No, she was an athletic fireball with a good dose of vulnerability thrown in for good measure.

And, it seemed, tenacity. Or, maybe it was loyalty. He wasn't sure yet.

Whatever her reasons, even three days later, Traci was still sticking to her promise. He shouldn't have been surprised, but he was. In his experience, most cops were overworked and underpaid. They didn't have time to continually visit a woman in the hospital. Especially a woman who was never happy to see them.

But Traci Lucky was proving that she wasn't like anyone else.

He wasn't the only person who thought that, either. The woman would probably be shocked to hear it, but she had quite a following around the hospital.

Matt wasn't surprised. Traci had an aura about her that caused everyone in her path to do a double take. She was assertive, athletic, and attractive, with her long brown hair poorly contained in a ponytail. But beyond all of those attributes, there was a whole other part about her that reeked of vulnerability. It made a guy want to step in front of her and shield her from the world — at least until she pushed him aside with a tersely uttered, "I've got this."

He walked down to Gwen's room, tapped on the door lightly, and then entered. Traci was sitting in a chair next to her. She looked as uncomfortable as he would feel sitting in a cell at the county jail.

Looking grateful for the interruption, Traci jumped to her feet. "Dr. Rossi, hi. We were just talking about you."

"Yeah?" He winked at Gwen. "Let me guess. You were wondering what time I was going to be making my rounds this morning?"

"Yep," Gwen answered, sounding and looking better than she had just the day before. "It's almost eleven. That's late for you."

"I had surgery first thing," he said as he approached Gwen's bed. He knew either Marissa or Dee would be joining them to go over Gwen's vitals, but he wanted to get a sense of how she was doing before diving into the specifics of her health. "How are you feeling today, Gwen?"

She shrugged. "Okay." After giving Traci a sideways glance, she said, "Better, I guess."

"Better is good. Marissa told me a bit about your bloodwork when I passed by the station. You're improving, Miss. I'm glad about that."

Gwen shifted, used the remote on the bed to help her get into a sitting position. "Officer Lucky says that I should be grateful to be stuck here."

"What do you think?"

She paused. "I don't know." As if she could tell that Traci wasn't happy with her honesty, Gwen added, "I mean, I'm grateful for the shower and the three meals and all, but I kind of feel like I just got a lucky break." She winced. "No pun intended, Officer."

"None taken," Traci murmured.

Fighting off a smile, Matt said, "But . . . ?"

"But, I don't know what to do about it." She shifted uncomfortably. "This isn't my home, you know? Not that I really have a home or anything."

"Of course the hospital isn't your home, but no one has expected it to be. Just take things one step at a time," Traci said in a brisk tone. "I've told you that."

Gwen looked at the police officer for the first time. "But I'm still gonna have to leave, right?"

Sensing that their conversation wasn't anything new, or anything productive, Matt said, "Let's start with the easy stuff then. What's been going on with the baby? Have you felt him move?" They'd done a sonogram the previous night and discovered that she was twenty-three weeks along and, though too small, the baby was otherwise surprisingly healthy. They had also learned that she was having a boy.

She placed a hand on her stomach. "I did. I mean, I do." Looking almost happy, Gwen said, "He seems like he's doing okay."

"You're having a boy?" Traci's look of wonder was adorable.

"Yeah. Go figure, huh?"

Dee popped in with Gwen's chart. "You ready, Dr. Rossi?"

Feeling a little bit like Traci had looked when he'd first stepped in, Matt said, "I'm ready. Will you excuse us, Traci?"

She was already on her feet. "Sure." After darting another look at Gwen, the corners of her mouth turned down. "You know what? I might just go —"

"Stay if you don't mind, okay?" Matt interrupted. "I'll be out in ten."

26

"All right." Pausing at the door, she said, "Gwen, you keep getting better. I'll come back tomorrow."

"Okay, bye."

After Traci left, Gwen relaxed a bit. "She kind of scares me sometimes."

It was all Matt could do not to burst out laughing. He knew what Gwen met. Traci was a pint-sized fireball, for sure. "I don't think she means to be scary."

"Maybe." She shrugged like she wasn't sure what to think about that.

Matt studied the charts and watched as Dee took Gwen's pulse and blood pressure. "It looks like your body needed some rest, young lady. It's responding really well to the hydration and meals."

Gwen looked away. "I've had the shakes but it hasn't been that bad."

"That should get better as you get healthier."

"I hope so."

"How are you feeling?"

"Better. I haven't slept so much in months."

He skimmed the nurses' notes. Noticed that Gwen had eaten every bit of all of her meals and had indeed, been spending most of her time sleeping. Not only was that good for her and the baby, but he took it as a positive sign that she hadn't been as hooked on drugs as he'd first thought. If her addiction had gotten really bad, she would have been going through withdrawal instead of being able to eat, drink, and sleep.

He needed to get a social worker involved, but in the meantime, he intended to keep her safe and healing.

"Gwen, I'm going to recommend that we keep you here until at least Wednesday."

"Two more days." Her voice was flat.

"I don't know if we'll have much luck keeping you longer than that. Do you have anywhere to go when you're released?"

"I'm not sure."

"Anywhere you want to go? Are you in touch with the baby's father?"

"No."

"And the place where you were staying?"

"I just kind of ended up there. I . . . Well, I don't know how to describe things. I wasn't exactly staying there because I was happy, Doc."

"I contacted Melanie Pendry this morning, Doctor," Dee said.

"Who's Melanie?" Gwen asked.

"She's the social worker assigned to the hospital."

"I don't need a social worker."

"You certainly do. You need as many

people as possible on your side."

When Gwen merely frowned, he turned back to Dee and gave her instructions to continue the IV drip and to monitor Gwen's blood pressure.

"Yes, doctor," Dee said as she walked out.

Sensing that Gwen was feeling even more confused, Matt walked to Gwen's side again. "I've never had a baby, but I've delivered dozens and I can tell you this. The world's a tough place."

"I know that."

"In that case, I'm sure you know that he's going to need you, Gwen. You owe it to him and to yourself to get into a better situation. I need you to be with me on this."

Gwen bit her lip and nodded.

Realizing that he wasn't going to get more of a promise than that, Matt nodded back and walked out to the hall. To his relief, Traci was still there, looking uneasy but determined.

Yes, they needed to talk about Gwen Camp, but that wasn't the only reason he wanted to see her.

Not by a mile.

CHAPTER 3

"When a body moves, it's the most revealing thing. Dance for me a minute, and I'll tell you who you are."
— MIKHAIL BARYSHNIKOV

Monday

Traci stood up the minute she spied Matt walking toward her in the hall. "How is Gwen doing?"

"Hanging in there. I'm going to keep her until Wednesday. I don't know if I'll be able to swing any longer than that." He looked frustrated about it.

She thought he should be pleased, though. Because of his concern, Gwen and her baby had received great care — badly needed medicine, food, and rest. They were doing much better than when Traci had first brought her into the emergency room. "Hey, that's huge. Wonderful."

"It's . . . good." His voice sounded as cautious as his words.

"No, by Wednesday, she'll have been here almost a full week." She smiled. "You must be a miracle worker."

His cheeks turned a little ruddy. "Hardly that. You know how it is. At least we're moving in the right direction. After our last conversation, I went ahead and got a meeting scheduled with Melanie Pendry. She's one of our best social workers on site. Have you met her?"

"Not personally, but the name sounds familiar. I'll ask Dylan if he knows her."

"Good. I like her. She doesn't give up."

Traci's eyes lit up again. "Neither do you. A lot of people, um, they don't always go above and beyond like you do. Thanks."

"I could say the same for you. You not only coaxed Gwen to come to the hospital, you escorted her, and then continued to visit every day. If not for you, that girl could've easily been forgotten."

"You're making it sound harder than it was. She wasn't actually kicking and screaming. I think she wanted to get help."

"She might have wanted help, but she was also complaining loudly and pulling at your arm." He laughed at her look of dismay. "Yeah, more than one person was talking about the way you shuttled that girl through

31

the waiting room last Thursday."

Yep, no doubt she had created a bit of a scene. Feeling even more uncomfortable, she looked away. "Bossing her around wasn't exactly my proudest moment."

He grinned. "It was awesome. I promise."

"If I can get her someplace safe when she gets out of here, *that* would be awesome. I hope the social worker can help." She couldn't put her finger on it, but she was fairly sure that Gwen was keeping something from her. Traci hoped that she wasn't actually thinking about going back to the loser she'd been with. As much as it didn't make sense, some women couldn't seem to stay away from what they knew. It was safer than the unknown.

"Hey, I've got about thirty minutes before I need to get to the office. Want to catch a cup of coffee?"

"Really? You have time for that?"

He glanced at his phone as if he needed to make sure. "I've got a little more than hour before I begin office visits. I always have time for coffee."

"Funny you should say that, because I kind of feel the same way."

"So, what do you say?"

"Sure." She smiled before getting her bearings again. It wasn't like it was a date.

They were talking about his patient, her albatross.

"Have you ever been down to the Mill?"

"Yep. It's my favorite."

"Mine, too. Come on."

Matt led Traci down the labyrinth of halls toward the east entrance. She kept up his pace but didn't talk as they walked. Instead, she seemed content to take in her surroundings. It didn't seem like anything went unnoticed. He wondered if that was a cop thing or a Traci thing.

"What?" she asked him, disrupting his thoughts.

"Hmm?"

She shrugged. "You're looking at me."

"I was just thinking that you're really observant. And it's obviously true, since you noticed me looking at you." Deciding he might as well tell her everything, he added, "Actually, I was wondering if you learned that as a cop or if it was something in your DNA."

She thought about it before answering. "Probably a little bit of both. I've always needed to have a pretty good feeling for my surroundings. It's come in handy with my line of work."

"I guess so." He held the door open for

her as they walked outside and got belted with a burst of hot air. "Ah, Cincinnati in spring," he joked.

Their town of Bridgeport lay just to the north of Cincinnati. Traci had slowly been coming to learn that the climate in the southern part of the state was far different than the northern. "It's taking me some getting used to."

"How come?"

"I was up in Cleveland. We had heat, but nothing like this. I might as well be in the South now, you know?"

"Nah. We might be just over the river from Kentucky, but our summers have nothing on the folks further south. *That's* like living in a sauna."

"Are you from the South and I didn't catch the accent?"

Matt knew she was joking since he was sure didn't have the slightest hint of a drawl. "Ha-ha. No, just went to medical school in Nashville and did my residency in Kentucky. I'm from the west side of Cincinnati."

"And here you are in a little place like Bridgeport."

"Yep." Thinking about all the factors that had weighed in his decision, Matt said, "I wanted to start a practice where I could get to know my patients. Someplace where I

34

would get to help women start their families, and then check in with them over the next twenty years."

"You really care about your patients, don't you?"

"Yep. I'm not jaded yet." Hoping to lighten the conversation, he said, "Plus, my mom would probably box my ears if I said anything less. I grew up with three sisters, you know."

"Wait a minute, there are four of you?"

"It's worse than that. I'm one of six. I have two older brothers, too."

"Your mother had *six* kids? Wow."

"It's not so impressive. The Rossis are a big Italian, Catholic family. Just like practically every other family on our street," he said as they walked into the Mill. They placed their orders, and after refusing to take Traci's money, Matt paid and then guided them to a table in the corner. The barista promised to deliver their coffees in a few minutes.

"Do any of your siblings still live nearby?" Traci asked, picking up their conversation just as if they hadn't just spent the last ten minutes getting settled.

"Every one of them does." As much as he grumbled about their interfering habits, Matt knew he wouldn't have it any other way. "We all get together on Sunday nights for supper."

"All of you?"

"Yep. My mom makes a big pot of spaghetti, and we catch up. It's pretty terrific."

"I bet." She smiled, but there was something else in her tone too. It sounded almost like wistfulness.

Their drinks were delivered, plain lattes for each of them. As he watched Traci take a tentative sip, smile, then take a longer one, Matt knew he wanted to know her even better. Anyone who took so much pleasure in something so simple was someone he wanted to learn about. In addition, he liked seeing her out of uniform. Today she had on a pair of faded jeans and a dark-green button down. She'd probably say it wasn't anything special, but he had noticed that both pieces fit her well. "What about you?"

"Me? Well, I don't have anything like that. When I was a toddler, my mom gave me and my sisters up for adoption. The social workers and the agency separated us, so I grew up without siblings."

He still couldn't believe things like that used to happen. "I bet that was hard." The moment he said that, he wished he could take it back. He had a feeling 'hard' was putting it mildly.

36

"For her? I have no idea." She shrugged. "I guess it was," she allowed after a slight hesitation. "I don't remember it though. I was little more than a baby. My sister Kimber wasn't even a month old. Even our sister Shannon, who was over a year, doesn't have any memories of that time."

Anxious to find a silver lining in a heart-breaking story, he said, "Did you see them much when you were growing up?"

"I didn't see them at all. I had no idea that I even had sisters until Shannon discovered it through one of those DNA tests you can take at home and search for relatives online. She contacted me out of the blue."

"And then?"

"And then, after almost a year of corresponding and talking on the phone, we decided to live together for a year, so we could all get to actually know one another. Kimber and I decided to move to Bridgeport because Shannon was opening up her dance studio here."

Gaping at her, he leaned back in his chair. "That's quite a story."

"Well, it's a story." Staring intently at the paper cup, she continued. "Shannon, Kimber, and I all grew up really differently. But, we each became people to be proud of."

"You should be proud. You're a great person."

Traci laughed. "You hardly know me. But thank you. I did all right, considering how I started out in life."

It was obvious now that she'd faced some challenges. Matt was curious about what they could be, but he wasn't sure whether he should ask for more details.

He didn't want her to feel like she was being interrogated when all he wanted to do was get to know her better. But, Traci didn't seem especially guarded, so he pushed forward. "You said you all grew up differently. How was it different?"

She smiled. "Shannon was in a small town in West Virginia and has a sweet country accent. Kimber grew up in New York, just outside the city." She paused. "I grew up in a group home in Cleveland."

"You were never adopted?"

"Nope."

"I'm sorry." This was about to go down in history as the worst "first date" conversation ever. Why hadn't he stuck to something safer — like movies or her job?

Her eyes widened. "Don't be. It made me what I am. And it wasn't horrible. But, it did make me more aware of how critical the consequences can be for someone like

38

Gwen, though."

"How so?"

"My mother took drugs when she was pregnant with me. I was born an addict."

He'd delivered babies who were born addicted to drugs. They were usually criers; some had trouble nursing, and others never slept. Some went their whole lives with the effects. Traci didn't seem to be one of them, though.

"That's why you're so concerned about Gwen."

"Yeah. Well, I was more concerned about her baby," she corrected. She winced. "Sorry. I know how that sounds."

It did sound harsh, but it also made her seem human. It took a strong person to admit their true feelings.

Now that he'd heard part of her story, Matt knew his interest in her was only going to grow from here. Traci Lucky was a maze of fascinating contradictions, and he was intrigued by each one of them.

All he had to do was find a way to see her again.

CHAPTER 4

"The Waltz is all about protection. It's a
dance that says I have you in my arms
my dear. Everything is right in the world."
— FRED, *CALL THE MIDWIFE*

Monday

She had until Wednesday. Roughly forty-
eight hours until she was put in some home
or room by a social worker, and then she'd
be on her own again.

No, she'd be at Hunter's mercy.

And that would be exactly what it was,
too — her at her crazy ex-boyfriend's mercy.
Not that he actually possessed any.

Hating to even think of the man she'd attached herself to out of desperation and had
remained with out of fear, Gwen shivered.
Hunter was one scary dude, that was for
sure.

Since she'd been stuck in this bed, she'd
had a lot of time to think about her relation-

40

ship with him — such that it was. A little over a year ago, she'd been living at home, hating every minute of it, and hoping and praying for a way out. Things hadn't been good there. They hadn't been good for a long time.

Gwen didn't know who her father was. Her only home had been a fifth-floor apartment with a mother who didn't have much to give anyone, and even less for her own daughter. Gwen had been in high school and flunking out. School meant breakfast and lunch, but also a whole lot of getting yelled at.

She skipped a lot and did anything to get through each day. Which was how she'd ended up hanging out with Valerie, who also skipped a lot and had a boyfriend named Rick. Rick was rich. Gwen had soon discovered that Rick's friend Hunter was rich too — since he did good business selling drugs in the neighborhood.

Gwen hadn't been into that, but she had been into his compliments, his gifts, and the fact that if she was with him and his friends, she didn't have to go home or to school.

A couple months after meeting Hunter, she'd dropped out and was living with him, Rick, and Valerie.

41

But then everything had gone to hell, which was saying a lot, because things hadn't been very good to begin with. Valerie's parents had pulled her out of the house and taken her across the state to live with her grandparents. Rick had gotten violent and Hunter had gotten lazy and sneaky.

Next thing she'd known, Gwen had been living with Hunter and a couple of guys who were even bigger losers than Hunter himself. She was pregnant, and he didn't care. No, instead, he was trying to sell heroin in Bridgeport, but had gotten so hooked on the crap that their place had essentially become a flophouse.

Then their neighbors had called the cops, and she'd ended up here. For the first time in months and months, she was clean, had three meals a day, and was actually thinking about more than how to get through the next two hours.

"Knock, knock!" an older, somewhat comfortable-looking woman named Dee called out before she rolled in a cart.

Lunch! "Hi, Dee. How are you?"

The woman smiled just as brightly as she always did. "I'm good, dear. Better now that you've got some color in your cheeks." After parking her cart on the side of the bed, she lifted up the covered plates. "Let's see what you've got here. Salad, chicken noodle soup, two wheat rolls, and a slice of apple pie."

Gwen's mouth was watering. "It all looks so good."

Dee grinned. "You're the first patient today who hasn't made a face about this lunch. You sure aren't a complainer, are you?"

"Not about hospital food. It's more than I've gotten to eat in a long time." *Like, years.*

Dee's smile faded. "You've had a time of it, haven't you?"

"Kind of." Wariness engulfed her. She shouldn't have said anything. She shut her mouth, reluctant to say more. She'd learned quickly that no one felt sorry for a girl who'd done the things that she'd done.

"You know, I don't just deliver meals around here. I help out with other patient services. Say, do you have any family that you've been trying to get a hold of? I can help you make some calls, if you'd like."

"Not really."

"What? Are you on your own?"

"Yes. I mean, I have a mom and a brother, but I don't think they're missing me much."

"You sure about that?"

"Very sure. My mom . . . well, she has her own demons. And my brother is fourteen

43

months older. He took off a while back. I wouldn't know where he was even if I wanted to try."

"That's too bad," Dee said softly.

"Other people have had it worse." Feeling increasingly uneasy, Gwen wished Dee would just move on. There wasn't a lot she could share about her life and even less that she felt good about or wanted to try to explain.

"I suppose that's a fact. Well, don't fret now. Tomorrow you'll get to meet Melanie. She's the social worker. She's real nice. I'm sure she'll have some ideas about where you can go after here."

"Hope so."

Dee stared at her a moment longer. Obviously, she was waiting for Gwen to spill some more information about her life. But what could she say? Gwen turned her head, looking out the window like there was actually something to see.

"Well, eat up, okay?"

"Yes, ma'am."

She kept her face averted until she heard the nurse leave. When she was alone again, she breathed a sigh of relief. It didn't make sense, but she almost preferred being alone with Officer Lucky. At least the cop didn't pretend to care about anything other than her baby. That was honest.

Shaking off her blues, she clicked on the television and flipped to some game show and started carefully pulling off the plastic covers of her soup and salad.

She'd just taken her second sip of the hot soup when a volunteer came in.

"Hey, mail call."

"Huh?"

The volunteer — a young, pretty teenager and was probably volunteering at the hospital just so she could say she cared about other people on her college application — held out a letter. "You've got a letter."

Just as Gwen held out her hand, she paused. "Wait. You are Gwen Camp, right? I was supposed to check that."

"I'm Gwen. You got the right room."

"Oh. Here you go, then." She smiled before grimacing at the soup. "That's your lunch, huh? Wow. I bet you can't wait to get out of here." She smiled again before flying out of the room.

Gwen shook her head at the volunteer before tearing open the envelope. Maybe Officer Lucky had found her mother?

All that was inside was a torn-off sheet of paper.

Baby, they wouldn't let me in to get you. Said you weren't allowing visitors. What's up with that?

Don't worry. They locked me up, but I got out since they couldn't pin anything on me. And they won't, as long as you don't talk.

You better not talk.

As soon as they let you out of there, I'll find you.

Then I'll make sure you and my baby don't leave ever again.

She shuddered. She supposed if someone read it one way, they might think that Hunter really cared about her. But he didn't. She knew more than anyone that he only cared about his reputation and his business. He was slick and a liar, and he was willing to do anything to make sure nothing hurt him.

Gwen wasn't even sure how she'd gotten involved with him.

It had happened almost out of her control — she'd been desperate. She'd had no clue where her brother Billy was, and she was frightened to go back to the apartment she shared with her mom. She had no money and was pretty sure she was about to get kicked out of school. Circumstances were dire.

And then she'd met Hunter. She'd been scared of him from the beginning, but she had been so glad to be away from her mother and off the streets that she'd done whatever he wanted. In a twisted way, she thought he'd saved her.

It was only during the last few weeks that things had gotten really bad, when Hunter had realized she was pregnant.

Then he began to get mean. He hit her a couple of times, withheld food until she did things he wanted. Then, the night before Officer Lucky found her, he'd forced her to smoke meth with him.

She wasn't sure how much time had passed, but by the time she was even halfway coherent, she was sitting in a hospital room getting an ultrasound.

Now all she knew was that she didn't want to be that person again. She might not ever be a woman to be proud of, but she sure didn't want to be that.

But now, holding that note, Gwen realized that she'd been fooling herself.

Hunter had found her in the hospital, contacted her, and he wasn't giving up.

It seemed like it wasn't as easy to run away from her life anymore. And . . . that

47

her luck had just about run out.

She didn't know what to do, either. She could already tell that Officer Lucky didn't really like her. She hadn't been mean or anything — but sometimes Gwen would catch the woman staring at her, and there was something in her eyes, like Gwen wasn't even human to her.

The sad thing was that Gwen didn't feel the same way about Officer Lucky. Actually, she kind of admired the police officer. She was tough, pretty, and walked with confidence. She also always spoke her mind. Best of all, everyone seemed to listen to her.

Gwen knew that they'd never be friends or anything, but she sure didn't want Officer Lucky looking at her like she was scum she'd discovered on the bottom of her shoes.

And that's how Officer Lucky would look at her if she knew the truth about Gwen's relationship with Hunter. Heck, the woman probably wouldn't even believe her if Gwen told her that she hadn't been communicating with Hunter, but he'd sent her a letter anyway.

No, it was a lot better to keep this note to herself. She was going to have to hide it and pretend nothing happened. And that might work out for her, too.

Until she was let out of the hospital.

48

Just imagining what would happen, no, knowing what would happen to her once she was discharged made her shiver. And feel nauseous.

Gwen barely grabbed the plastic bowl on her bedside table before losing the contents of her stomach.

CHAPTER 5

"There are shortcuts to happiness,
and dancing is one of them."
— VICKI BAUM

Tuesday Night

"This isn't very much fun, Shannon," Traci muttered. "Like, I don't think it's fun at all."

They were standing at Shannon's barre in her dance studio. They were also kind of, sort of stretching.

Correction, Shannon was stretching. Her sister looked like the ballerina she used to be, dressed in pink tights and a black leotard, with her long hair contained in a messy bun on the top of her head.

Traci, to her disgust, was wincing from the effort as she tried to follow her sister's lead. Their third sister, Kimber, clad in a tank top and black leggings, was quietly going through the motions, though she performed each movement only about halfway. Kimber seemed perfectly happy about her progress and wasn't even breaking a sweat.

Traci, on the other hand, in her gray sweatpants and old band T-shirt, was starting to look like she'd just stepped out of a sauna. Honestly, she would've thought being flexible was a genetic thing. Or, maybe it wasn't, since it hurt to touch her toes.

"Oh, come on, Traci. You've just got to give it a chance." Shannon smiled at them in the reflection in the mirror. "This is one of my favorite things to do to relieve stress. There's nothing like a good stretch to make a girl feel like she can do anything in the world."

"Right now I feel like I'm not going to be able to do anything at all. I know for a fact that I'm not going to be able to move tomorrow morning. Every bit of this hurts."

"It's not that bad," Kimber said as she lifted one of her feet on the barre and followed Shannon's lead. "You've just got to stop fighting your body, Trace. You need to think of positive images."

After barely getting her foot on the barre as well, she groaned. "Positive images? Who taught you that? Your fancy-pants model girlfriends?"

Kimber, to her credit, didn't look fazed at

51

all by her nastiness. "Ah, yeah."

Shannon chuckled. "She's got you there, Traci."

Kimber smiled, too. "See?"

Traci rolled her eyes in the mirror at both of them. Kimber was not only thin, tall, and graceful, she was a bona fide super model. She'd appeared on the covers of magazines, been featured in fashion shows in New York City, Milan, and Paris, and who knows what else. "You're one to talk. Your body is just used to not eating and looking good."

"No, it's more like I take care of myself. I saw those fast food wrappers in your Subaru, girl. You've been eating junk food on the sly."

"I wasn't hiding it, Kimber."

Shannon cleared her throat. "Oh, for heaven's sakes. Y'all are enough to drive a girl to drink. Now listen up and do what I do. Raise your right foot, set it gently on the ground, and move into first position." While Kimber and Traci followed, she smiled. "Good. Good job! Now, plié."

Traci groaned again as she moved her feet into position and sank into some awkward knee bend.

"Slowly, Traci!" Shannon called out.

"I'm trying to go slow." She was also now

trying to get up without making a fool of herself.

After another ten minutes of torture, she stepped away at last. "I'm sorry. I can't do this anymore. I'm going for a run."

Shannon paused in her latest movement, which involved one arm stretched out to the side while she bent her torso backward. "Are you sure?"

"So sure."

"Okay. Well, at least you tried, right?"

"Right. Um, you're not mad that I hate this with every fiber of my being, are you?" Shannon was constantly trying to get all of them to do fun, bonding things together. Traci didn't want to hurt her feelings.

"Mad that you don't want to do ballet with me? Not at all."

"Thanks. Um, you can go running with me one day if you want."

Shannon looked alarmed. "Thanks, but no thanks. I'll stick to sweating indoors."

"Fair enough. Well, girls, I'm outta here."

"Hey, Trace!" Kimber called out before she got to the door.

"Yeah?"

Kimber lowered her voice. "Hey, are you okay? You seem a little more on edge than usual. Are you still worried about Gwen?"

She *was* on edge, even though she'd been

doing her best to pretend she wasn't. Gwen had seemed particularly stressed when she'd visited her that morning. She'd even been short with Dr. Rossi, which she never had been before. Something was up with her. But Traci knew better than to worry about her too much — Gwen Camp had multiple issues that one concerned cop couldn't fix in just a couple of days. "I'm all right."

"Are you sure?" Shannon asked.

"Yeah. I'll be fine." Gwen might not be, but that wasn't her problem, right? She was a cop, not a social worker.

After giving her sisters another half smile, she ran up to her room, put on a pair of shorts, a tank top, and her favorite running shoes, and then headed over to the kitchen to grab some water and her earbuds.

Their newest roommate, Jennifer, was chopping up vegetables at the counter. She grinned at Traci. "You clocked out of barre ballet, too?"

"Too? Shannon tried to get you to do it?"

"Well, she offered. I told her that I was not quite ready to get on board with that."

"At least she listened to you. I tried to get out of it, but it didn't go over too well."

"Shannon has been dancing so long that I think she's forgotten how the rest of us mortals feel when we enter her classroom."

"Hopelessly clumsy?"

"I was thinking more like a little flabby and a lot intimidated."

"No worries, I feel the same way when I watch you cook. You can make anything taste good. What are you making for dinner, by the way?"

"Stir fry."

"Oh, yum. With pork?"

"No. Tofu."

She groaned. "Really?"

Jennifer smiled. "Come on. It's not so bad. Plus, you said you liked it last time."

"I also liked stir fry with pork. Or beef. Chicken. You know, real food."

"Tofu is real. Well, real enough." She went back to slicing peppers. "Anyway, it's as a favor for Kimber. She asked for it. She's leaving on Friday for another photo shoot."

"I forgot about that." Now that she realized how many accommodations Kimber had to make in order to look good in tiny pieces of designer clothes, she shrugged. "Tofu stir fry is fine with me."

"I am also making a coconut cake."

Jennifer could both cook and bake like a dream. But no matter how many things she did well, she created the most amazing cakes. "Get out. Why?"

She smiled. "Dylan and Shannon are joining us for dinner before they go back to their place. He asked me to make it for him."

Shannon's brand-new husband was Jennifer's older brother and Traci's partner on the police force. It was a lot of connections, but it seemed to work. "You are the best sister."

"I'm his *only* sister," she said with a laugh. "I don't mind, though. He's done so much for me."

"You know he'd say that you don't owe him a thing." Jennifer had been stalked by one of the members of a gang who had attacked her, and Dylan had supported her through all of it.

"It doesn't mean that's the way that I feel, though." She winked. "I'm trying to own my emotions, just like my therapist has been encouraging me to do. What do you think?"

"I think I need to take some lessons from you. I seem to own everyone's emotions." And problems.

Jennifer's easygoing smile faltered. "That's not good."

"I know." She kicked out a shoe. "That's why I'm going for a run. I've got to get a handle on it." Like, before she exploded.

"Have a good time."

Traci grabbed earbuds, slipped on her

CamelBak, and began a slow jog down to the bike trail that ran along the river through the middle of Bridgeport. The moment she reached the trail, she felt her body relax.

She wasn't a ballet barre type of woman, no matter how much Shannon wanted her to be. Traci needed space and good old-fashioned push-ups, sit-ups, and four-mile runs. Sure, it was probably a product of her upbringing. Desiree, one of the women who ran the group home had been a terrific runner and had encouraged all the kids to join in and keep her company.

But even if it was just a product of how she grew up, she'd take it. Desiree had been awesome and had encouraged her to do things she didn't think were possible. Like entering the police academy and accepting the toughest job she could get — working for the Cleveland police force.

Her steps slowed as she remembered how tough that woman had been, and yet so giving. A perfect combination for Traci. Desiree had changed her life.

Sometimes Traci really believed that God had put her there to give Traci a head start in life.

Which made her wonder if He had done the same thing with her and Gwen.

CHAPTER 6

"Listen to my feet and I'll tell you
the story of my life."
— JOHN BUBBLES,
FATHER OF RHYTHM TAP

Wednesday

Gwen had come into the hospital with a bad attitude and was leaving with a suitcase of clothes for herself and a big box of personal items — everything from toiletries to a pretty purse to a stack of books and even a couple of gift cards.

She couldn't remember a time that so many people had done so much for her. It was beyond humbling, especially since everybody knew that she couldn't give anything back.

"Thanks everyone," she said through choked tears. "I love everything, I really do. I . . . I don't know how to tell you how much I appreciate everything."

"You already said it," Dee said with a smile. Looking at the other staff members surrounding them, she added, "We're all just really happy for you and that baby boy."

Gwen curved her hands around her belly. Thanks to the week in the hospital, she had put on some weight and now she had a good little baby bump. "I wouldn't have gotten through this week without all of you."

Dr. Rossi, who was standing in his white coat next to Dee, picked up one of the shopping bags that was near the door. "No need to thank us. Don't forget, you're not going to be a stranger. I'll see you in a week."

"I've got to come back to the hospital?"

"Oh, no. I'll be bringing you to his office," Officer Lucky said.

"It's not far. Just across the street," Marissa added. "And, if your appointments are ever on Tuesdays, we'll get to see each other. I work in the clinic on Tuesdays."

"Plus, we'll be asking the doc about you, too," one of the orderlies said.

"Yep, you're stuck with us now," a resident joked.

Gwen turned to the group of people who had not only helped monitor her health, they'd also taken time to talk to her so she wouldn't feel so alone. Even though they probably only helped because it was their jobs, she thought, it still felt good. "Thanks," she said again.

After exchanging hugs, everyone started moving out of the room. Soon, it was just her, Dee, Melanie, Dr. Rossi, and Officer Lucky. Gwen had a lot of regrets about things she'd done, both with Hunter and to herself. But one of the things she most regretted was that she didn't know what she'd done to offend the cop. It wasn't like they were destined to be best friends or anything, but she'd hoped by now that Officer Lucky would have begun to thaw a little bit toward her.

It didn't look like that was going to happen, though. The last two times Officer Lucky had stopped by, she'd hardly stayed ten minutes, and she'd spent most of the time on her phone.

Gwen had tried not to let her feelings get hurt, but they kind of had been. If they had been alone, she would have tried to apologize, but now it wasn't the time.

"Ellen is waiting for you, so we better get on our way," Melanie, the social worker, said.

"Yes, ma'am." She picked up her suitcase.

"Nope. Now put that down, Miss, and get in the wheelchair," Dee ordered.

"Really? I can walk."

"I know, and I can follow the rules." She wheeled the chair in front of Traci. "Hop on, and I'll hand you your flowers."

"I think we're all set," Melanie said as she picked up Gwen's new backpack, which was stuffed to the gills. "Officer, want to walk out with us?"

Traci nodded. "Sure. And, um, I'll get your suitcase, Gwen."

"You don't need to," Gwen said in a rush. "I bet we can perch it on my lap, too."

Officer Lucky gave her a chilly look. "Hey, you're supposed to take care of yourself, right?"

"Yes, ma'am." She faced forward, stung by the words. It was obvious that Officer Lucky was going to make sure she never forgot that she'd been doing a pretty poor job of taking care of herself until now.

At last, they began their procession onto the elevator. As Dee continued to push her along, Gwen couldn't help but contrast with how much difference a week had made. She now had a cop guardian, a doctor, a social worker, and was on the way to a women's center where her room and board was going to be completely taken care of. After being essentially alone for most of her life, she now kind of had her very own team. Who would ever have thought?

When the elevator dinged and they exited the building, Melanie led everyone to a bright-red minivan.

"Here we are," Melanie said.

"Wow," Gwen said. She'd thought Melanie looked more like a classic sports car kind of person.

"Yep. It's really cool, huh?" She chuckled. "Back when I was twenty-two, I swore I'd never drive a minivan, but now here I am." She patted the side of it. "Even worse, I picked it out. My husband wanted me to get an SUV, but this is a whole lot easier when you're transporting kids and clients."

Traci grinned. "Now that I'm driving around with my sisters so much, there's been plenty of times when I've wanted more room. You're rocking the minivan."

Melanie playfully bowed. "Thank you. Thank you, very much." Clicking her key fob, she smiled at Gwen. "All right, dear. Are you ready to begin again?"

Gwen nodded slowly. She had no idea what the Bridgeport Women's Center was going to be like, but she figured it couldn't be any worse than what she had already been through.

"It's gonna be okay," Melanie said, as if reading Gwen's mind. She gestured toward the passenger door. "Hop in and I'll put your things in the back."

As Gwen was climbing into the vehicle, she glanced across the parking lot and suddenly found herself under Hunter's gaze. He looked like he always did — a little cocky, almost like he had a right to be standing in the middle of a parking lot in a black hoodie, with a phone in his hand. He was also staring at her so intently, it almost burned.

Even from a distance, she could tell he was mad at her. She inhaled sharply. Boy, she *really* should have told someone about his letter. But who could she trust?

"Gwen?" Officer Lucky stepped closer. "What's wrong? Is something happening with the baby?"

"No. It's just . . ." Feeling Officer Lucky's gaze on her, Gwen shrank. No, she wasn't ready to mention Hunter. She was going someplace else, someplace safe. Plus, Hunter was looking especially scary. If she told everyone he was there, he might even get madder at her.

"It was what?" Officer Lucky eyed her curiously.

"It was nothing. I, well, I just thought I saw someone I knew."

Melanie turned around and scanned the area. "Who do you think you saw?"

"No one. Just a girl I used to know. I was mistaken, though. When I looked again, I realized it wasn't her. Sorry."

Officer Lucky didn't move. "Are you sure that was all that happened?"

"Yes, ma'am."

Melanie opened her driver's side door. "I think we've got this now, Officer. Thanks for your help."

Officer Lucky didn't look inclined to leave, but after a long pause, she stepped back. "Anytime. I'm uh, glad to help." Turning to Gwen again, her smile faded. "Don't forget, I'm going to visit you in two days."

"I won't forget. And, um, thank you Officer Lucky. Thank you for helping me so much."

"Anytime. That's what I'm here for, right?"

Officer Lucky's words rang in Gwen's ears as Melanie drove out of the parking lot. She wondered if that was indeed the truth, that the cop who had done so much for her was only doing her job.

For some reason, Gwen thought there was more to it than that, she just wasn't sure what it could be. Maybe she'd offended Officer Lucky when she had found her? She'd been so out of it that it could have happened and she wouldn't remember.

Or, Gwen thought, it was even more likely that Officer Lucky didn't trust her and didn't think Gwen was ready to turn her life around. Maybe Officer Lucky was afraid that she was going to have to deal with more of Gwen's problems and she was annoyed about that?

If that was the case, the police officer might be exactly right.

Gwen was afraid that a whole new set of problems was just beginning.

CHAPTER 7

"When you dance, your purpose is not to get to a certain place on the floor. It's to enjoy each step along the way."
— WAYNE DYER

Every time he walked into the back door his parents' house, Matt was struck by how some things never changed. His father would have opera blaring just a little too loud, the kitchen would smell like fresh tomato sauce and lemons, and his mother would always stop whatever she was doing to greet him, often with some kind of dishcloth tied around her waist.

And, if he didn't arrive on time for Sunday supper, he could count on getting chastised like he was eight years old again.

"Hey, Mom," he said as he tossed off his jacket and put his cell phone and car keys on the kitchen counter. "Supper smells good."

"Thank you, Matteo." Looking pointedly at the brass, old-fashioned clock over the sink, she added, "You're late, son."

"I know and I'm sorry. It couldn't be helped, though. Mrs. Nelson's baby had a mind of its own."

As he'd hoped, her expression softened. "Ah, you were delivering a baby. It took its own sweet time being born?"

"Oh, yeah." He smiled. "It was worth it, though. Mother and baby are doing fine."

She popped a hand on her hip. "Well, don't keep me in suspense. What did Mrs. Nelson have?"

"An eight-pound baby boy with blue eyes. He looked at me, stretched his arms out like he was glad to have more room, then let out a piercing cry." He grinned. "It was beautiful."

She chuckled as his father joined them in the kitchen. "That's a miracle, indeed."

Looking pleased, his father slapped him on the shoulder. "You did good. I'm proud of you."

"I'd say thank you, but Mrs. Nelson did most of the work."

"Come on into the family room," Dad said as his mother went back to the pot on the stove. "You can say hello to everyone else and I'll get you a drink."

Scanning the crowded room, Matt said, "Is everyone here tonight?"

"Everyone but Bennie." Looking pleased, his father said, "Your mother is glad you're all here. She's been holding court in the kitchen most of the afternoon."

He spied Vanny, two of his aunts, and a handful of neighbors from down the street. But not his older brother. "Where's Anthony?"

His dad shrugged. "That, I can't answer. He and Marie could be anywhere showing off that ring."

"So, that's why there's so many people here tonight."

"Engagements are a blessing." Eyes brightening, he grinned. "Or so your mother says."

Matt shared a grin with his dad before weaving his way through the crowd.

His parents were good people. Old world in a lot of ways. Unpretentious with items but exceedingly showy with their kids. Matt couldn't recall the number of times he'd been asked to be his parents' show and tell, they were so proud to have a doctor son.

Anthony was a doctor as well, but a research one. Ramon was career Navy and on a ship somewhere in the Pacific. Their two younger sisters had gone in different directions. Vanny was a real estate agent and Bennie was a newlywed and financial consultant. She had also just gotten pregnant.

They also all lived nearby because their parents were the best people on the planet. His mother and father had raised them to be hardworking. They'd also given them a huge respect for faith and family.

And that was why Matt was at Anthony and Marie's impromptu engagement party instead of heading directly home and collapsing after delivering two babies on a Sunday and volunteering at a clinic for most of Saturday.

Nothing mattered as much as family. Nothing — though a new baby in the world was close.

He loved his brother. He was glad he and Marie were tying the knot. But he was not too excited about the swarm of people. As he weaved his way to the kitchen, stopping often to shake hands and say hello, he tried to figure out when he could sneak out. Hopefully within couple hours. Ninety minutes if he got lucky.

"Matt!"

And there went his best intentions, out the window. "Hey, Amy." He lifted his arms automatically when she veered in for a close hug. "It's so good to see you. Isn't it great about Anthony and Marie?"

"So good." He stepped back to put a few feet in between them. "Great."

"I heard they want to get married in three months."

"I kind of doubt that. My sister Bennie's wedding took a whole year to plan."

Amy frowned. "I don't think I got that wrong." Instantly, her frown turned upside down. "They're already talking like it's going to be a great party."

"I'm sure it will be. If my mom gets involved, she'll be calling the caterers and the priest at nine o'clock tomorrow morning."

"You know, I'm not dating anyone special right now . . . You aren't either, are you?"

"No. I've been working a ton."

"Hey, maybe we could go together? Going with an old friend would take some of the pressure off, you know?"

Amy might have had a point, but she was kind of freaking him out. "Thanks, I'll keep it in mind." He'd also reminded himself to keep his distance from her. "Sorry but I need to go find Anthony and Marie. I've been here almost twenty minutes and I haven't even talked to them yet."

Her eyelashes fluttered. "Are you sure you have to go?"

"Very sure." He backed up another step. "I need to go find Bennie too. See you later."

Amy looked taken aback, but she recovered quickly. Flashing a bright smile, she tossed a lock of her hair over one shoulder. "Oh. Well, I'll catch up with you later, Matt."

He turned and walked toward the kitchen faster. Amy and he had dated for two months in college. That girl could make plans faster than most people could drink a cup of coffee.

His mother, stirring sauce at the oven looked up and grinned when he walked in. "You're back already?"

"It's a zoo out there." After dutifully hugging two aunts and one niece, he kissed her on the cheek. "You're better company than most."

She pressed a hand to his cheek. "That's why you're my favorite."

She said that to all of them. After briefly chatting with his aunts, he leaned back against the kitchen counter next to his mother. "So, this little get together has gotten pretty big."

"What can I say? Twenty people turned into fifty in a heartbeat."

It looked like the number was closer to seventy. "How are you feeling? You haven't

71

been cooking all day, have you?"

"People helped, don't worry." She smiled. "You know I'm happiest when everyone comes over. And today is such a good day, don't you agree?"

"Of course. Especially since you're happy."

"Of course, I'm happy. We're going to have Marie. She's the perfect woman for Tony."

With anyone else, he would have said something snarky about her being the only woman to put up with his brother. Instead, he just smiled. "I need to go find them."

"They're in the basement."

"On my way."

Just as he turned, she said, "Matteo, get ready."

"For what?"

"They're planning a fast engagement, son. Three months."

"For real?" Amy had been right.

She nodded.

"There's a story there, yes?" He stepped closer and lowered his voice. "Mama, is she pregnant?"

"No. Well, not that I'm aware of. It's a different story, and one that's just as good."

His mother's eyes were sparkling and there was something in her voice that sounded pretty fishy. He didn't exactly appreciate that. "Mama, you know I don't like surprises."

"I do know. But, this isn't about you, is it? It's Anthony's news." She paused, "Well, his and Marie's."

"Sounds like I better go find them right now."

She held out a hand. "Don't go charging over and pester them with questions. Let your brother give you his news in his own time."

If he hadn't been fairly certain that she'd whack him with the end of her wooden spoon, he would have rolled his eyes. Instead, he simply turned and headed toward the basement.

It took another fifteen minutes to get to his brother and future sister-in-law. But when he did, he had to stop for a moment to take in the sight. His normally all-business brother was lounged in their father's favorite chair and laughing with two of their cousins. Marie was perched on his lap and giggling, too. They looked happy. Exuberant.

Like they were meant to be together.

Marie caught sight of him first. "Matt! Hi!"

Anthony glanced his way and smiled. "I was wondering when you'd get here."

"Sorry. Work," he said simply, not wanting any baby news to interfere with their celebration. "Now are you going to let go of your girl for a second so I can congratulate her properly?"

After pressing a kiss to her temple, Anthony dropped his hands. Marie scrambled off of Anthony's lap and gave Matt a hug. "Can you even believe it? We're engaged!"

He hugged her back and kissed her forehead. "Anthony is a lucky man. You're the best thing that's ever happened to him."

Her cheeks pinkened. "I say the same thing about Tony."

It took some effort, but he only smiled at Marie's shortening of Anthony. Until he started dating her, Matt couldn't remember him ever being okay with the nickname. Only their mother had ever been allowed to use it before Marie came along.

When Anthony held out his hand, Matt bypassed it and pulled him into a hug. "I'm happy for you. Really."

"Thanks." After checking to see that their cousins had drifted off to another conversation, he added, "I'm hoping you'll be our best man."

"Of course. I'm honored."

He held out a hand for Marie. "There's something else you need to know as well."

"Yes?" Inwardly, he was giving a sigh of relief. Matt had been half afraid that Anthony would wait to share the news about the quick wedding.

"There's a reason that we decided to get married right now. We want a quick wedding. And no, it's not because we're expecting a baby or anything."

"Okay . . ."

Anthony looked at Marie. When she nodded, he continued. "We've got a new adventure planned. It's as amazing as it's unexpected."

Amazing and unexpected? He hadn't thought that those two words were even in his brother's vocabulary. And what did that even mean, anyway? "You two are starting to scare me. What are you talking about?"

"Marie, it's your news, love."

"I know." She nibbled on her bottom lip. "But, I still think you should tell him, Tony."

"But —"

"One of you tell me!" When he realized about eight people were now staring at him, Matt lowered his voice. "Sorry, but come on. Spit it out."

Anthony shrugged. "All right. Here is our news. Marie was asked to join the Budapest Symphony for two years."

"Say again?"

"We're moving to Budapest so Marie can play the violin for them," Anthony said slowly. "You know, in Hungary?"

"I know where Budapest is. But why . . ." he allowed his voice to drift off. Wanting to get some answers now but not wanting to sound completely disrespectful of Marie's news.

"I haven't been real happy in the orchestra here. It's a good orchestra, of course. One of the best. But there are a lot more violinists who have seniority over me. It's been pretty apparent that I wasn't going to ever get to be highlighted or receive more opportunities anytime soon. Plus, now's the time to go to Europe if we're ever going to. We don't have a mortgage or children. I've been wanting to do something like this for a while," she said. "We both have, actually."

They had? "But Anthony, you've got a great job at UC Medical Center. And, just saying . . . there are plenty of orchestras in the United States."

Anthony shrugged like his job was easily replaceable. Like he'd been stocking shelves at a discount store instead of being one of the top researchers at his hospital. "They have hospitals in Hungary, too. And they even have a need for some physicians with experience in family medicine and oncology."

"Wait. You're going to work with patients?"

His brother stiffened. "I did rotations, just like you did."

"I know." But his meticulous, uber-organized brother always seemed happiest in a research lab. "I just never heard you talk about wanting to get out of the research side." Or go to Hungary, for that matter.

His brother's voice hardened. "You know, now would be a real good time to tell us congratulations."

"Sorry. Of course." He smiled at Marie. "That's wonderful. Congratulations! I'm sure everyone in Budapest will be lucky to have you."

"Thank you." Her eyes lit up. "We're really excited. The only problem is that we've got to hurry this wedding along. We need to find a place to live, Tony needs to do another round of interviews, and then we'll need to put half of our lives in storage here and move the rest halfway across the world."

That was a lot. Like, a whole lot. "How much of a hurry?"

"Six weeks."

A lot sooner than three months. "Wow. That is really soon."

Anthony grinned. "Yep, which means you'd better figure out who you're going to be bringing as your date, Matt."

He wasn't sure why that even mattered. "Because?"

"Because in honor of Marie, it's going to have an old-world feel."

"Okay . . . care to clarify that?"

"That means it's going to be an evening wedding in the foyer of the Music Hall," Marie said excitedly. "Someone else's reception fell through so I was able to get the space for a steal. And, some of my friends are going to play during the ceremony and the reception."

"Wow. I'm impressed."

"I can't wait. It's going to be so beautiful, just like the wedding I always dreamed about. Plus, we're all going to waltz."

Matt grinned, sure that they were playing a joke on him. "Anthony . . ."

"I'm serious. You're going to have to bring a date and waltz at my wedding, Matteo."

He laughed. "Sorry, I don't know how to waltz."

"Then you best get to finding a date to teach you. You've got six weeks." Just as Matt was about to protest some more, his brother continued, his voice like iron. "Consider it your wedding gift to us."

Wedding gift, indeed. It sounded more like a prank.

Wedding gift, indeed. It sounded more like
a prank.

CHAPTER 8

"Nobody cares if you can't dance well.
Just get up and dance. Great dancers are
not great because of their technique, they
are great because of their passion."
— MARTHA GRAHAM

"You are continually surprising me, Lucky,"
Dylan said as they exited the middle school.
"Who would've ever guessed that you would
be so good with thirteen-year-olds?"

"Uh, me?" She grinned at him. "I told you
I had experience working with teens,
Lange."

"I know you did. But I just figured you
were talking about delinquents."

"Not every teenager I came in contact
with in Cleveland was in trouble. A lot of
them were really nice kids."

"Point taken," he said as they approached
the cruiser. "How about this — I hadn't realized that you would be so good at talking

about personal safety. You had those kids eating out of the palm of your hand."

"Hardly that," she said as they got in. Dylan was driving today so she was riding shotgun. Usually, that was something that annoyed her. She liked driving, liked being in control. However, since she had a lot on her mind, she appreciated Dylan picking up some of the slack. "So, back to the station?" she asked after checking her phone.

"Nah. I thought we'd go get lunch downtown. What do you say?"

She grinned. Being able to grab a quick lunch in the middle of a shift was a huge perk. "Hmm, I say that depends. What are you thinking?"

"Tina's?"

"Tacos again?"

"Tina's food truck is the best around here. She's always near the bike trail on Tuesdays."

"Go ahead. I don't mind."

Dylan grinned as he headed down the road. As was their habit, both kept an eye out for speeders, but the roads were fairly quiet. Their radios were quiet today, too. Though she knew that was the case in small town life, she couldn't help but feel it was just the calm before the storm.

"So, I heard you shot down Shannon's attempt to make a ballerina out of you."

"Ugh. Did she tell you about our barre class?"

"Not in detail. Just that you took off running." He grinned. "Was she that tough?"

"Ah, yes." When he grinned, she rolled her eyes. "You better watch out, I'll make her give you a barre class."

"Don't you dare. I'm already having to fill in for her rumba class."

"Every time I think about you rumbaing with your wife I crack up."

"At least one of us does." Pulling into an empty space near the trail, he shrugged. "I don't love it, but I do love Shannon, so there you go."

That said it all, Traci reflected. He loved her and was willing to step outside of his comfort zone to make her smile. Maybe that was what was missing in her life. She felt a prick on the back of her neck again.

What was going on?

"Lucky?"

"Hmm?"

"You're looking tense again. What's up?"

"Sorry. I keep feeling like something is about to happen."

Dylan studied her. "Like what?"

"I don't know. I keep thinking about Gwen and that house we raided."

"What about it?"

"She says she hasn't heard from anyone there. I want to believe her, but what if her baby daddy wants her back?"

Dylan shrugged. "When Emerson and I booked them, neither of those guys acted like they even remembered Gwen was there." He frowned. "I think she was just a convenient —"

"I know what you meant, but don't say it, okay."

"Okay. You're right."

"Dylan, what if she was something more to one of those guys? What if one of them is the father of her child?"

"I thought you said she wasn't positive who the father was."

"That's what she said, but she could've been lying. There's something about the guarded look in her eyes that worries me. What happened to that Hunter guy, by the way?" She'd been so busy with Gwen and her other duties she'd lost track of the guy after a few days.

"He bailed out."

"I was afraid of that."

"Since we didn't have enough evidence to prove that he'd been selling, we could only put some drug charges on him." Dylan frowned. "I believe in the law, but in cases

like this, it sure doesn't work in our favor."
Dylan continued. "If it was my guess, I
don't think Hunter is going to even think
about her again. She's a liability to him."

"She is. But, I can't help but think that he
might want to have her, just to make sure
she doesn't talk."

"Yeah." Dylan's whole tone and expression was how Traci knew hers should be.
Detached. Professional.

"Hey, don't look so worried. You, of all
people, know that you can't ever try to guess
what some of these drug dealers are thinking — or what their motivations are. If the
guy reaches out to Gwen, then she'll let you
know and we'll go from there."

She nodded.

"Hey, Trace. I know you care about the
girl, but settle down. You got her in a good
place and she's getting medical attention.
No doubt this guy has found a new girl
already."

"Maybe so." Everything Dylan was saying
made sense, but she felt like they were making it all sound too easy. They were also
counting on Gwen trusting Traci enough to
confide in her. So far, Gwen hadn't exactly
given off a "let's trust each other with our
secrets" kind of vibe.

"Traci, I know you've got a good heart,

but this time I think your worry is misplaced. Sometimes a duck is just a duck, right?"

"Right." She shook her head. "I bet I'm making too much of this. I guess sometimes I can't stop for problems where there aren't any."

"There you go." After getting out, he waited for her to do the same before gesturing at the bright yellow food truck parked on the side of Memorial Park. At least a dozen people were lined up in front of the cashier's window to order and another twenty were sitting on various benches and curbs balancing cardboard containers of tacos on their laps. The scent of grilled onions, garlic, and chili peppers filled the air. Dylan breathed deep. "Ah, heaven."

"Heaven in the form of a taco truck?"

"Absolutely." Moving to the back of the line, he grinned at her. "Lucky, you're going to love this place."

"I'm sure I will." She squinted, trying to read the descriptions on each of the five types of tacos on the menu. "The California taco sounds good." It was full of chicken, pico de gallo, avocado, tomatoes, and lettuce.

"No way," he said as they moved up in

line. "What you need is a Tina's taco special."

The ingredients consisted of shredded pork, green chilies, onions, peppers, sour cream, and some kind of cheese sauce. "If I don't drip it all over my uniform, it would be a miracle. Plus, it probably has over thousand calories in it."

"So?"

"So, it will also likely give me heartburn all night."

"Oh, stop. You run all the time. You'll burn those calories off before you know it."

"Maybe that's what I ought to do." Actually, when was the last time she'd gone out for a decent run? She couldn't remember. "Remind me to register for a couple of 5- and 10Ks."

"A couple?"

"Oh, yeah. I used to enter at least four a year when I was up in Cleveland." All that running and training had been good for her, too. It had relieved her stress and enabled her to rarely worry about what she ate.

Dylan nodded slowly. "You know, I might hound you to do that. You should get a hobby."

"Because?"

"Because it will keep your mind busy and

you'll be ready to eat out with me at every shift."

"And . . . it all comes back to *you*," she teased. "You know what, Lange? I'm surprised Shannon puts up with you."

"Me, too. She's everything classy and graceful that I'm not. But, what can I say? I was born under a lucky star."

"Next!" the cashier called out.

As they stepped up yet again, Traci grinned. These tacos might have a thousand calories in them, but being able to spend a few minutes with her partner doing nothing but standing in line and talking was priceless.

CHAPTER 9

TANGO: *Ballroom tango has a 2–4 time signature, and it is thirty-two bars per minute. While ballroom tango can certainly be romantic, sensual might be a better word to describe this popular dance.*

One week later

Gwen had been in the cozy room with the plum colored walls, massive bookcases, and two sets of blue velvet chairs for almost an hour. She and Ellen Landers had been talking for a while. It was nice, but weird.

It was the second time she'd been summoned for a visit in the director's swanky office, but it didn't feel any more comfortable than it had the first time. Not only was the office fancier than any place she'd ever been before, the sixty-year-old director had a way of speaking to her like they were equals.

Gwen knew they were anything but that.

Ellen leaned forward, her chin-length bob swinging forward. "Gwen, like I said at the beginning of our talk, no one here is judging you. Actually, we're doing the opposite of that. We're all on your side."

"Yes, ma'am."

"All you need to do is take things one day at a time," Ellen continued in her soothing voice. "Now that the restraining order is firmly in place, we can concentrate on your health and plan for your future."

Future. She wasn't exactly sure what that entailed. How did a person start over when she never had much to begin with?

"Do you have any questions?" Ellen asked.

"No, ma'am."

"All right then. I'll see you later."

She was dismissed. After smiling awkwardly, Gwen scooted out of Ellen's office and headed to her room on the third floor.

She'd been in the women's center for one whole week, and it didn't feel any more comfortable than it had the afternoon she'd arrived.

Gwen suspected that it wouldn't ever feel very comfortable, at least not anytime soon. Everything was so completely different than what she was used to, she hardly knew how to handle it.

She wasn't used to being the center of anyone's conversation. She sure wasn't used to focusing so much on herself. That was part of the problem, she guessed. She actually couldn't remember the last time that she'd concentrated on herself at all. She'd always been more worried about Hunter and not making him mad. Before that, it was her mom she'd worried about upsetting.

Then, she'd been *so sure* that things were going to turn *even worse* that she'd gotten high the night before Officer Lucky had found her on the floor.

Though her body didn't seem too harmed by her recent poor choices, she was wracked with guilt. She wouldn't know for sure until she gave birth if her selfish behavior had hurt her baby. But she thought it must have. How could it not?

The worst part was that she'd *known* it wasn't good for her baby, yet she'd done these bad things anyway. Her time with Hunter had pulled her into a black hole of regrets — regrets that she was likely going to be paying for for the rest of her life.

"Hey, you don't look so bad," her roommate Zara said when Gwen opened the door. "Did the meeting go all right?"

"I guess." She sat down on the bare mattress of the third twin bed in their room. Gwen liked how it had been just her and Zara in the room, but Ellen had been quick to let her know that they would probably have another roommate within a few days. Empty beds didn't last long here.

"Well, what did she say?"

"Not much. She just asked how things were going."

Zara frowned. "That's it?"

"Well, there was a little bit more."

"I swear, getting you to talk is like pulling teeth. What else did y'all talk about?"

"Well, um, first she asked how we were getting along. I told her fine. Then she asked if I was doing okay with the chores. I said yes." Looking at Zara warily, she said, "Why? Should I have been worried?"

"No. Not really." Zara gingerly walked to her dresser in the back corner of the room. "I guess I always worry about stupid stuff."

Gwen crossed her legs and watched Zara dig through a drawer full of T-shirts and shorts. She debated pushing further, and decided to go ahead and say more. She was learning that it didn't pay to be ignorant around the center. People expected you to do your part . . . even when you weren't sure what that was, exactly.

"Why? Does Ellen get mad if I say the

wrong thing?"

"No. She only gets upset if you keep things from her."

"Sounds like you know that from experience."

"I do. When I first got here, I was still drinking a lot on the sly."

"How did you get alcohol? Plus, didn't they they make you sign a contract before they assigned you a room?"

Zara rolled her eyes. "Come on. You don't think everyone here actually means what they promise, do you?"

Gwen actually had. Feeling embarrassed by her naivete, she said, "Well, what happened?"

"Late one night I snuck out and forgot to lock the front door behind me." Zara turned from the dresser and pointed to the mattress Gwen was sitting on. "Angel's ex walked right in."

"This was her bed?"

"Yeah. We were roommates."

"What happened to her? Where is she living now?" Wracking her brain, she tried to remember more of the other women's names. "Did she move rooms? I don't think we've met."

Zara turned away again. "You wouldn't have met, 'cause she's dead."

"What?"

"You heard me." Zara's voice sounded hollow. "Angel's ex was as bad a man as they come, and even though she ran away he found her. He searched the whole place, woke her up, and when she fought him, he shot her."

"Oh my gosh!"

Nodding, Zara pulled out one of her shirts and refolded it. "Yep. It was all my fault, too. I cried like a baby when I told Ellen what I'd done. I'm surprised they didn't kick me out."

"Zara, you didn't kill her."

"No, I sure did not. But that doesn't mean I shouldn't have taken my spot here more seriously." She popped a hip out. "The thing, Gwen, is that for whatever reason, you've been given a second chance. But it don't come without consequences, you know? Ellen might be full of rules, but she's what's keeping that bun in your oven safe. You've got to step up, be honest with yourself and her, and realize that nothing in your life starts changing until you do."

"I hear what you're saying."

"I hope so, 'cause I don't know if I can take another late-night visitor like Angel's ex." She stuffed the shirt she'd just folded in her purse. "I'll see you later. Ellen found me a place to work. I'm going to go interview."

"What kind of job is it?"

"Kitchen help. If I get the job, I'll be working in the back of a restaurant. I'll have to wash dishes at first, but Ellen says the people are fair and if they like what they see, they'll start teaching me other things. I aim to have a good job as a cook one day."

"Good luck." Gwen offered a smile that she hoped was encouraging.

Zara stopped at the door with a grin. "Thanks."

When she was alone again, Gwen thought about Ellen and the social worker and even the cop who seemed like she really cared. Each one of them had given her a chance. No, a second chance. Now it was up to her to try to figure out what to do with that. Did she want to merely survive and stay off drugs, then give up her baby?

Or, did she maybe want to do something worth thinking about? Worth being proud of?

Either option was going to be a big step for her, but only one of them would make her feel proud.

CHAPTER 10

INTERNATIONAL LATIN SAMBA: *A bouncy dance that is partnered for competitions, but as the national dance of Brazil it is performed solo.*

"Thank you for taking me to the doctor today," Gwen told Traci as she pulled into the parking lot outside Dr. Rossi's offices. "I was really in a bind when Ellen had an emergency come up."

"I was off today, so your timing was perfect." Looking over Gwen, Traci felt like she was almost a different woman. Already Gwen's eyes and skin looked better. She'd obviously gained a few pounds, too. She was still extremely thin, but now, at least, she didn't look like she'd been starved in some prison camp. "I wanted to check to see how you were doing anyway."

"I'm doing all right."

"Everything going well at the center?"

"I think so. Most of the other women are nice and easy to get along with."

"Only most?"

"It's a houseful of women who are going through hard times," Gwen said with a shrug. "I guess no matter where you're at, there's always a couple who like to stir things up."

"When I hear statements like that, I'm always glad I work with a lot of men," she joked. "I can steer clear of *their* kind of drama." She laughed.

Gwen smiled back, but it was tentative. It was obvious that she was waiting for Traci to get to the reason she was looking at her like that.

Traci figured stalling any longer wasn't going to make her news easier to bear. "Gwen, I not only wanted to take you to your doctor's appointment but I also needed to tell you some news." She glanced at the clock on the dash of her car. "Since we've got a little bit of time before your appointment, I thought we could talk about it right now."

"What's happened?"

"Let me back up a sec. The night I brought you to the hospital, my partner and a couple of other officers arrested Hunter, as well as the other men in the house."

Studying Gwen, Traci noticed that none of that was a surprise for her. "To continue on, we ran their fingerprints, locked them up because they were under the influence and in possession of assorted illegal drugs, and set bail. Unfortunately, every one of them made bail before you even got out of the hospital."

Not looking surprised, Gwen nodded.

"Last night, one of our informants hinted that Hunter is not real happy that you're at the women's center." She sighed. "There's no better way to say it, Gwen. He wants you back."

"I know he does."

Everything inside of Traci told her that there was more to these four words than a gut feeling. "Care to explain why you know that?"

"Because he sent me a note when I was in the hospital, and I'm pretty sure he was waiting for me the day I got out."

"And you're just now telling me this?"

Gwen's blue eyes looked even more pained. "I'm really sorry I didn't tell you."

She was beyond furious. "You're *sorry*?"

"But, um, before you get even madder, I should tell you that he sent another note yesterday. He wants me to leave the center and move in with him." She grimaced. "Like

97

I would ever do that."

"No one should have given you that letter, Gwen. They're supposed to screen your mail."

"It was addressed from a woman." She bit her lip. "And addressed to me in a woman's handwriting."

As Traci processed this news, she had to keep reminding herself that Gwen was just a girl. Just an eighteen-year-old who'd likely been abused and mistreated for months or years. "Why didn't you tell me this all before? Why didn't you call me last night after you received the letter?"

"I don't know. I guess . . . I was afraid you wouldn't believe me."

As frustrated as she was with Gwen's secrets, there was a part of Traci that was also breathing a huge sigh of relief. Gwen wasn't cowering or crying. She was telling the truth now.

This girl was getting stronger. That was a good thing. "Gwen, Officer Lange and I tried to find Hunter last night, but we couldn't find any sign of him. We won't give up though, okay?"

"Okay."

"All right. Let's go inside."

Ten minutes later, a nurse was calling Gwen's name.

As Gwen stood up, she looked in Traci's direction with a sense of panic.

"I'll be here waiting for you," Traci promised.

Two minutes after Gwen disappeared from view, the receptionist called Traci over.

"Yes?"

"Dr. Rossi asked if you could step into his office for a moment. We needed to draw some blood from Gwen, so he has a minute while she's in the other room."

"All right." Traci got to her feet.

"Come back this way, please."

Traci followed the older woman inside, past several examining rooms, to a spacious office.

"Have a seat. He'll be right in." She walked back out, leaving the door opened behind her.

Traci sat down in one of the gray leather chairs across from his desk, waited a few seconds, and then stood back up. She was curious about Dr. Rossi, and the photographs displayed around his office were impossible to resist. At least twenty photos of families and tiny babies covered a large bulletin board on one wall. Dr. Rossi was dressed in scrubs in at least half of them. But in each one, he was wearing such a look of delight and pride that Traci felt her heart melt.

She had a feeling that these babies weren't the only ones he'd delivered. Not by a long shot. Had he put them up for a special reason?

On another wall was a set of three photos. In each, he was surrounded by a group of men and women about his age. Her favorite was the one where they were all wearing graduation gowns that were unzipped and blowing in the wind. They all had their arms around each other and not a one of them was looking at the camera.

But the pictures that really stole her heart were the ones behind his desk on his credenza. There were six photographs in all, each encased in a silver frame. The people in the pictures all had olive skin, dark hair, and dark eyes — obviously members of Matt's family.

She studied them more intently, but only managed to spot him in one. That photo showed a far younger Matt Rossi. He was standing on a dock with a fishing pole in one hand. Next to him was an older man who she guessed was his grandfather. They were both laughing at something in the distance. Right at that minute, she would have given anything to see what they were looking at too.

"Sorry, Traci . . . ah, what are you doing?"

Feeling like a nine-year-old caught shoplifting, she turned in a start. "I'm sorry. I have a hard time sitting still, so I was looking at all of your pictures." She hurried back around his desk. "I guess I got carried away."

Instead of sitting right down, he pointed to the framed picture she'd been staring at when he walked in. "That's my grandfather and me."

"What did you two see that made you laugh?"

"Hmm?" He looked again. "Oh." He shook his head as his expression softened. "We were laughing at my sisters trying to fish with my dad."

"Trying?"

"You couldn't even really call it that, to be honest. Dad kept telling them to bait the hook and they'd squeal every time he tried to hand them an earthworm. My father was very annoyed with them."

"He got mad? What did he do?"

"Do? Well, nothing, really. I mean he told them that they would have to eat peanut butter and jelly for dinner instead of fresh fish." He grinned. "That was their plan, I fear."

She smiled back at him, swallowing the fierce sense of longing that had just risen up in her. Biting it off, she said, "I heard you wanted to see me?"

He blinked. "Oh. Yes. Can I have your phone number? I want to talk to you about something, but I don't have much time."

"You have my card . . ."

"No, I meant your personal number." For the first time since she'd met him he looked discomfited. "I . . . it's nothing bad. I promise."

"Doctor?" the nurse prompted from the doorway.

"Coming." Walking to the door, he said, "Grab a Post-it from my desk and write your number down, would you please? Thanks," he threw out over his shoulder before striding down the hall.

"Gwen shouldn't be much longer," the nurse said, letting Traci know that she might be a cop but that gal still didn't think Traci should be in Dr. Rossi's office by herself.

"I'll be right out," Traci said. Then, because she didn't ever want to be thought of as a gal who doubted herself, she pulled off a yellow Post-it Note, carefully wrote down her name and phone number, and then applied it to the top of a leather appointment calendar that was embossed with his initials.

She hoped he'd call soon, because she had no idea what he could want to talk to her about.

But when they did talk, she'd be sure to let him know that she didn't like surprises much. In fact, not at all.

CHAPTER 11

"The only way to make sense out of
change is to plunge into it, move with it,
and join the dance."
— ALAN WATTS

After returning Gwen to the women's
center, Traci went back to the station and
did some paperwork. Then she went with
Dylan to do a talk at a retirement home.
They ended their shift by patrolling Bridgeport, which was always her favorite activity.
She liked the unexpectedness of it.

Well, the unexpected ease of *these* patrols.
Back in inner city Cleveland, she and her
teammates rarely had time to do more than
grab a protein bar before racing to the next
emergency. On top of that was a general air
of hostility that greeted them around the
city. Oh, not every person hated the police.
Not by a long shot. But there had been
enough people who did that she had needed

to constantly put up her guard.

Her days in Bridgeport had more to do with serving the community than with protecting the population from those intent on doing them harm.

After the first couple of rocky interactions, she'd begun to get the hang of simply talking to citizens and learning about their needs. For her there was nothing like walking along the bike trail and talking to folks, visiting the local parks and helping redirect teens who looked like they were a little too bored, and the various house calls they often did together.

She had been in Bridgeport a year now and it was amazing how much she'd gotten used to the slower pace of her job. Oh, there was still stress. And it definitely wasn't Mayberry. But she also hadn't pulled her gun in weeks, and she and Dylan had begun to have a friendly banter about where to eat during each shift. Back in Cleveland, she'd just been trying to keep up with all the calls. It was definitely a change of pace that she appreciated.

After showering, she went to their loft's spacious kitchen, which had become their go-to place to reconnect. To her surprise, her three roommates were all gathered around the table, glasses of rosé in hand.

"What's going on?"

"We're choosing dresses for the party Shannon's parents are throwing for her in Spartan," Kimber said. "If you want a say instead of all of us picking something out for you to wear, go grab a glass a wine and join us."

"When is this again?"

"June," Jennifer said.

"Am I the only one who thinks it's a little crazy to be worrying about what we're wearing two months in advance?"

Kimber lifted her chin. "Yes."

"Come on."

"It's actually only about six weeks from now, Traci," Jennifer said. "The party is the second week in June and it's already near the end of April."

She still thought it was early, but she wasn't willing to argue that point. "Fine. I'm in, though I thought this was going to be a low-key event," Traci said as she bypassed the wine and grabbed a beer.

Shannon's smile faltered as Traci sat down on the couch next to her. "Well, um, I know I told you that." She started talking faster, her accent thickening with every third word. "To be fair, this kind of thing is low-key for my mother. But since Dylan and I had such a small wedding here, I'm afraid my mom has gotten it into her head to make it kind of a big deal."

"What does her low-key, big deal event mean, exactly?" She held out a hand before Kimber got all testy and told her that she was being selfish. "I promise, I'm not trying to be difficult. I just don't have any experience with this. We didn't have fancy parties at the group home and I hang around mostly male cops all day. They talk about sports."

"It means the party is at a country club," Jennifer said.

"And we're all going to be wearing cocktail dresses."

Warning bells started going off in her head. "Please tell me that we aren't wearing matching gowns or anything."

"No," Shannon said. "Of course not." Pushing the fashion catalog they'd all been looking at to one side, she added, "But, um, my mother wanted everyone to know right away how special you girls are to me. She kind of asked if all our dresses to be a little alike. Like all the same color or style."

"That sounds like bridesmaids dresses to me."

"Oh, who cares if they are?" Kimber asked. "It's just a dress for one night."

Traci put down her beer. "Shannon, I

107

want to go and all, but don't you think your mom is being pretty pushy? This party is supposed to be about you and Dylan, not her."

Looking pained, Shannon added, "For some reason, my mother feels bad that she didn't adopt all three of us instead of just me."

"She shouldn't, though. The adoption agency is the one who separated us, not your parents."

"I know, but sometimes even when your head tells you one thing, your heart says another," Shannon said. "I know getting dressed up isn't really your thing, but maybe you could look at this party as my parents' way of welcoming everyone into the family? Would that help at all?"

Not really. Traci was about to ask how much these not-dressy dresses were going to cost when she caught sight of both Jennifer and Kimber giving her death stares.

Then she had to admit that the cold, hard, truth was that she was jealous. Shannon had grown up with people fussing over her. Wanting to spend thousands of dollars to celebrate her. The comparison pinched, but it also wasn't anything that she hadn't tried to come to grips with before.

She took another sip of beer instead and

pasted what she hoped was an interested smile on her face. "So, what color are all of you thinking of?"

"Since it's in June, we were thinking red," Shannon said. ""What do y'all think of that?"

"You want us in red?" Traci wore grays, ivories, and black. Red was not in her comfort zone.

"Mom suggested yellow but I wasn't up for that," Shannon said. "I wanted something bright and cheery." She smiled at Jennifer. "Besides, I think red would be flattering on all of us." Glancing at Traci again, that smile faltered. "Or, maybe pink? I do like dark pink."

"I like either color just fine," Kimber said.

"Kimber, you aren't allowed to have a say. You look good in everything."

"Not everything."

Kimber was a model. People paid her money to wear clothes. Of course she could do red.

"What about you, Jen?" Shannon asked. "Tell me honestly."

"This is such a sweet idea of your parents. I'll wear whatever you want me to."

"Traci?" Shannon asked at last.

Even that one word was filled with tension, which she felt terrible about. Deciding to make a joke, she said, "Even though I think I look best in navy blue, I'll be happy in red."

"Believe me, I might have chosen navy but Dylan would have grumbled. He doesn't want to wear his dress uniform or anything resembling that."

"Show Traci the designs we've been looking at," Kimber prodded.

Shannon pushed over a two-inch-thick magazine with about a dozen pages dog-eared. Looking excited again, she started flipping through pages. "First, I was thinking about strapless, since my gown is strapless, but then I saw these halter-style dresses. Those look more comfortable. What do y'all think?"

Gesturing toward her curves, Jennifer said, "I vote for the halter."

"That's great with me," Traci added.

"Me, too, sweetie," Kimber murmured to Shannon. "This party is gonna be great. I'm looking forward to it."

"I can't wait," Shannon said. "It's going to be so pretty. And I'm so excited about my mom being so supportive, too. We're talking on the phone every day now."

Traci had long since resigned herself to not having parents, but there were moments like this when she realized just how much she envied Shannon's good fortune in getting adopted. Usually, she pushed her envy to one side. But there were times, such as this moment, when she wondered again why her two sisters had gotten adopted so quickly but she never, had.

Had she really been that terrible of a baby?

"Traci?" Jennifer prodded. "Did you hear my question? Do you want to have pork tenderloin tomorrow night?"

"Sure. That sounds good," she replied.

"What do you think about roasted asparagus? It's in season now. Or we could have Brussel sprouts," Jennifer continued, just like spring vegetables really mattered. "Do you like them? Some people don't."

She couldn't do this now. She couldn't talk any more about vegetables and matching dresses. Just as she was feeling like the walls were closing in, her cell phone chirped.

She reached for it like the house was on fire. "Sorry . . . Oh! I've got to take this." Walking to the other room, she wondered if she was being saved from her dark thoughts or about to be thrown into another round of insecurities.

Because Dr. Matt Rossi was on the phone. He'd called after all.

"Hello?"

Matt breathed a sigh of relief. For a moment, he'd thought she was going to let his call go straight to voice mail. "Traci, hi. It's Matt. Matt Rossi." He stopped himself in the nick of time from saying he was Gwen's doctor. Jeez, he was nervous.

"Hey. I was wondering if you were going to call."

"I was wondering if you'd answer when I did."

She laughed. "What's going on?"

He leaned his elbows on the railing of his deck and smiled. He kind of loved how she was always business all the time. Did the woman ever just relax and kick up her heels? "Well, it's not work."

"What is it about?"

"My brother is getting married in six weeks. My whole family is in full wedding mode."

"Mine, too. I mean, my sister Shannon is having a ceremony in June. Your call just saved me from another fifteen-minute discussion about bridesmaid dresses."

He chuckled. "Not your favorite thing to talk about?"

"No. Not even close. But, it's kind of fun, in a strange way, I guess. Shannon is happy."

"My sister loved wedding planning. Most girls do, I guess."

"Not this one. When I get married, I'm going to vote for a justice of the peace."

"My mother wouldn't talk to me for a month if I did that." He cleared his throat. "Anyway, here's why I called. Would you be my date for the wedding?"

"Planning ahead, are we?"

"Not so far. They're hoping for a quick wedding. In six weeks. Plus, there's actually something else involved."

"Which is . . ."

"Dancing is involved. Waltzing."

To his surprise, she burst out laughing. "I cannot even believe this."

"What?"

"Until I moved to Bridgeport, I was hardly aware that people outside of *Dancing with the Stars* actually did those dances. But now I live above a ballroom dance studio. I'm surrounded by it."

"So, you know someone who teaches ballroom dancing?"

"I sure do," she said. "My sister Shannon."

"That's great. Do you already know how to waltz?" He closed his eyes. Wow, he sounded annoyingly hopeful.

"Uh, no. Waltzing isn't really my thing."

"Oh."

"But, um, I could give it a try, I guess."

Now her voice was sounding kind of hopeful, too.

"Traci, would you consider taking a few lessons and waltzing with me at my brother's wedding?" He knew he sounded needy, but what could he do? He was in a bind. Plus, he wanted to get to know Traci better. There was something about her that he found refreshing.

"Um, I don't know, Matt."

"Is it the dancing or me?"

"Whoa. Well, that was direct."

"I figured you'd appreciate directness. Am I wrong?" As one second passed, and then two, he looked out at his backyard. It was adjacent to a pretty good swath of open space, the majority of which had a creek. He loved looking out at the narrow stretch of water and seeing what animals had come to visit.

"I'm starting to realize how you got to be a doctor. You don't mess around, do you?" Her voice had a smile in it. He could practically see her expression. Traci had a way of smiling that was a little faint and a little on edge. Almost like she was amused in spite of her best efforts not to be.

Her question caught him off guard. Not necessarily because she was wrong, but he'd never thought of himself as coming across as especially driven. "I wanted to be a doctor because I wanted to deliver babies. I wanted to do something with my life that was positive. And it is. I've never looked back." He took a breath. "But I'm not as independent in my personal life. The fact is, I love my brother and I know I'm going to love having Marie as a sister-in-law. Just as importantly, I love my parents and try not to disappoint them if I can help it. They want me waltzing at Anthony and Marie's wedding."

"So you're going to waltz."

"Yeah, I am. It's not that big of deal in the grand scheme of things. Just a couple of hours of lessons. Plus, it will make them happy, Traci. I'm not going to be the guy to cause any type of disappointment on their wedding day." Realizing that he needed to give her time, he said, "Will you think about it and give me a call in a day or two?"

"No."

No. Damn. "Well, okay. So, th —"

"Matt, I meant: no, I don't need to think about it. I'll do it."

"Whew. You had me worried there for a minute. Are you sure, though?"

"Dr. Rossi, you might not be able to say no to your parents and siblings, but I sure am not going to be the woman who helps

115

you ruin your brother's wedding day."

"We'll probably have to take a couple of lessons."

"Like I said, I have a sister who can help us out. I'll ask Shannon about her schedule and let you know."

"Thanks."

"No, thank you. I'm not exactly sure why you thought of me when you thought of dancing, but I appreciate it."

Staring out at the creek just beyond his house, he grinned. Traci Lucky was a woman who didn't know her own appeal. It was yet another way that she was refreshing. "Anytime, Traci. I'll look forward to your call."

"I'll be in touch. Bye."

She hung up before he had a chance to respond.

But Matt was fine with that. He was already learning that when it came to Traci Lucky, it was better to take what he could get.

And where she was concerned, that was more than enough.

CHAPTER 12

"There is a bit of insanity in dancing that does everybody a great deal of good."
— EDWIN DENBY

The kitchen at the Bridgeport Women's Center was huge. It was also outfitted with all kinds of modern equipment, thanks to a grant that Ellen had received a couple of years ago. There were stainless steel counters, a walk-in freezer, a huge pantry, a gas range, two ovens, and something called a dish pit, which was essentially a dishwasher.

It was also fairly hot inside. Even though three of the windows were cracked to let in fresh air, it was by far the hottest room in the center.

Gwen was so glad she had on simple black leggings, Keds, and a flowery loose-fitting short-sleeved top. At least she was going to stay relatively comfortable and cool.

"Don't forget to take a break every hour,"

Ellen warned. "You need to take care of yourself and the baby."

"I won't forget," Gwen replied, sharing a look with Dawn. "Thank you, ma'am."

"Of course, dear. I'll see you at dinner." She winked. "I can't wait to taste your creation!"

After the director left, Gwen and Dawn smiled at each other again. Sometimes the things that happened around this place were un-be-*lieve*-able. Never had she been treated with such concern. "Do you ever stop and wonder if Ms. Landers is for real?" she asked.

"All the time. The first two weeks I was here, I could hardly believe the things she was promising me. I was sure she was playing a trick or something."

"And now, here you are. Working in the kitchen."

"Yep. And I even got myself a helper." She braced her hands on her hips. "What do you think? Are you ready to make a King Ranch Casserole?"

Gwen still wasn't sure what that was, but she was willing to help as much as she could. "I'm as ready as I'll ever be."

"That's what I wanted to hear. Now, first things first. You need to boil this chicken." She pointed to two whole birds on a plastic cutting board. Cut them up like I showed you yesterday and put them in the pot with the celery and onion. Got it?"

Gwen wasn't going to lie — those twin naked chickens, raw and wet, made her want to throw up. But she wasn't going to let a little thing like queasiness stop her from learning some skills. Or from earning her keep around the place. "Okay."

Dawn gave her an encouraging smile. "All right, then. Now, while you do that, I'll get started on the sauce." She walked to the pantry and started pulling out items, leaving Gwen alone with a pair of disposable kitchen gloves, a sharp knife, pot of water, and those two chickens.

Taking a deep breath, Gwen put on the gloves, took hold of that knife, and started cutting up those birds. When her stomach lurched as the knife slid into the skin, she breathed deep and forced herself to think of other things.

Things like her progress over the last two weeks.

In some ways, she could hardly believe all the changes that had occurred. Just two weeks ago she'd been living with Hunter, feeling like she was at the end of her rope, and barely getting by.

None of Hunter's friends had seen her as

anything other than a waste of space. They'd treated her like it, too.

And Hunter? When he hadn't been berating her for getting pregnant in the first place, he'd been either forcing himself on her or yelling at her to wait on him hand and foot. Her only relief had been when he was too high to care about anything.

To her shame, she'd begun to be grateful for his drug habit.

She'd hit rock bottom the day before Officer Lucky and her partner had raided the building. After months of refusing Hunter's offers of drugs, she'd given into his pressuring, hoping to escape her life one way or another. When Officer Lucky had tried to get her into that ambulance, all she'd wanted to do was cling to anyone who could help her. Even a cop.

Since arriving at the Bridgeport Women's Center, she'd been taking baby steps. Two days ago, Ellen had asked her to help Dawn in the kitchen, even though Gwen had confided that she had next to no cooking skills. She'd been prepared to be talked down to, but Dawn hadn't cared about her lack of experience. At first, Gwen had only chopped vegetables and washed dishes. But to her surprise, no one seemed to mind that she needed a lot of instruction.

Yesterday afternoon, Dawn had announced that it was time for her to break down a chicken. After getting over her first bout of squeamishness, she did all right. And now, here she was, doing that same task by herself twenty-four hours later.

"Uh-oh," Dawn exclaimed. "I caught you smiling. You must not hate it this job as much as I thought you did."

"I think raw chicken is still gross but I was just thinking that I'm in here doing something productive." Because she caught herself about to put herself down, she stopped and took a deep breath. She didn't have Hunter in her life anymore. She didn't need to be so negative. "I know it's a small thing, but it's a huge step forward for me."

Putting down the wooden spoon, Dawn turned to her. "You do realize that I was brought in here by the police too, right?"

She shook her head. "Really?"

"Every woman in here was brought in here either by the police or a social worker. Everything you are going through now is what half the population of this place has gone through."

The way she phrased it seemed strange. "And the other half?"

"The other half gives up and goes back where they came from, honey."

"That many?"

"Sobriety is hard. Leaving a bad situation for something new and different? Well, some people find that just as difficult to do."

Remembering the complete sense of despair she used to feel, Gwen shuddered. "I really don't want to be in the group that goes back."

"Good."

"Any advice?"

Dawn laughed quietly. "You don't need anything from me."

"Maybe I don't need anything, but I'd appreciate hearing what you have to say. Please?"

"All right, then. Here's my tip. Just keep doing what you're doing. Even when it feels like staying here is too hard, just keep at it. Think of your baby. That's all you can do."

"One step at a time." She plopped the last piece of chicken into the pot of hot water and pulled off her gloves. "It sounds easy but it's how it's done, right?"

"Yep." She picked up her wooden spoon again. "Come over here and I'll show you how to make a roux."

After rinsing off the board and setting it in the sink, she switched places with Gwen.

"First thing, measure —"

Three bells chimed.

"Oh, Lord."

Two bells chimed again, followed by a sharp beep.

Gwen looked around the room. "What's going on?"

"We're in lockdown, sister." Dawn's voice was calm but firm. "Turn off the burners, okay? We've got to go up to our rooms."

Gwen did as she asked. "What did someone do? Oh my gosh, did a woman try to escape or something?"

Dawn stopped in the doorway. "Gwen, no one is going to ever stop you from leaving. That alarm is because someone is trying to force their way in."

"Ladies, now," Ellen called out. "This is not a drill."

"Come on," Dawn said. "We've got to hurry."

Gwen's stomach sank as she hurried up the stairs with the other women. Everyone was completely silent and their expressions were terrified.

Only then did she realize that there was a real good chance that Hunter could be the man who had broken in. He wasn't one to take no for an answer.

And he had a whole lot of reasons to want her silent, especially since he knew she'd do almost anything to save her baby.

123

CHAPTER 13

"Dance first. Think later.
It's the natural order."
— SAMUEL BECKETT

Traci had the lights flashing and the sirens blaring before Dylan had time to end the call with the dispatcher. As she took a right turn with a little too much gusto, her partner cursed under his breath.

"Calm down, Lucky. Getting us killed on the way to the center isn't going to help anyone. Especially not me."

Barely braking through an intersection, she didn't bother to spare him a look. "You know what's going through my mind. That piece of crap Hunter is out on bail. And, remember, I told you that he contacted Gwen last week."

"There's a lot of women there, Traci. Gwen isn't the only one who has a danger-ous ex. Get your head on straight and slow down," Dylan said before getting back on his radio.

Dylan was right. She knew he was right. Traci also knew she was way too involved. She couldn't fix Gwen, only help her get connected with the people who could help her get back on her feet.

But, that didn't mean she was ready to stand to one side if Gwen was in danger.

"Emerson already arrived. We're close, right?"

"Yeah." Finally, she heeded him and slowed.

"Thank you." He mumbled something else under his breath that was probably good that she didn't hear. "Are you good?"

"Yeah."

"What's with you and this girl, anyway? The first time I saw you visiting her at the hospital, it looked like you would've rather been getting your teeth pulled."

He wasn't too far off the mark. "She reminds me of me."

"How so? I didn't know you had a drug problem."

"I didn't."

"So, what? You have an abusive ex?"

Realizing that he wasn't going to give up, she said, "My birth mother experimented with drugs and alcohol when she was pregnant with me. I was born an addict."

"Shannon, too?"

"No. I mean, I don't think so. Not with Kimber either. I was part of her experimental phase, I guess."

"I'm sorry."

"I'm fine. But that's the answer to your question. I started out wanting to help this girl's baby. But now . . . I kind of want to help her too." At last, she pulled to a stop in front of the center.

Two other squad cars were there, illustrating that her partner had been right. The situation was urgent, but there hadn't been a need to drive like a bat out of hell.

Dylan opened the door. Traci did the same.

Emerson met them as they approached the building.

" 'Bout time you got here, kids."

"Don't egg her on," Dylan warned. "I had to tell Lucky at least five times to slow down."

"Never mind that. What's going on?" Traci asked. "Where do you need us?"

"Nothing to do," Emerson replied. "Somebody's ex decided to force his way in. When the guard questioned him, he took off."

"That's all you know?"

"No. Suspect was a white Caucasian male,

126

likely between twenty-four and twenty-eight years of age. Looked strung out, but it could just be his normal way." Turning more serious, he gestured toward the front entrance. "Filmore is looking at the tapes with the administrator right now."

"See? Lucky? It could be anyone."

Her partner was right. That description could fit a lot of people. However, it also didn't rule out Hunter Benton. "We'll see."

"I was just about to go in and talk with some of the women," Emerson said. "Traci, would you mind coming in as well? They might say more to you."

"That works for me," Traci said. "Dylan, you good?"

"Yeah. I want to stay out here until Filmore gets an ID."

"It might be a minute," Emerson warned.

Dylan grinned as he pulled out his phone. "That's okay, I need a minute. Shannon texted me when we were on our wild ride. I need to call her back real quick."

Traci smiled as she hastily followed Emerson inside the Center. Shannon was in full party planning mode. Kimber had said that their girl was on the phone most of the night before talking to her mother about food for the party. She was fairly certain that discussing chicken versus pasta was the last thing that Dylan was going to want to talk about — though, who knew? He was putty where Shannon was concerned.

"Officer Lucky!"

She turned to see Gwen approaching. Today, she was wearing a loose, printed blouse, black leggings, and white Keds. She looked adorable and pregnant. She also looked scared to death.

Hoping to calm her down, Traci smiled. "Look at your shirt! Tiny daisies on your clothes suits you."

"Someone donated this." She ran a hand along the edge of her top. "I wouldn't have thought it was me, but I think it kind of is."

"I definitely think it is." Turning serious, she said, "How are you doing? Hanging in there?"

"I would say pretty good but now I don't know. The alarms went off when I was working in the kitchen with Dawn. Next thing I knew, we were in lockdown."

"That'll wake you up, huh?"

"It about gave me a heart attack." She gestured toward Emerson who was talking with two women. "That cop said that an officer and Ms. Landers are looking at tapes right now."

Traci nodded. "That's correct. Officer Filmore is really good, Gwen. He'll find out who was here."

Gwen lowered her voice. "Officer Lucky, what if it was Hunter?"

"We don't know it was."

"But what if it was?"

"If it was him, then we'll deal with it, right? You're not alone anymore." Traci waved a hand, gesturing to the long table in the dining room and the soft, comfortable couches in the room where they were sitting. "This place is really nice. You've got people here to support you, three meals a day, and top of the line security. I can't think of a better place for you to be."

"I guess."

"I *know* I'm right."

Dylan came up behind her. "Modesty isn't Officer Lucky's strong suit," he teased. "I'm Officer Lange. I don't know if you remember, but we met a while ago."

"I remember." She eyed him warily.

He pulled out a chair. "Let's all sit down."

Gwen sat immediately.

After double-checking with Emerson to make sure he didn't need her help, Traci joined them. Noticing that Gwen looked pale and tense again, she spoke to Dylan first. "So, what did Shannon want?"

"She wanted to know what I thought about pasta primavera. Why?"

"No reason."

He narrowed his eyes. "Wait a minute. You knew that's why Shannon was calling, didn't you?"

"I could say no, but I'd be lying."

"You could have warned me." He turned to Gwen. "I'm engaged to Officer Lucky's sister."

"Really? That's cool."

Traci smiled too. "It really is . . . except that now I hear about the party to celebrate their wedding from both my sister and my partner."

"Don't listen to a word she says. Officer Lucky loves it," Dylan retorted just as Ellen Landers and Officer Filmore walked out of her office. Both looked serious.

Dylan stepped forward. "Do you have a name?"

"We do," Filmore said before looking at Gwen.

Gwen jumped to her feet. "Oh my gosh! Was it Hunter? Was he here?" Tears formed in her eyes. "What was he trying to do?"

Ellen Landers shook her head. "It wasn't Hunter Benton, Gwen."

"Are you sure?" Gwen swiped a tear that had fallen down her cheek.

"I'm positive." The director sighed. "But that doesn't mean someone else here wasn't affected. I'm afraid you're going to have to head back to your room, dear."

Gwen seemed frozen. "I'll walk her to the stairs, Ellen," Traci said. Wrapping an arm around the girl, she half-guided, half-pushed her into the hall.

When they were alone, Traci looked at her in the eye. "Calm down."

"But I was so sure."

"To be honest, I was worried, too. But tonight isn't your nightmare. It's someone else's." She lowered her voice even further. "Do you hear what I'm saying?"

At long last, Gwen nodded. "He didn't find me. I'm safe."

"That's right, honey," Traci soothed. "Now go get some rest. I'll call you in a couple of days."

Still looking shaken, Gwen nodded then slowly ascended the stairs.

Traci wondered if the girl felt any better or if she believed she was safe. She hoped Gwent felt secure, because Traci didn't believe she really was very safe. As long as Hunter was still in the area, Gwen was going to be on his radar. If he didn't know where she was already, he was still looking for her. Men like him didn't disappear easily.

CHAPTER 14

"Music is an agreeable harmony for
the honor of God and the permissible
delights of the soul."
— JOHANN SEBASTIAN BACH

The Next Day
He didn't want to answer his cell phone, but experience had taught Matt that it was better to get some things — like a flu shot — over with and move on with his life. "Hi, Mama," he said as he continued to drive down the windy roads of Bridgeport.

"Matteo, what is this girl like?"

That's how his mother was. She didn't believe in small talk with her kids. No, she went right for the jugular every time. "I've told you about her already. She's a cop."

"That tells me nothing. I hardly know anything at all about this girl. What's her name?"

"Traci."

"No, her full name."

"Traci Lucky."

His mother's voice rose. "Lucky?"

"Yeah, Mama. You know, like a four-leaf clover," he added as he came to a stop.

"Lucky-like-a-clover isn't Italian."

"You're right. It isn't, because she's not Italian."

"What nationality is she?"

"I'm not sure. That hasn't come up yet."

"Really? I find that hard to believe."

He mentally rolled his eyes. "Mama, of course you would. But, I promise, no one else would think such a thing. People don't go around asking personal questions about other people's heritage."

"Saying you're Italian isn't exactly personal. What is her religion? Is she Catholic?"

Oh, for Pete's sakes. "Mama, I don't know that either. And no, I am not going to ask."

"So all you know about her is that she's a cop. That doesn't seem like enough information. She's going to be your date at your brother's wedding, you know."

"First of all, it's a wedding, not a family reunion. Secondly, I know that she's a cop, she lives in a house with her sisters and that house is also a dance studio. I also know that she cares enough about other people that she goes above and beyond to help

133

them. Isn't that enough?"

"I suppose so. Those are very good qualities," she said grudgingly.

"I thought so too, Mama." Yes, he was being sarcastic.

"You haven't told me what she looked like. Is she a pretty girl?"

"Yes. She's about five and a half feet tall, has brown hair, brown eyes, and she likes to run."

"So, she could be a little Italian."

Matt was glad he was on the phone. There was only so much of this round and round conversation that a man could take. "Sorry, Mama, but I've got to go now. I'm almost at the dance studio."

"Oh. Oh!" Her voice turned warmer. "That's good. Well, call me when you leave."

"No, I'll call you tomorrow."

"But —"

"Good night, Mama."

"All right," she said around a sigh. "Good night, Matt. Have a good time."

When he hung up, he breathed a sigh of relief. She was both his greatest love and his greatest source of exhaustion. She always wanted more information than he could give her, which always left him feeling as if he was letting her down. Of course, it was better than how their conversations used to go — back in the day he would reveal too much and then come to regret it.

One woman he'd dated had said she'd felt as if his mother was in their bedroom, she knew so much. Of course it hadn't been that bad, but that sly comment had given him reason to guard his tongue more often.

Just as he was walking to the door of Dance With Me, his phone buzzed again. He wasn't on call, but he checked his phone anyway. The hospital staff knew there were a few of his high-risk patients who he would want to talk to no matter what.

When he saw who it was, he rolled his eyes but answered it anyway. "Hey."

"Are you there yet?" his sister Bennie asked.

"I'm about to walk in. What's up?"

"I'm calling to give you warning that our mother wants to know all about this police-woman."

"Policewoman? I believe that term ended at the end of Angie Dickensen's show. The correct term is police officer."

"Whatever. Has our mother called you yet to give you the third degree?"

"I just got off the phone with her. You know she wasn't going to wait to get information."

"Oh. How did it go?"

135

"About how you would expect. I left her wanting more."

"She seems to think that a cop isn't the right girl for you," Bennie said.

"I got that idea too, but I have no idea why she would think such a thing."

"Um, I believe she said something to the effect that you bring babies into the world while she locks them up."

He felt like hitting his head against the wall. "So, our mother has officially gone crazy."

"Pretty much," Bennie agreed. "I'll run interference as much as I can."

"I appreciate it."

"I do have your best interests at heart here."

"I know you do, which is why I know you're going to understand when I tell you that I've got to go. Bye, sweetheart," he said as he entered the front door of the building.

He walked in, closed it quietly behind him, and took a cleansing breath.

And when he opened his eyes, he found three women sitting on a window seat side by side. Every one of them was watching him with an amused expression.

"Hey," he said, feeling embarrassed. "Have you all been sitting here a while?"

"Long enough to see that you talk on your

phone more than most girls I know," a wholesome looking woman with bright blue eyes said.

"Long enough to hear you call that person sweetheart," a strikingly beautiful woman with warm bronzy skin said.

"That was my sister."

"You call your sister sweetheart?" that was from a pretty blonde in an emerald green flowy dress.

"She's my little sister. Bennie."

"Bennie?" the blonde asked.

"It's short for Bernadette," he explained. Boy, it was really ironic. He'd hated giving his mother any information about Traci, but here he was telling these three strangers all about his sister.

"I'd go by Bennie, if my name was Bernadette, too," said Traci who had just appeared in gray slacks, low heels, and a black sweater.

After taking a moment to appreciate how pretty she looked, he turned to the women again. "Since you now know all about my sister, I should probably introduce myself. I'm Matt Rossi."

"Dr. Matteo Rossi," Traci corrected. "Matt, please meet my sisters Kimber and Shannon and my sister-in-law Jennifer."

"My brother Dylan just married Shannon," Jennifer explained.

"Dylan is also my partner in the police department," Traci added.

"I see." He stuffed his hands in his pockets, since he was sort of feeling like he was on display.

"It's nice to meet you as well," the woman in the green dress said. "As Traci said, I'm Shannon, and I heard that you two need to learn to waltz for a wedding."

"We do." He smiled at Traci. "It's in six weeks."

"I think it's time we got started, then. We've got a lot to do." She held out a hand. "Traci, Matt, shall we dance?"

Matt didn't know whether to take Shannon's hand, take Traci's, or turn and walk away.

But then Traci solved the problem. "We've got this," she whispered before taking her sister's hand, winking at Kimber and Jennifer, and beckoning him to follow them into the dance studio.

Like a duckling following his mother, Matt followed along.

He had no idea what was about to happen, but he was now ready for anything.

Including holding Traci in his arms very soon.

CHAPTER 15

PASO DOBLE: *The man dances as if he were the bull, and the woman as if she were the bullfighter.*

There had been a number of times in her life when Traci had stopped, looked at herself in the mirror, and wondered how she'd gotten to such a place.

It had happened during her fourth or fifth foster home, when she'd realized that her foster parents weren't very smart or very hands on. They'd simply done the minimum that was expected of them so they could get checks from the government.

It had happened when she'd gotten into the group home — the place that she'd been terrified of being sent to for most of her life — and realized that it was a better situation than she'd ever dreamed was possible.

She'd had that same feeling of awe and confusion when she'd graduated first in her class from the police academy. And, of course, when she'd gotten off the phone with Shannon for the first time.

And now, here she was, feeling that same tingly, confusing sensation again.

Because she was literally looking in the mirror and seeing how she was dancing with Matt Rossi. Though they didn't know the steps, were hopelessly clumsy, and weren't very good at listening to directions, there was something special between them. It was evident in the way they stood together. In the way Matt curved his hand around her waist. In the way that they laughed more than corrected each other. In the way that they looked so good together. Like they fit.

"One last song and then we'll call it a night," Shannon said as "Save the Last Dance" came on. "Don't forget to start on the second beat. Here we go. And . . . one," she said, waving her hand to the beat.

As Shannon continued to count, hovering around them like a hummingbird, Traci looked up into Matt's eyes. "I think we're actually dancing."

His lips quirked. "In a matter of speaking," he said.

"No, I looked at us in the mirror. We look pretty good." She smiled. "You should look. Go ahead."

"No, you should both count the steps," Shannon corrected. "Wait, now, one, two-three, one . . . two-three. There you go. You're back on the beat."

"I didn't even know we had left it," Matt said.

"Me, neither." She giggled. *Giggled!*

"Umph." Matt grunted.

"Sorry!" she exclaimed, realizing that she'd just stepped on his toes.

"You're little. I didn't feel a thing."

"Really?" She lifted a brow.

"Okay, hardly anything."

"Next time, when I'm wearing real high heels, I'll be more careful."

"High heels, huh?"

"Hey, what is that tone for?"

"Nothing. I'm just trying to imagine you all dolled up."

"I'll look okay."

She looked so sweet, he leaned closer. "I'm thinking better than that, Traci."

And, her heart just melted . . . as they drew to a stop.

"We're done for the night," Shannon called out. "Thank goodness."

Matt dropped his hands like he'd been lit on fire. "Were we that bad, Shannon?"

"Not at all. But you two together are a challenge. You don't listen."

"Wow, Shannon." Traci was kind of hurt.

"Don't wow, me," she said as she turned off the ballroom beats program. "You know what was going on." She turned to face them. "Matt, it was a pleasure. Traci, turn off the lights when you're done, would you? I'm going upstairs to get a glass of wine."

"Oh, uh. I think we drove your sister to drink."

"Don't worry about it. Shannon's just a little high-strung right now. That's all."

He laughed. "Do you really believe that or do you just want me to?"

"Neither. I'll go apologize to her after you leave. But I promise, this isn't anything too new. She's already tried to teach me to dance before — with disastrous results. I'm hopeless, can't touch my toes, and forget dance steps minutes after she tells them to me."

Matt walked to the doorway. "For the record, I don't think we're that hopeless."

"Oh?"

"I did what you suggested and looked in the mirror. We do look pretty good together. You weren't wrong about that."

She knew a different girl would have a better comeback, or at least a cute thing to reply. She simply smiled. "I'll see you next time I bring Gwen by your office."

"Yeah. If not before. Get some rest, officer."

"You too, Dr. Rossi. Thanks."

He waved a hand and walked out of the building. When he got into his car, she turned off the studio's lights, then walked to the window to watch him back out and then turn left onto the street.

She was still thinking about him while she walked upstairs to the loft — and came right smack into Shannon, Jennifer, and Kimber all sitting on the barstools at the kitchen. All three were watching her.

"So, we heard it went great," Jennifer said.

Traci darted a look at Shannon. She was sipping her glass of wine.

"It didn't actually go *great*. I'm afraid Matt and I aren't real good listeners."

"Y'all hardly listen at all," Shannon groused. "I've taught thirteen-year-olds with more control over themselves."

"We had control."

"No, you were flirting," Shannon said.

Kimber chuckled. "I guess this dancing thing is working out for you, Trace. Who knows, maybe you just snagged yourself a doctor."

"Oh, shut up. It's not like that." Well, she might not care what his occupation was, but she couldn't disagree with Kimber's assessment of their chemistry. There absolutely had been something *perfectly* hot between them.

"You two, leave her alone," Jennifer said. "I thought they looked sweet together."

"How did *you* see us?"

"I went down and spied on you," Jennifer said with a grin.

"Now who's acting like she's thirteen?"

"Nothing wrong with that. I was a *great* teenager."

"I'm sure you were. I bet you were perfect," Traci retorted as she opened the refrigerator. "Hey, do we have anything to eat? I'm starving."

"Look in the second shelf," Jennifer said. "I saved you and Shannon plates."

Finding the plastic container with her name on it, Traci grinned. Jennifer had made chicken piccata again. "I love you, Jennifer!"

"I know. Eat now. You, too, Shannon."

"Okay. So, does everyone want to look at the flower arrangements I decided on?"

Kimber, Jennifer, and she all shared a look. But because they were good sisters, they all smiled weakly.

"I can't wait," Kimber said.

"Oh, yay! You're going to love the bouquets."

And Traci's heart warmed again at the look of delight that shone in everyone's eyes.

CHAPTER 16

"Dancing: The highest intelligence
in the freest body."
— ISADORA DUNCAN

"I can't thank you enough, doctor," Mr.
Davidson said as he shook Matt's hand for
the third time. "We were scared to death
there for a while."

"Alaina is the one who did all the work,"
Matt said. "It was a tough delivery but your
little girl is a fighter. And so is your wife."

Roland Davidson grimaced as he turned a
little paler. "I don't think I can go through
this again."

Matt tried not to smile but failed miserably. *Every* new father didn't say such
things, but a lot of them did. And it made
him grin every time. Women really were
tougher than men.

"You did great. You were very encouraging. I'm sure Alaina will be singing your praises for months."

"I don't know about that. I'm sure going to be singing hers, though," he said with a fond look at his wife.

Matt smiled. "You two take it easy, and I'll stop by on my rounds tomorrow morning."

"Then we can take Kylie home?" Alania asked with a look of hope.

"I don't see why you wouldn't. She's doing great. All we have to do is make sure Alaina gets a little rest during the night." After reminding them both about some things to watch out for, Matt left the room.

Once he stepped into the hallway, he paused and took a deep breath. The delivery had been a little touch and go for a while. No delivery was textbook, but Alaina's had been especially problematic. He wanted nothing more than to get to his car and collapse at home.

"Dr. Rossi, is everything going all right in 4A? Do you need help?"

He lifted his eyes to see Dana heading toward him. Dana was new to the obstetrics floor. She was also a recent nursing school graduate, slightly ditzy, and had made it known from the moment they'd met that she wouldn't be opposed to the two of them dating.

He didn't often date medical personnel, but he wasn't interested in anything with her, and he didn't like the looks she'd been sending him. There was just something about an overly flirty woman that had never appealed to him. She tried his patience like little else.

"Alaina's doing well. Her husband might need some checking up on, though. I thought he was going to pass out on me for a hot minute."

She grinned. "That's when I wish I could hand out a shot of bourbon to these new dads."

He chuckled. "You're right, Dana. Sometimes all these dads need is a shot of liquid courage. Course, there are times when I might be tempted to partake, too." He glanced at his phone and realized another hour had passed since the last time he'd checked. It was now closing in on 1:00 A.M. "I'm out of here. Don't forget that Nemeitz is on call."

"Yes, doctor." Just as he turned away, she said, "Oh, when are you on-call again, Matt?"

Matt? If Marissa heard Dana call him by his first name while they were on duty, she'd give her a real talking to. He didn't mind the use of his name as much as the flirty tone in which she said it.

Instead of replying, he kept walking. He hoped she would think that he hadn't heard her. Because if she pressed him again, he would probably put her firmly in her place, and he didn't want to do that.

Taking the stairs down to the parking lot instead of waiting for the elevator, he fought a yawn. Then, just as he was walking out, he spied a pair of cops walking by a pair of EMTs and a man on a stretcher.

One of the cops was Traci.

He paused, caught her eye.

She blinked, smiled slightly, then returned to the team she was walking with.

There was something about Traci's single-mindedness that he loved — it was actually only one of the many things he really liked about her.

CHAPTER 17

*"Love is two people
dancing in the kitchen."*

"Was that your doctor buddy you've been dancing with?" Dylan asked Traci as they walked back to the cruiser.

"Yes, that was Dr. Rossi."

"Come on, I know you don't always call him that. What's his first name, again? Mark . . . or something?"

"It's Matt. Matteo, actually. He's Italian."

"Shannon said he's a nice guy."

"He is." Thinking of how Matt was continually going above and beyond for pretty much everyone in his life, she added, "He's taking waltzing lessons because his future sister-in-law asked him to. Who does that?"

"Probably a guy who doesn't want to get on his sister-in-law's bad side."

Getting in the passenger side of the vehicle, she said, "Ha-ha, Lange. But listen, I'm being serious. Between those dancing lessons and how kind he was to Gwen, he's making me rethink the male half of the population."

"Have you had that many bad experiences dating?"

"No, not dating. Just in general, I guess. It comes with the territory, I think."

"Which territory? Cop territory or growing up in a group home territory?"

Ouch. She was so used to everyone pussyfooting around her past, she sometimes forgot that good friends like him didn't see a need to. "Both. But, mainly growing up in a group home."

He was driving back to the station house. They'd agreed to eat there, catch up on paperwork for an hour or two, and then head back out until the end of their shift.

Dylan glanced her way as he drove down West Bridgeport Ave. "What was it like? Were you scared all the time?"

"No." Remembering how scrappy she'd been, she chuckled softly. "I had a hell of an attitude."

He looked pleased. "You were a tough kid, huh?"

"Oh yeah. Looking back, I think I had a chip on my shoulder from the time I was four or five. I went around practically daring anyone to look at me the wrong way." When he merely glanced at her again, she continued. "By the time I got to Mrs. Henderson's, I'd been in something like ten foster homes. The social workers knew it was stressing me out, and not all of those foster families were great, you know?"

He nodded. "In my experience, few can be called *great.*"

That had been her experience as well. Hating that she sounded so pitiful, she lifted her chin. "My social worker was a really nice guy. He used to take me out to breakfast once a month — at six-thirty."

"Early."

"It was so early! I would get really annoyed about it, too. I used to always whine and complain that no one else's social worker made them eat before eight. Now of course I realized that was the only time he could fit me in — because it was off the clock. The truth of the matter was that no one else had a regular breakfast date with their social worker." She sighed. "Anyway, one day Charlie said that Mrs. Henderson had an opening and he wanted me to go visit the group home with him the next day."

"I guess you went and that was that?"

"I wish it had been that way, but it wasn't. Like I said, I had a chip on my shoulder. I kept acting like I was sure someone was going to adopt me and I wouldn't need to be in that home. But, of course, no one adopted me."

"Damn, Traci. Sometimes you break my heart."

"I'm a success story, Officer. Don't cry for me. But, to answer your question, through the years, I met a lot of people who I didn't have much time for. Then I met Shannon and Kimber."

"And Dr. Rossi."

"Yeah. And you. You're a good one, too."

"Now you're going to make me blush."

"At least it's dark, so I won't have to see it."

Just as they were about to pull into the station's parking lot, their radio squawked. "Better turn back around Dylan," she said as she picked up the handset to report in. "Our mountain of paperwork is going to have to wait."

Dylan flicked on the lights as she started calling out directions. They were off again.

CHAPTER 18

"Classical dancing is like being a mother:
if you've never done it, you can't imagine
how hard it is."
— HARRIET CAVALLI

Ten Days Later
Gwen had been living in her own fantasy
dream world. There was no other explana-
tion. After her false alarm — which had
involved a lady named Stacey, Gwen had
decided to simply live her life. She'd begun
to work more in the kitchen with Dawn and
spent her spare time napping and dreaming
about being a mom.

But then she'd started to get letters again.
To her shame, every time she got another
note from Hunter, she'd simply shredded it
and thrown it out. The last two she hadn't
even bothered to open.

Even worse, she hadn't let Officer Lucky
know about the additional letters and

hadn't said a single word to Ellen.

But then she opened this morning's note and realized she had been a fool. Denial wasn't going to work anymore.

"I really wish you would have told me about these notes and sightings from the very first," Ellen told Gwen. "Your refusal to share information honestly and openly has put a lot of people in danger."

Standing in front of the administrator's desk like a kid in trouble with her teacher, Gwen clasped her hands behind her back. Each word felt like a sharp pin pricking her skin. "I'm sorry, Ellen. I kept thinking Hunter would lose interest and he would forget about me and go away."

"Men like him rarely do that, especially if you don't respond. Predators like Hunter thrive on seeing you scared. If you don't respond, they miss out on that little thrill."

"Oh boy. And here I thought ignoring him was the best thing to do."

"I'm afraid all ignoring his notes did was make him angrier — and gave you a false sense of security while you put your head in the sand."

Gwen didn't exactly think she'd been doing that, but she couldn't deny that she had hoped that eventually Hunter would have moved on. "I really am sorry. I realize that if he shows up here, I'm going to put everyone in this place in danger."

"You already have, dear." Ellen frowned at the sheet of paper she was holding, Gwen's eighth or ninth letter, and by far the most threatening. "From what you told me about his first notes, he's certainly escalating."

"Yes, ma'am."

"He doesn't want to let you go," she continued, her voice hard. She raised her chin. "You know that, right?"

"Yes, ma'am."

Ellen eyed her for a long moment before picking up her cell phone. "Have a seat, dear."

She wasn't going to kick her out. "I really am sorry."

"I know you are." She smiled weakly. "This is hard but it isn't anything we haven't gone through before. Plus, we have friends in high places, right?"

"We do?"

"I'm going to call Officer Lucky and see what she thinks."

Gwen didn't really think Officer Lucky was going to put her neck out any further for her. "She's going to think the same as you, Ellen. That I made a really bad mistake."

"Yes, she is. And you're going to be lucky if she doesn't give you a real piece of her mind." Ellen raised her eyebrows. "You know what I'm talking about, right?"

"I've already been the recipient of one of her lectures, Ellen."

She groaned and punched in the number.

Gwen could hear it ring four, five, six times before clicking into voicemail.

"Officer Lucky, it's Ellen Landers over at the women's center. I'm sitting here with Gwen Camp, and we think you need to see something she just received. Please call or stop by when you can."

After she hung up, she studied Gwen again, her expression piercing. "Maybe we should talk for a minute about why you didn't tell anyone that these letters continued."

With any other person, she would have probably made up some story but she couldn't lie to Ellen. Not after everything she'd done for her. "At first, I wasn't sure if I wanted to stay away from Hunter."

"I see."

Did she? Gwen wasn't even sure she did herself. Her dependence on the guy embarrassed her, but now that she'd heard from other women in their group meetings, she knew she wasn't alone in her feelings. "He

157

treated me bad. I know he did."

Ellen held up a paper. "Does, right?"

Conceding with a nod, Gwen added, "He *does* treat me bad. I know that. But I was alone, right? Even though Officer Lucky and Melanie and you have been telling me that things are different now, I didn't believe it." Plus, there had been a part of her who had thought that she didn't deserve anyone better. She wasn't special, and she'd made a whole lot of dumb mistakes. Why would she deserve better? Though her mouth had gone dry, she forced herself to continue. "I also kept thinking that maybe he was changing. Or, um, that he could change, if he wanted to."

"Why?"

"Because I've changed."

"What's changed for you?" Ellen asked slowly. "Or do you still feel the same way about Hunter that you used to?"

"I don't. I haven't felt that way for some time. Maybe I never did. But what's changed is me and this baby boy. I don't want to be the type of woman who puts up with bad because she doesn't want to see any good."

"I'm proud of you."

"Nothing to be proud of. Though, do you

think there's anything Officer Lucky can do?"

"He's threatening you. You've got a restraining order against him. Yes, there are things the police can do."

"Then I'll listen to whatever she tells me and apologize about ten times."

Ellen smiled. "She might only make you apologize five times. Eight at the most."

"I hope so." Boy, she'd really messed up. Again.

"Gwen, don't leave the building."

Ellen's warning sent a chill down her spine. If she hadn't already been so on edge, their conversation would have made her take Hunter's notes seriously. "I won't."

After studying her for a long moment, Ellen continued. "Gwen, if Hunter texts you on your new phone, don't respond. Give the phone to me."

"I will. I promise."

"One last thing. And this is most important."

"Yes?" Was Ellen going to remind her that she could be kicked out of the shelter at any time, especially for putting the other women in danger?

Her voice softened. "Don't give up hope, or stop believing in yourself, dear. Things are going to get better for you, Gwen. I promise they will."

"I don't know how you can promise that."

"I can promise because you're worth it, Gwen. You are special and important. I promise you that," she said as she walked around her desk and hugged Gwen tight.

Gwen hugged her back just as tightly. The words were so sweet, and the praise so foreign to her ears that she didn't want to let go.

CHAPTER 19

"Dance is meditation in movement, a walking into silence where every movement becomes prayer."
— BERNHARD WOSIEN

Traci had rarely seen Shannon so irritated. Standing in the middle of her dance studio, all decked out in a black wrap dress with matching heels, Shannon looked like she had just walked off an episode of *Dancing with the Stars*. She even had black eyeliner and red lipstick on.

She would have looked striking if, say, she wasn't scowling at the two of them.

"You know, the three of us can't get much accomplished if you two continue to cut up," Shannon warned. "I thought our first class was frustrating, but you two aren't acting any better tonight."

"Cut up? Who says that anymore?" Traci asked.

"What should I have said? Goof off? Ignore me?" Her eyebrows raised.

Shannon Murphy stood barely taller than five foot two inches in bare feet. In heels, she was maybe five foot six, if she stood up really straight and puffed up her hair. Traci imagined that Shannon's look was exactly opposite of a typical drill sergeant's.

But now, looking at the way she was standing, with her hands on her hips and her tone chilly, Traci decided that Shannon could give those drill sergeants a run for their money.

"I'm sorry," Matt said. "Everything you're saying is exactly right. I'll try to do better."

Shannon's voice softened. "Thank you, Matt. I'll try to explain the steps better too." She glared at Traci. "And, what do you have to say for yourself?"

"I'll try to stop laughing and cutting up, Shannon." Lifting her right arm onto Matt's shoulder, she said, "I think we're ready now."

Shannon glared at her but turned on her heel and strode toward her iPad. "Let's start this again, then."

As Shannon fussed with her iPad, Matt leaned closer to Traci. "You are incorrigible."

"I'm not."

"You are. You're having way too much fun and making me mess up," he whispered.

"Don't put this all on me," she hissed in his ear. "You haven't been a saint either, Dr. Rossi."

"True."

"The music's on, you two. Now, here we go — one, two-three. One, two-three. Hold her firmly, Matt. I promise, she won't break."

Just as Traci was going to say something rude, Matt shook his head. "Come on now. Dance with me, Traci."

Maybe it was that smile. Or the way his dark eyes pulled her in like little else had in her life, or maybe even the sappy words that sounded like the sweetest invitation coming from his lips. Whatever the reason, she kept her arms locked, her eyes on his, and finally listened to her sister guide them around the room.

She and Matt were well proportioned together. She hadn't put on a dress, but she had worn two-inch heels with a pair of dark skinny jeans. Now she was only about four inches shorter than her dance partner. Tall enough to look easily in his eyes and follow him around the room, short enough to feel feminine while she did it.

They took a brief break, then Shannon

put on "Save the Last Dance" again and made them pick up the pace and do a couple of turns.

Slowly, Matt's look of concentration turned warmer. By the time the song ended, she could feel that she was smiling broadly. In spite of everything, they were having fun.

When they drew to a stop, Shannon clapped softly. "When y'all stop joking around and fighting me, you dance well. You two make a lovely couple."

Traci turned to her in shock.

"On the dance floor, Trace." Her voice softened and her West Virginia drawl thickened. "I wish I could have videotaped y'all. Then y'all could've seen what I did. It was beautiful!"

"You're a great teacher, Shannon," Matt said. "If we started looking good, it was because of your patience. I'm sorry about the way we were behaving at first."

She laughed. "Don't worry about it. I think most teachers would say that it's harder to teach family members."

"At least we are family, Shannon. Right?"

"Right." Linking her fingers together, she stretched her arms above her head. "You two were my last class of the night. I'm going to go upstairs and put on sweats. Would you turn off the lights, Traci?"

164

"Yep. Thank you."

Shannon waved a distracted hand as she walked out of the room.

When Traci turned back to Matt, he was smiling at her.

"What?"

"Nothing. Only that the two of you are kind of cute together."

It was on the tip of her tongue to remind him that grown women didn't especially like being called cute. But coming from him? It kind of made her happy. "Cute, huh?"

He nodded. "Shannon is all femininity and you are the opposite."

"Are you saying I'm masculine?"

"No! Hell no. I meant . . . athleticism. Together, the two of you make a good pair."

"Thanks. Even though I was giving her a hard time tonight, I think she's pretty terrific. I love to watch her dance, too."

"Does she ever practice with a partner?"

"No. Sometimes with Dylan, but to be honest, he doesn't pay too much more attention to the steps than I do." Of course, when Shannon was with Dylan, she didn't look like she cared too much about perfect dance steps, either. Instead, she was always looking up at him with shining eyes and standing so close, Traci feared they were going to start making out in front of the big windows lining the street.

"I meant, sometimes, she'll put on her toe shoes and dance ballet."

"She was a ballerina, huh?"

"She says she's a dancer who took years of ballet classes, but she looks like a real ballerina to me. She's so petite, it's fun to see her twirl. Kimber and I kind of think she looks like one of those ballerinas in a musical jewelry box. Well, she would if she would ever put on a tutu, like we keep asking her to."

"If she does, I hope I'm there to see it." He walked over to his jacket and shrugged it on. "In the meantime, how would you feel about joining us for dinner on Sunday?"

"Joining . . . who?"

"My family. Remember how I told you that every Sunday my mom makes a big pot of pasta? Why don't you join us this week?"

"Why?"

"Why not? The food is good, great, even. Plus, it will be great for you to meet everyone."

He wanted her to meet his family? "Matt, just because I'm going to be your date for the wedding, I don't think it means that I need to meet your family, does it?"

"Why wouldn't you want to?"

Because it sounded like a date. Because it

sounded like a serious date. Like a relationship. But she didn't want to be that honest. "Let me double check my schedule and I'll let you know."

"You might be working?"

"Bad guys don't take breaks, Matt." Boy, she hoped Dylan never, ever, ever heard what she just said. He'd give her grief for sounding so cheesy for the next twenty years.

His eyebrows lifted. "Oh. Well, um, I guess you're right. Let me know when you can."

She smiled as she walked to the door. "Have a good night. Fingers crossed that no babies are born tonight."

"Babies don't take breaks either, Lucky. But I should be good since I'm not on call." Before she knew what he was about, he leaned over and kissed her cheek. "Night."

"Night," she whispered as she watched his silhouette disappear down the street.

Hearing noise above her, she sat down on Shannon's chair and thought about their class. The way she'd been so happy in Matt's arms.

And, yes, the way she'd kind of melted into him, then had backed up like a scared, wet cat when he mentioned eating with his family.

Even though he knew a lot of her back-

167

ground, she was sure he didn't really know what his invitation had meant to her. Where he saw family fun, good food, and a girl he was sort of seeing in the middle of it, she saw stumbling blocks.

She would have to answer questions and interact with family members, and she didn't have much experience doing that. And she'd need good table manners, which she hadn't exactly mastered.

What if she failed so badly at one of those things that his family decided to tell him to invite someone else to the wedding?

And then she would be left on her own. Able to do an almost decent waltz.

But would be without a partner to dance it with.

She couldn't think of anything sadder at all.

CHAPTER 20

RUMBA: *Many people consider the rumba to be the most passionate and romantic dance in ballroom. It can be incredibly complex and involves many different hip movements.*

It had been a mistake to confide in Kimber. Traci could only blame it on a moment of weakness. They'd been sitting together at the Corner Café, Traci sipping a double shot mocha latte and Kimber drinking her usual iced black coffee, when Kimber's phone rang. While Traci watched, Kimber had gone from excited, to disappointed, to looking like she wanted to throttle the person on the other end of the line. When her sister had hung up, Traci hadn't been able to resist.

"Who was that?"

"Griffin." Kimber took a fortifying sip of her drink, grimaced, and set it down abruptly. "Griffin Carter."

"Who's — Wait. Isn't he an actor on that show, *What's My Number?*"

"Yes." Looking annoyed, Kimber crossed her legs, fiddled with her drink, then shifted yet again.

Traci was beginning to learn that a lot of movement in her usually cool-as-a-cucumber sister meant that she was seriously agitated. "What did he want?"

"He found out I'm going to be in Palm Springs next week. He wants to drive out and meet me."

Kimber talked about going to Palm Springs the way other people talked about going to the hardware store. "What's wrong with that?"

Kimber's dark-brown eyes flicked toward hers. "First of all, I'm going there to work. I won't have time to see Griffin Carter."

"Is there a second of all?"

"Yes. The only way Carter could have known that I was going to be there is if my agent told him. And that just brings up a whole *other* hill of beans."

"A hill of beans, huh?"

"Stop. It's a good phrase."

"It sounds like a Shannon, West Virginia phrase."

"My mother's mother was real fond of

saying that. I must have picked it up." She stirred the straw in her coffee, then dropped her hand again. "The point is, my agent shouldn't be telling people where I'm gonna be. That isn't right."

"You're right. Are you going to talk to Adam about it?"

"I am." She rolled her eyes. "And then he'll probably pretend he didn't talk to Griffin, and I'll have to pretend that I believe him."

"If you weren't modeling bathing suits and such . . . would you have wanted to see this movie star?"

"He's not a movie star. Just an actor," she corrected. "And, just for the record, I won't be modeling bathing suits, it's ready-to-wear and evening gowns. And, finally . . . no, I wouldn't have wanted to see him."

"Why not? He looks really cute on TV."

"I promise he's not that cute in real life, honey. He's also a lot of work."

"Like how?" She wasn't going to lie. Kimber's high fashion-movie star world was pretty fascinating.

"Griffin is the kind of man who doesn't eat anything that has eyes."

"Pardon me?"

"You know, fish, chicken, cows. He is morally opposed to that."

"He's not the only person to feel that way." Growing up the way she had, Traci was morally opposed to going hungry, but she supposed everyone had their likes and dislikes.

"Furthermore, Griffin doesn't go to places where he isn't gonna get noticed. That means, that he never looks directly at me. He kind of looks right above my shoulder, just in case someone recognizes him."

"Sounds irritating."

"It is. And the worst part of it is that I can't even get a decent free meal out of him while he's ignoring me."

"You eat lots of tofu and vegetarian dishes here."

"I know I do. I like it all just fine, too. But that doesn't mean I don't want a steak or a piece of salmon when I'm out on a date."

Traci wasn't going to touch that. "Other than that . . . is he nice?"

Kimber blinked. "Traci, I just essentially told you that the man talked about me to my agent, is narcissistic, and has views on my love of meat."

"So . . . yes?"

Her lips curved. "You are something else, Lucky. No wonder you're a cop. You never give up." She sighed. "Okay, fine. Yes. I suppose Griffin is nice, in that California, polished man, kind of way."

Looking like she was doing Traci a favor, Kimber added, "He's kind of funny, too. He's got a lot of good stories. And even though we haven't eaten anything decent the two times he's taken me out, he always pays. Not all men can say that."

"I didn't know you've been dating actors when you're on the road."

"I haven't been dating that much. Just every now and then. It's nothing serious. Not like Shannon and Dylan."

Traci heard a note of wistfulness in her voice. That was something she didn't need Kimber to explain. Sometimes, she felt the same way. It wasn't that she *liked* Dylan, it was that Shannon had found a person to love who was perfect for her. They suited each other.

It also didn't hurt that she knew for a fact that Dylan was a real stand-up man. He was kind and treated their sister like she was the best thing he'd ever seen.

"Well, we all can't find a good guy like Shannon has."

"You've gotten close though, right?" Kimber asked.

"I'm not dating anyone. I mean, not anyone seriously."

"You're going to that wedding with Dr.

Charming and spending your free time dancing with him."

"That's true, but . . . I don't know."

"What's wrong with him? He's handsome, takes dancing lessons for his brother, and is a doctor. You'd be set."

"He's not perfect."

"He's not?"

"Oh, stop. And listen. Even if he was perfect — which he isn't, by the way, we're too different." She frowned, thinking of his Sunday dinner invitation that she still hadn't responded to. "Actually, I kind of don't know what to do about him. Matt invited me over to his parents' house on Sunday night."

"He already wants you to meet his family?"

"Kind of. I mean, I guess if would be good since I'll be seeing everyone at the wedding and all."

"What's bad about it?" Her voice softened. "Are you worried that he's getting too serious too fast?"

"Not exactly. I'm uh, worried about eating a meal with them."

Her eyes widened. "Do they not eat meat either? Geez. What's this world coming to?"

"They eat meat, Kimber. It's just that, um, I don't really have company manners,

174

you know?"

Kimber stared at her blankly. "No."

"Matt's a doctor. So is his brother. His parents have money."

"And?"

Even though she knew was sounding a little crazy, she continued. "And, I don't know, what if they put out a bunch of forks and spoons? I'm not going to know which one to use!" And then they'll know that she shouldn't have anything to do with him.

"You know that you're a cop, right?"

"I haven't forgotten."

Kimber stirred her iced coffee with a look of distaste before looking directly at Traci again. "I'm trying to tell you that you have a pretty incredible job. Traci, you are tougher than most people I've ever met. And I've met a lot of people."

"I might be tougher than Griffin." She winked.

"Honey, your big toe is tougher than pretty boy Griffin. What I'm trying to say is that you have nothing to be ashamed of. I went with you to target practice, remember? You are a good shot. A really good shot."

"Being able to kill someone from fifty paces isn't exactly a point in my favor, Kimber. Especially if I pick up the wrong fork or say something completely uncouth to his mother."

"Uncouth?" Kimber laughed. "Where you get these words, I don't know. But seriously, all you need is some practice. That's all."

"By Sunday?"

"We'll practice at home. You've got me; Jennifer, who's eaten with all sorts of fancy chefs; and Shannon, whose mother practically made her go to charm school. We've got this."

"Thanks." Traci smiled at her, though she was now secretly cringing inside. She had a feeling that this upcoming lesson was going to give her a run for her money. "Hey, can I ask you something?"

"Of course."

"Why do you always get those iced coffees? You never drink more than a couple of sips."

"I don't like them all that much but I get tired of drinking water." She leaned back. "One day I'm going to get a new job and do something else."

"Like what? Do you know?"

"Nope. Maybe use my mind for a change? That would be nice." She shrugged. "All I do know is that whatever I do, no one is going to care about how much I weigh. And it's going to be great."

CHAPTER 21

"On with the dance!
Let joy be unconfined."
— LORD BYRON

Matt looked around at his family. They were all — by his estimation, at least — looking far too relaxed about the arrival of their upcoming dinner guest. Anthony and his fiancée Marie were looking at travel magazines, Vanny was playing on her phone, and his dad looked half-asleep.

Even his mother looked a bit on the sluggish side. She was on the couch cuddling Lady M, her prize Persian who nobody else liked. When he entered the room, she looked up at him and smiled. Then looked at him more closely.

"Matteo, what's wrong?"

"Mama, what's wrong is that Traci is coming over here in fifteen minutes."

"I know that. We're having manicotti, re-

177

member?"

"But the table isn't completely set."

Vanny looked up from her phone. "And this is a problem because . . ."

"Because she's a guest."

Marie and Bennie walked to the dining room. "We'll finish up," Bennie called out. "All it's missing is water glasses and napkins."

"Thanks," Matt said. "I don't want Traci to think we forgot about her coming over."

"Why would we do that?" Vanny asked. "It's all you've been talking about for the last week."

"That's not true."

"Sorry, but it is," Anthony said. "You've brought up this cop's visit every time we've seen you."

"See, that's what I'm talking about. Don't call her that."

Their father opened his eyes. "Don't call who what?"

"Don't call Traci a cop, Dad."

He blinked. "But that's what she is. Isn't she?" Before Matt could answer, he turned to his mother. "Teresa, I thought she was a policewoman."

Still petting that cat, his mother murmured, "She is, Bruno. I'm certain of that."

"But we're not supposed to call her a

policewoman, I don't think Daddy," Vanny said.

"How come?"

"It's sexist."

"Really? But didn't there used to be a tv show called *Police Woman*?"

"Yeah . . . back in the dark ages. Now you need to say police *officer,* Daddy," Vanessa said. "Or, I suppose you could call her a cop."

"Not according to Matt here," his dad said.

Matt interrupted. "Oh, for heaven's sakes. Everyone, just call her Traci."

After arranging Lady M on the couch, his mother walked to his side and curved a hand around his cheek. "Matteo, you are getting yourself too worked up. Don't worry so much. Everything will be fine."

"No one is going to ask her to dance," Marie said with a small smile. "At least not yet."

"But I do want to ask her about those lessons," Anthony said.

"Don't. Don't ask her about those lessons. Or about being a police officer." He snapped his fingers. "Or about her childhood or family."

"Why not?"

"Because she doesn't have a family."

His father got to his feet. "Teresa, I thought you told me that her sister was teaching her to dance."

"I did!"

"I was talking about her new sister," Matt said.

"She can't be that new if she's teaching dance classes," Anthony said. "Can she?"

Just as he was about to argue that point, the doorbell rang. "She's here. Where's Bennie?" Before anyone had time to reply, he glared at the lot of them. "Now, everyone, *behave,*" he added as he opened the door.

And, there was Traci, wearing black slacks, a silky looking top with a geometric pattern on it, and black patent leather heels. Her hair was down around her shoulders, and she had silver hoops in her ears.

"You have on earrings," he said.

She touched one of them lightly. "You're right. I do." She smiled nervously. "Is that okay?"

"Yes." The laughing he heard behind him brought him out of his daze. "I'm sorry. Won't you please come in?"

Traci stepped into the entryway and then looked behind him, her eyes widening.

Because standing right there was his whole family. Practically in a receiving line. All of them were grinning.

Matt frowned. For a guy who had graduated at the top of his class, inviting her over had been a really stupid idea.

"If I apologize in advance for all of them, will you still go out with me again?"

Her eyes widened. "Uh, sure?"

And, he'd done it again. So far, he'd made it clear that they were just friends. That they were only taking dancing lessons for his brother. That it wasn't personal. But with one plaintive question, he'd completely pushed that out of the water.

He swallowed. "What I meant to say was will you not hold this evening against me?"

Before she could answer, his parents approached like gleeful puppies spying new friends.

"Traci Lucky!" his father boomed. "We're so honored you could join us tonight. "I'm Bruno, and this is my wife, Teresa." He held out a hand.

Traci blinked, then smiled up at him. "It's nice to meet you. I haven't heard a thing about either of you, so I hope you'll talk a lot."

His mother frowned in his direction. "Matteo, are you embarrassed by us?"

At the moment, yes. "Of course not, Mama."

"He's a handful," Teresa said as she shook Traci's hand. "He always has been, I'm afraid."

"I bet."

Just as he walked to Traci's side, his mother slipped a hand around her elbow and guided her to his siblings.

"Everyone, as you heard, this is Traci Lucky." Then she started pointing down the line, just like that was a normal thing to do. "Now, this is Anthony. And that is Marie, his fiancée. Marie is from Baltimore. Have you ever been there?"

"No, ma'am."

She brightened. "I haven't either! Now, next to Marie is Vanny. That's short for Vanessa. She doesn't have a boyfriend right now, so if you know of any nice men who have jobs, let us know."

Vanny winced. "Mama."

"I'm sorry, but it doesn't hurt to ask. Next to Vanny is Bennie, which I know sounds like a boy's name, but it's short for Berna-dette."

"Which is why I go by Bennie," his sister said. "And before my mother tells you, I'm married to Stephan, who is home tonight. I also happen to be pregnant, which no doubt makes you a little bit uncomfortable, seeing as its kind of personal information, but I'd rather tell you than have my mother do the honors."

His mother shrugged. "Bennie here is a financial consultant."

"Nice to meet you," Traci said.

His mother sighed. "Finally, do you see the empty spot between Vanny and Bennie?"

"Pretend you do," Matt said. "It will go easier for you."

"Ah, yes?"

"That is for Ramon, my youngest."

"Where is he?"

"Serving in the navy. He's an officer," his dad supplied.

"Yes. We're very proud," his mother said as she gave the sign of the cross.

Traci turned to Matt, stricken. "Was he killed in action?"

"No, we just pretend he's in danger whenever we speak of him," Vanny said under her voice. "Now, Mama, that's everyone, yes?"

His mother looked around the room before smiling broadly. "Ah, I knew I forgot someone. It's Lady M."

Traci scanned the area. "I'm sorry, where is she?"

Mama picked up her feline. As usual, Lady M looked pissed to be disturbed. "Here she is. Do you like cats, Traci Lucky?"

"Um, sure. I mean, they're okay."

His mother paused. "Pardon me?"

Traci looked taken aback but then quickly gathered herself. "I'm sorry, Teresa. I mean, yes, I do like cats. Very much."

"Good," she replied. "That's very good."

"Now that the cat has been introduced, may we all please go to the dining room?" Bennie asked. "I'm starving."

For a moment, their mother looked like she was going to correct Bennie's poor manners, but then she pointedly looked at her stomach. "Oh. Of course." She turned and started walking.

Traci leaned toward Matt. "What do we do now?"

His father answered that one. "Now, Traci Lucky, we eat."

CHAPTER 22

"We're fools whether or not we dance,
so we might as well dance."
— JAPANESE PROVERB

Traci assumed dinners like this went on every night in every family all over the world. But supper at the Rossi house wasn't like anything she'd ever experienced before.

As she sat down to the pure white tablecloth covered in raised white embroidery, she felt like she'd walked into a scene from *The Godfather* — but without all the murders and swearing.

The family seemed steeped in tradition and love, and they all crammed around the table that would have comfortably seated six but held the eight of them just fine.

Kind of.

Each place setting included a china plate, silverware, and a cloth napkin. Crystal glasses perched above the knife and spoon at each place, and bottles of wine rested on the sideboard.

But what really caught her attention were the serving platters. They were piled high with olives and bread and salad and some kind of filled pasta dish.

"Boy, there's a lot of food." When everyone chuckled, she realized that she'd spoken her thoughts way too loudly. "Sorry. I don't mean to sound rude."

"You're not being rude at all, Traci. There is a lot of food," Marie said. "There always is."

"My mother likes to cook," Matt explained. "She likes it a lot."

Traci looked up at Mrs. Rossi. "Everything looks wonderful. Thank you again for having me over."

"It was Matt's doing," Bennie said.

"But we were happy to have you over and get to know you better, since all we know about you is that you . . ." Mrs. Rossi stopped, looking flummoxed.

"That I'm a cop?"

"I didn't think we were supposed to say that," Vanny said.

"I'm sorry, but why not?" Traci looked confused.

Bruno spoke. "I wanted to call you a policewoman, but that's only for Angie

Dickinson."

Traci turned to Matt. "What have you been telling them?"

"Nothing."

"Which is the problem, Traci Lucky," Anthony said. "We don't know anything about you. Besides your name, that is."

Was that why they kept calling her by her first and last name? "Um, there's not much to tell." They were all looking at her the way she looked at people she was interrogating when she knew they were lying. "I'm sorry, but it's true. I grew up in Cleveland, went to the police academy right after high school, and then served on the Cleveland's police force for five years. Now, I'm here."

"I thought you recently found your sisters," Mrs. Rossi said.

"Well, yes. That's true. My sisters and I were given up by our mother when we were little more than babies. I grew up never knowing about Shannon and Kimber. We have Shannon to thank for getting one of those mail order DNA tests and tracking us down."

"What did your parents think when you told them?" Mrs. Rossi asked.

She put her fork down. "Pardon?"

"She means your adoptive mother, not your birth mother," Marie said. "Was she

187

supportive of your desire to get to know your sisters?"

"Traci doesn't need to talk about that," Matt said quickly. "Actually, I don't think she needs to answer any more personal questions. Let's eat." He picked up the dish of olives next to him and placed four on his empty plate.

Traci watched the black olives roll around on the china, practically taunting her to keep more of her past a secret. But she was done pretending she was something she wasn't. She was really done attempting to shepherd Gwen while pretending that she had a past to be proud of. "What Matt doesn't want me to say, I guess, is that I don't have an adoptive mother." Just as she was taking a breath, figuring out the best way to tell her sad little story, Teresa spoke again.

"Oh, honey, she died?"

"No. I was never adopted. I grew up in foster care and then in a group home."

"No one wanted you?" Vanny asked. She slapped a palm over her mouth. "Oh my word. Please forgive me. That just slipped out."

Maybe even a year ago, Traci would've been hurt. But now? She had to laugh at Vanny's artlessness. "I promise, there's nothing to forgive. Just because the truth isn't pretty, doesn't mean it shouldn't be told. You're right. For lack of a better way of putting it, you're right. No one wanted me."

Matt muttered something under his breath that sounded a lot like a string of curse words.

She peeked at him. His expression was as stoic as she could ever imagine him to be. Around the table, everyone was staring at the full serving dishes.

"Boy, what a buzzkill, huh?" She smiled. "Would you please pass the manicotti, Mr. Rossi?"

He picked up the pasta dish, handed it to Anthony, who served himself and Marie, then passed it to her.

"Thanks. This looks great. I'm so hungry."

Mrs. Rossi's eyes filled with tears. "I feel so terrible for you, honey." Turning to her husband, she said, "Don't you wish we would've adopted her?"

"No, because then she couldn't date Matt."

Traci almost choked.

"Mama, Dad, stop, yeah?" Matt said.

"He's right, Mama. You're making things worse," Vanny said. "Now pass the salad and bread, too."

Little by little, the air in the dining room cleared, dishes were passed, Mr. Rossi said a blessing, and then, at last, everyone started eating.

"I showed some folks twelve houses today," Vanny said out of the blue. "And guess what? We went in one place that looked like it had just had a party in it." Her eyes lit up. "Then we found a pair of teenagers naked in one of the beds."

"Vanny, that's not a suitable topic."

"Mama, come on. You can't say it wasn't gossip-worthy."

"I'm interested," Marie said. "What did they say when you found them?"

"Not much. They were passed out." Eyes shining, she added, "My poor clients looked like they were afraid to touch anything, like there were cooties all over everything or something."

"There probably were," Anthony said.

"When we got to the car, I called the real estate agent, who called his clients. And guess what?"

Traci grinned. "What?"

"The parents were on vacation and their son was watching the house."

Traci grinned. "Sounds more like he was having a real good time while his parents were away."

x

Anthony smiled. "Bingo."

"I guess you've seen that a time or two?"

"At least a time or two," she admitted with a grin. "I'm usually called to the house, though. Not showing one to clients."

"I didn't know whether to slam the door, wake them up, or burst out laughing," Vanny said with a chuckle. "It was awful."

"I would've laughed," Matt said. "You can't make that up."

"You're right, you sure can't."

"Did your clients find a house, honey?"

Vanny looked at her father and smiled softly. "They sure did, Daddy. They put an offer on the most expensive house we looked at, then and there. And it has already been accepted."

"Congratulations!" Bennie lifted her glass of water.

"Yes. Salut!" Mr. Rossi said.

Traci picked up her glass of red wine and toasted Vanny with the rest of the Rossi family.

While everyone continued to toast, Matt rested a hand on the back of her chair and leaned close. "I bet you're regretting ever agreeing to this dinner."

"Actually, I was just thinking that I can't wait to come again."

He grinned at that. It was a million-dollar
smile, for sure.

CHAPTER 23

FOXTROT: *This is an all-American dance set to jazz music and can be fast or slow, depending on the band.*

She'd done it. She'd survived her first Rossi family dinner, and the only member who hadn't seemed to like her much was Lady M, the cat. Traci was just fine with that, too, since she didn't care much for that stuck-up cat either.

"I don't know how to apologize any more than I have," Matt said to Traci as he backed out of his parents' driveway. "My family has no filters." Matt was giving her a lift home, since Jennifer had dropped her off on the way to meet some friends — Traci had been too nervous to drive, so she'd tagged along for a ride. Now, not nervous anymore, she was just happy for a few minutes alone with Matt.

"I thought they were fun. I mean it, too,"

she added. "They weren't rude. Just inquisitive. There's nothing wrong with that."

"They were nosy."

"Matt, I'm a pretty blunt person. If I was sitting here thinking that they'd been rude or mean to me on purpose, I would tell you. Stop making a big deal out of something that I'm not upset about."

"You're right. Sorry."

"Honestly, I wish my sisters and Jennifer could have been there. I had a mini-breakdown last night about table manners. They tutored me for a good hour about which fork to use and how to twirl pasta with a spoon."

He smiled for the first time since they'd gotten in the car. "And we didn't even have spaghetti."

"I know! I was pretty disappointed not to show off my new skills," she teased.

Going over the bridge toward downtown Bridgeport, he said, "For the record, officer, they all really liked you. Every person in my family cornered me after dinner just to let me know that they hoped I'd bring you around again."

"That's sweet of them. I'm not even Italian."

"They don't care about things like that." Glancing at her sideways, he said, "And . . .

that pretty much clinches this date as one of my clumsiest. Here I'm trying to ask you out again, but I do it by saying you've got my parents' approval."

He was asking her out? "Is that what you're trying to do?"

"I'm trying. Not very well, obviously," he added as he parked his car in front of her building.

"So, will you ask?"

He unbuckled his seat belt and turned to face her. "Traci, thank you for going over to my parents' house, even though as a first date, it was a poor choice."

"You're welcome."

"Are you busy next weekend? I'm not on call."

"I'm off on Saturday night."

"Traci, may I take you out to dinner, just the two of us?"

She smiled at him. "Yes."

"Thank you. Stay there and I'll walk around to help you out."

She was a cop. She'd grown up fending for herself. No one had ever opened her car door while she was sitting in the passenger seat. She would've thought it would be awkward, just sitting and waiting.

But when Matt opened her door, leaned forward, and held out a hand for her to take,

195

she realized that just because she hadn't been treated like a lady before, she didn't *not* like it.

Actually, she liked it a lot.

Liked it so much, she hoped he'd keep doing it.

He held her hand, their fingers linked together as they walked toward the door. The lights near the front door were lit, but the first floor looked quiet.

He looked up at the windows. "I see a couple lights on the third floor, but not many."

"Kimber's out of town, and Shannon's probably already home with Dylan. Jennifer might be with Jack, I'm not sure."

"Would you like me to walk you inside?"

"I love your chivalry, but I've got this one."

"Okay then. Even though you're a cop, let me make sure you get inside all right."

Dutifully, she got out her keys, inserted one in the lock and turned — just as her work phone rang.

"Come in. What awful timing. I've got to get this, though. It's work," she said, already digging into her purse.

"I'll wait," he said, just as she answered.

"Lucky here."

"Traci, hey," Dylan said, all business. "Sorry to bother you on your big date, but

196

we've got a problem over at the women's center."

"What happened?"

"Somebody broke in and fired a gun. He took off before we arrived, but things are pretty chaotic around here."

Though her heart was pounding, she kept it together. No way was she going to lose it on Dylan again. "I'll be right there."

"Wait. Are you still with your doctor?"

"He's not *my* doctor . . . but yes."

"Bring him, along, okay? The guy was after Gwen and she's looking pretty bad right now."

"Was she shot?"

"No. No one was actually hit, but she's rattled."

It took her a second, but her voice was firm when she spoke again. "Understood. See you soon."

She clicked off and looked at Matt. "Any chance you can do a house call?"

"What happened?"

"Our girl Gwen is in trouble. The ex found her, broke in, and fired his gun. She didn't get hit, but she's having some issues."

"What do you need before we get back in the car?"

"My badge and gun. I'll be right back," she said as she strode inside. Running upstairs, she unlocked her safe and pulled out her gun and badge.

Just as she was putting on her holster, Jennifer peeked into the room. "Traci?"

"Jen, hey. Sorry, I just got called out. I've gotta go."

"Be careful."

Traci smiled at her gratefully. "Always."

By the time she got back downstairs, Matt had on his game face, too. "Dr. Rossi, let's go see if we can help this poor girl."

"I'll drive," he said.

Since she knew she had to get a better grip on herself, she walked to the passenger side of his SUV. "Thanks," she said simply. "I appreciate it."

CHAPTER 24

"Dancing is creating a sculpture that is
visible only for a moment."
— EROL OZAN

Gwen didn't know where she would be safe,
but it wasn't here. Standing in the middle
of a dozen flashing lights, ringed by four
officers in uniform and Ellen, she'd never
felt more alone. Or more vulnerable, and
that was saying a lot.

Officer Lange was standing next to her as
two other officers combed the area.

She couldn't believe she had even heard
that phrase used in real life. She shuddered
again.

Officer Lange noticed. "Emerson, see if
someone can bring Miss Camp a blanket,
would you?"

"I'm okay," she said quickly.

"I know. But it is kind of cold out, yeah?
A blanket never hurts."

199

She was just about to refuse again but stopped herself just in time. She wanted to say that she didn't want to be any trouble. Standing here like she was! She was currently nothing but trouble.

A tall policeman wearing jeans, a black T-shirt and a wind-breaker that said "BPD" on it, handed her a blanket. "It's cleaner than it looks."

She hugged it to her chest. "It's softer than it looks, too. Thank you."

After nodding at her he turned to Officer Lange. "I don't think we're going to find much now. It's getting late."

"Yeah, anyone who might have seen something from a window would have told us by now. I'll stay here."

"Sure?"

"Yep. Lucky's on her way."

"All righty then." Nodding to Gwen, he murmured, "Ma'am," then headed to the other officer who was standing by one of the cruisers.

A lot of things were running together in her mind, but one thing was standing out. She mentally grabbed hold of it like a lifeline. She turned to Officer Lange. "Did I hear right? Did he say that Officer Lucky is coming over here?"

He folded his arms over his chest. "Yep,

she's on her way right now." He paused, then added, "She's coming over here with Dr. Rossi."

Gwen was shocked. "You called my doctor? There was no need. I'm shaken up, but I don't think the baby is in danger or anything."

"I didn't call him on my own. They just happened to be together."

"Happened? So, they weren't working?"

"Nope. He took her to meet his family." He smiled slightly and raised his eyebrows, like he was amused.

It was unbelievable, but that bit of news, coming from the officer she'd once been so afraid of, made her smile. "It's kind of nice that they're dating, huh?"

He chuckled as a shiny black SUV with silver rims pulled up. "Since I've probably already said too much, I think I'll take the fifth on that. My advice to you is not to mention it either."

"Noted," she replied as they watched Officer Lucky and Dr. Rossi get out of the vehicle and head their way. "Wow," she whispered. Both the doctor and Traci looked real fine.

Officer Lange winked at her before heading their way.

Officer Lucky kept watching her. Even

though so much attention usually made her uncomfortable, Gwen was finding the officer's concern made her feel better. It had been a horrible night, one that she was going to be living over and over again for a while. But someone was looking out for her, and that was comforting.

After another minute or two, Officer Lucky and Dr. Rossi joined her while Officer Lange turned to talk to Ellen.

"It seems you had a bit of excitement tonight, Gwen," Officer Lucky said. "How are you holding up?"

"Okay, I guess."

Dr. Rossi frowned. "We need to have you sit down." He looked around. "May I take her inside now?"

"Yep. Dylan's telling Ellen that everything's clear. How about you to go sit in the living room? Will that work, Gwen?"

"I guess." Gwen didn't want to step one foot inside. But what choice did she have?

Dr. Rossi held out his arm. "Come on, Miss Camp. Let's get you someplace calmer."

She wrapped her hand around his elbow and walked with him to the side door. "It's really nice of you to come out here," she said. "Especially since you look all dressed up."

"You're just used to me wearing scrubs and a lab coat," he teased. "I promise, coming over wasn't a problem."

She was tempted to ask about his date but she knew better than to pry. Instead, she directed him to the side door, which led to a small sitting area for the residents. She preferred it over the big living room that had a television. The space was rarely used so it was a perfect place to sit and read or just think.

"Good, it's empty," Dr. Rossi said. "Do you want to lay on the couch or sit on a chair?"

"Sit." She sat down in her favorite spot, a brown leather chair with a matching ottoman.

After taking a metal chair from the card table, Dr. Rossi picked up her wrist and started taking her pulse. She stayed quiet while he glanced at his watch.

"It's a little high, but not out of the normal range. How's the rest of you?"

"Okay." She placed a hand on her belly.

He studied her. "Any cramping? Bleeding?"

"No. I mean, not that I'm aware." Looking down at her hard stomach, she shrugged. "I feel okay. I mean, my body does. The rest of me is shaken up."

"I bet. When everyone leaves, take a shower if you think it might help you relax. Then, you need to try to get some rest. That's the best thing for you and the baby."

"I will. Thanks."

He stood up as Ellen, Officer Lange, and Officer Lucky walked inside. "Gwen is holding up like a champ," he said.

"Good. That's real good," Ellen replied.

Gwen noticed that the director didn't seem especially at ease. Getting to her feet, she said, "Do you have any news about Hunter?"

Traci shook her head. "After he broke the front window, yelled at everyone, and tried to grab you, he took off."

"You saw the other cops looking for him," Officer Lange added. "He ran. I'm guessing that one of his buddies had a car waiting for him a block or two away."

Thinking about how close she'd come to getting yanked out of the safe house, she shuddered. She'd tried to tell herself that Hunter was going to forget about her, but it was now obvious that she was still on his mind. "I don't know why he still wants me."

"You don't think it's the baby?"

She shook her head. "He was really mad at me when I told him I was pregnant. He wanted me to get an abortion." She

204

frowned. "I didn't want to do that, but even if I had, I couldn't have. I didn't have a car and didn't have any money for it." Now that her head was so clear, she realized that she'd been even more dependent on him than she'd realized.

"He may be simply thinking of you as his possession, Gwen," Officer Lucky said. "Some guys get into that."

Gwen shrugged. "He was really mean tonight." Looking at her wrist, black marks from Hunter's fingers already forming, she added, "If our security guard Clyde wasn't on duty tonight, I wouldn't have stood a chance."

"Clyde is a hero, for sure," Ellen said. After taking a breath, she said, "Gwen, when we were outside, I told the officers that you're going to need to leave the center."

"You don't want me here any longer?" Her chest tightened. Her stomach rolled.

"It's not that I don't want you, it's that your being here is a danger to the other residents right now. As you know, this women's center isn't technically a safe house; it's a place for women to get themselves back together. To heal."

"I understand." Well, she could understand Ellen's point of view, but it didn't make her life any easier. She didn't know where she was supposed to go. But it wasn't their problem. "Do you want me to leave tonight?"

"No, dear. Tomorrow morning is fine." Looking at Officer Lucky, she said, "How does nine work for you?"

"I can do nine." She smiled at Gwen. "I'll see you in the morning."

"Why?" Suddenly she put two and two together. "Are you taking me to jail?"

"Jail? Oh my gosh, no. Gwen, Officer Lange and I talked, and we came up with a plan. A better place."

"Where is that?"

"Gwen, you're going to come live with me."

Gwen was glad she was sitting down because she'd just gotten the wind completely knocked out of her.

CHAPTER 25

"Everything in the universe has rhythm.
Everything dances."
— MAYA ANGELOU

Traci and Matt had agreed to meet Dylan
and Shannon at their building so the four
of them could talk with Jennifer and Kimber
at the same time. Dylan had gone to pick
up Shannon soon after Traci had dropped
her bombshell on Gwen.

She had walked Gwen up to her room
while trying to convince her — and maybe
herself — that this was for the best.

Matt had stayed downstairs since no men
were allowed up in the dorm rooms. He'd
offered to help Ellen clean up a little. She'd
refused, saying she was too tired to do much
except make a cup of hot tea and retreat to
her room.

When Traci had come downstairs, she'd
found Matt sitting just about where she'd

found him when he'd been checking Gwen's vitals. Except now he was looking lost in thought.

"Sorry," she said as she joined him. "That took a little longer than I expected."

He stood up. "Is she okay?"

Traci nodded. "I think she's more shell-shocked by the whole evening's events than anything. She had a pretty big scare."

He held the door for her then made sure it closed completely after he exited. The door had an automatic lock for the outside. Walking to her side, he reached for her hand. "You gave her some pretty big news too."

"I know. It's necessary though."

He wasn't sure it was. He was coming to learn that Traci Lucky might be a really good (and definitely tough!) police officer, but that didn't mean she didn't have a soft heart underneath that bullet proof vest. And nothing about her being so close to Gwen felt safe to him. Gwen triggered a lot of emotions for Traci, forcing her to relive some of the worst parts of her past. That was bad enough, but now add on top that she was going to put herself in danger in her own home?

He was beyond frustrated with her. And her partner. Was there really nowhere else they could put Gwen?

He was still stewing on the situation as he unlocked the passenger-side door and helped her into his vehicle.

"Thanks," she said, smiling sweetly.

Because he couldn't resist, he reached down and quickly brushed his lips against hers before heading to the driver's side.

After he'd backed out and was driving toward her house, she smiled at him. "What was that for?"

"No specific reason. Maybe I decided I was tired of waiting."

"You've been waiting to kiss me?"

"You couldn't have been that surprised." He glanced at her again as he stopped at a red light. "Or, are you?"

"I don't know. I am a little." Taking a deep breath, she pressed a hand to her face. "You know? Never mind. Forget I said anything. I sound like we're in eighth grade and you're my first boyfriend."

"I could do that." Holding out his right hand for her to take, he said, "Do you want to go steady, Traci?"

"Stop. Now I'm totally embarrassed."

He kind of liked this flustered side of her. It was unexpected and cute. "You're a puzzle, Traci. Every time I think I've got a handle on what type of girl you are, you go and surprise me again."

"I think that's supposed to be a good thing. You know, that way there's an air of mystery about me."

"There's already that." Deciding that he was impatient for a lot of things, he added, "For example, why, out of all places in the area, did you decide that Gwen Camp needs to go into hiding in *your* house?"

She pulled her hand from his, brow furrowed. "You sound like you're angry."

"That would be because I am."

"Why are you angry at me? I'm trying to do the right thing here."

"No, the right thing would be to put that girl in a safe house. Or in another house. Anywhere, say, but *your house,*" he said as he parallel parked in front of her building.

"Maybe you should just drop me off."

"No. I want to hear what you and Officer Lange have cooked up." When she reached for the handle, he barked, "No. Sit there for a minute until I come get you out."

She sat, but she was fuming.

He figured if Vanny or Bennie or even his mother was sitting in the vehicle, they'd be angry at him too. He was acting like a chauvinistic jerk, and he knew it.

But someone had to take care of her. And at dinner tonight, while she was fending off

CHAPTER 26

"Socrates learned to dance when he was seventy because he felt that an essential part of himself had been neglected."

What had she done? Looking into her sisters' eyes, Traci began to second guess every rationale she'd had while sitting in the living room of the Bridgeport Women's Center. She'd thought she'd been thinking about Gwen. But what if she'd really been thinking about herself?

What if she'd somehow transferred all the pain, all the worthlessness she'd grown up feeling and wound it up into a ball of excuses to do a good deed?

If that was the case, she didn't know if she could possibly be more embarrassed.

After staring at her a good long minute, Shannon turned to her husband. In a crisp tone, she said, "As much as I like all of us getting together on the spur of the moment at ten at night, I think we need some explanations, Dylan."

Looking at Traci, Kimber nodded. "What do you have to share that's so all-fired important?" Narrowing her eyes, she said, "Or is it about you two?"

"Me and Matt?" She knew she sounded as incredulous as she felt.

"That's the only other couple I'm looking at."

Ouch. She felt her cheeks start to heat. "Um, this is not about Matt and me."

"Really? Because we all saw you two kissing outside."

"I didn't know that." What was happening to her tonight?

This time is was Jennifer who spoke. "It's late. Will someone please tell us what's going on?"

"All right." Taking a deep breath, Traci said, "I invited Gwen to stay here for a while."

Shannon threw a hand in the air. "Gwen? Who's —" She gasped. "Oh my gosh, are you talking about the pregnant drug addict girl you pulled out of that shack?"

"Way to put it all out there, Lucky," Dylan chided.

"Oh, stop. You know your first impression of her wasn't any better," she said before turning back to Shannon. "Yes, that's her."

"Gwen is pregnant, but she's not a drug addict," Matt said.

"Are you sure about that?" Kimber asked.

"Positive. She did have a crystal meth in her system when she arrived at the hospital, but we later learned that it had been her first time to do that. She was mostly malnourished and exhausted."

"And you believed her?" Shannon asked.

"We did," Traci replied, her voice hard. "I'm not saying I approve of what she did, because I don't. But that's the truth." She looked at her sisters. "Look, this girl has been barely subsisting for months. She's been really alone and in a tight spot. She needs to be someplace safe."

Jennifer crossed her legs. "I feel really bad for her. I really do. But I don't understand how it went from her being in a home to needing to come to *our* home."

Dylan answered that one. "There was a problem tonight. Gwen's ex-boyfriend broke into the place and fired two shots at her. When he missed, he attempted to remove her by force."

Kimber's whole expression changed. "Oh my gosh! Is she okay?"

"She's shaken up and scared to death," Traci said. "If Clyde, the off-duty security guard hadn't been there, he would have abducted her."

"How did he stop this guy? Is he dead?" Jennifer asked.

Jennifer's matter-of-fact way of asking such a thing made Traci even more aware of her past. She'd been attacked in a parking lot by three men a couple of years ago and was still dealing with the after-affects. That, plus the fact that she was a cop's sister, gave Traci even deeper concerns about her spur of the moment decision. "No," Traci finally answered.

"What happened to him? He's in jail?" she asked.

"No. He got away," Traci finally admitted.

Dylan continued. "That's why we need to put her someplace safe."

"But this isn't safe," Shannon countered. "Jennifer and Kimber live here. I have high school girls who take lessons here. This is a really bad idea." She glared at her husband. "You know how much finding my sisters has meant to me. How could you just put us all in jeopardy?"

Dylan reached for her hand. "Honey, it wasn't like that."

Shannon snatched her hand away. "How could it be any other way?"

"You're forgetting that Traci's a damn

216

good cop and she lives here."

"But she's working. You're working. And I don't want to start taking shooting lessons to have to defend Kimber."

"You won't have to defend me," Kimber retorted. "I can take care of myself." With a pointed look at Dylan, she added, "Not that I'm real happy about this little setup either."

"She had to go somewhere safe," Traci said again.

"Couldn't you have put her in a cell or something?" Kimber asked. "At least then she'd be safe."

"Gwen is eighteen years old and pregnant. She's been through hell," Traci added. "What she needs is someone to care."

"So you decided it would be you two," Shannon said.

"Yes, Shannon. And listen, before you get mad at Dylan, you need to know that he didn't come up with this idea. I did."

"I think it's a good option," Matt said.

Shannon eyed him warily. "I'm sorry, but I don't understand why you're here."

"First, because Traci and I are dating, so I care about her health and safety whether she thinks I should do that or not. Secondly, because Gwen's my patient and I can honestly say that putting her in a jail cell would not only do damage to her, it might

217

even harm the baby."

"And third?" Shannon asked, a hint of a smile appearing on her face.

Matt leaned back. "I don't have a third reason why this is a good idea. To be honest, Traci took me by surprise, too. I'm not real happy about her putting all of you and herself in danger. I told her that as well."

Jennifer stood up. "That settles it then."

"What is settled?" Dylan asked.

"You and Traci are going to have to go back and tell Gwen that she can't stay here. We don't want her."

We don't want her. Boy, how many times had she heard that phrase? It hurt her almost worse than anything she could imagine.

Traci inhaled, trying to keep a grip on herself. "Jennifer, Gwen's mother kicked her out of her house. She's been yanked around by an abusive boyfriend. When she finally finds a safe place to live, someplace where she could actually get healthy and learn something, her ex breaks in. Then, because he's a danger to the others, she was asked to leave. And it's just not herself we're talking about. She has a baby on the way."

"You're not being fair, Traci," Kimber said. "I'm sorry if this girl has had a crappy life, but we can't save her."

"That's where you're wrong. *Believing in her* is going to save her. She needs that. Please, you guys."

"I asked Shannon over here tonight because I want us to move in here for a while too," Dylan added. "That way either Traci or I can always be here."

"But you two are partners," Shannon said. "Is that even allowed?"

"We can split up for a few weeks. We're also going to find this Hunter guy and make an arrest."

Traci nodded. "That's our priority."

Shannon pressed her hands to her face. "I don't know what to do. If I was reading about this in a magazine or a newspaper, I'd say that people should absolutely take her in. But this affects not just me, but people I love. This isn't easy."

"I know it isn't," Traci murmured.

Kimber leaned forward. "What if she goes back on drugs? Or gets back together with this guy and steals our things?"

"I don't think that's going to happen."

"Traci, I'm sorry, but it can happen," Kimber said. "I grew up in New York City and have traveled all over the world. Sometimes people do relapse or go back to the life they once knew. It happens to people even when they have the best of intentions."

Matt held up a hand. "Everyone, for what it's worth, I believed a lot of the same things you all do. As a matter of fact, I spent most of the drive over here telling Traci that I thought she was wrong. But now, I have to admit that I was wrong." His voice softened. "Listen, I know this girl. Gwen isn't perfect — not by a longshot. But she's not going to rob you or bring in this ex-boyfriend. I'm ninety-nine percent sure that she's not that girl."

"But what if you're wrong?" Jennifer asked.

"But what if I'm right?" Traci countered as she looked at each of them. "What if all she needs is someone to believe in her? Someone to give her some slack so she can take the lead?"

"I can't believe I'm saying this, but . . . okay," Kimber said.

"Really?" Traci had been sure that, out of all of them, Kimber would be the hardest to convince.

"Really." Looking reflective, Kimber spoke again. "Look, I'm not saying that I'm not a little worried, but if she's had as hard of a life as you say — who am I to decide that she doesn't deserve someone to sacrifice something for her? I am who I am because of my parents."

Jennifer nodded. "Dylan, I believe in you. You've been a cop for years and helped a lot of people. If you believe in this woman, than the least I can do is believe in you."

"I'll have officers patrolling around here more often. I promise."

"I'll get Jack to come over more often too."

"That's good. Next time I see him, I'll fill him in."

Jennifer walked to Traci's side and gave her a quick hug. "I know this conversation wasn't easy for you. Thanks for doing it, though. Night."

"Night."

Kimber walked to her side. "Hold up, Jen. I'll walk up with you. Good night, everyone. See you in the morning."

Traci sat down next to Matt and gazed at Shannon. Of all the women in the house, she would've thought that Shannon would be the first to help Gwen. She'd sure been wrong. "Is there anything I can do or say to help you?"

"To help me what? Come around to your way of thinking?" She shrugged. "Traci, I'll go along with this, but I don't feel good about it. I realize I'm not being very kind or understanding, and I know I've disappointed you. I'm sorry."

"You can't help how you feel." Thinking

about it, Traci realized that of all of them, Shannon had had a bit of a charmed life. She'd been adopted by a well-to-do family who doted on her and gave her a wonderful life. She'd had some success in dance. And, while her career path hadn't been exactly easy, it also hadn't involved a lot of hardship.

Of course everything about Gwen sounded foreign and a little frightening to Shannon.

"I promise you're going to be pleasantly surprised by this girl."

"I feel sorry for her, but I'm still worried. I just found all of you. Jennifer, too. What am I going to do if this guy hurts one of you?"

"He won't."

"You can't promise that, though."

Dylan took her hand. "Honey, life isn't made up of promises. Life is made up of days and nights and survival and hope."

"And love."

"Most of all, if we're lucky, love." He kissed her brow before standing up. "We're outta here. I'll call the captain in the morning, Lucky."

She nodded. "I'll stop by and speak to Ellen and Gwen."

"Sounds good."

Traci walked over and stood in front of Shannon. "Please don't be mad at me forever."

"Oh, you." She wrapped her arms around Traci and hugged her tight. "I'm not mad. I love you."

After they told Matt good night, they walked out.

Matt gazed at her. "How are you doing?"

"Better now. Thanks for standing up for me."

"I wanted to. I thought you were right."

"Have I even thanked you for taking me to your parents?" He laughed. "To be honest, I've been afraid to mention that dinner. I prepped them so much, they were ridiculous."

"Did you really tell them they couldn't call me a cop?"

"It didn't sound respectful."

"Or policewoman?"

"I didn't think you were allowed to say that anymore."

She burst out laughing. "Oh, Matt. One day I'm going to make you hang out with all my cop buddies. Then, you'll know that cops are a pretty hardy lot. We've got thick skin. It takes a lot to offend us."

"You might have thick skin, but you're a sweetheart underneath, Lucky," he said before he kissed her.

Realizing that he was exactly right — and that she didn't mind it one bit — she kissed him back.

CHAPTER 27

QUICKSTEP: *This dance is inspired by the foxtrot, but it has a much quicker tempo, which is where the name of the dance originates.*

"I still can't believe I'm moving in with you," Gwen said as Officer Lucky drove them to her house in her Subaru. "Are you sure it's okay?"

"I wouldn't have offered if it wasn't."

Gwen figured that. Officer Lucky didn't seem like the type of person to do anything she didn't want to do. But that said . . . "It seems like a lot to ask of your sisters."

"Don't worry about it. I told you that it isn't a problem."

"I'm still going to feel guilty, though."

Officer Lucky shrugged, which made her look even more at ease. That was kind of weird, since she had picked up Gwen in a pair of jeans, flats, and a gray fitted T-shirt.

Gwen had done a double take the first time she'd looked at her.

After she turned left at a light, then made another left, she spoke. "Look. I see your point, but there's nothing to feel guilty about. I talked to my sisters and they feel for your situation. Plus, if it makes you feel any better, we decided to take you being at our house one day at a time. Until things calm down, it's the best solution for you and your baby."

As if he heard the mention, her baby shifted. Gwen placed the palm on her hand on her belly, half to reassure her little guy that he wasn't alone. Half to reassure herself of the same thing. She would have never guessed it, but this baby had already changed her life. She wasn't alone in the world anymore.

It might even be the first time she'd ever felt that way.

Realizing that Officer Lucky was probably waiting for her to say something, Gwen cleared her throat. "What do you mean by things calming down? Until when?"

"Until Hunter is picked up and we're sure neither he nor his friends are a threat to you." She glanced at Gwen as she took a right turn. "Or until we can find you some-place better to stay."

"Who is here again?"

"Me, my sister Kimber, and my sister-in-law Jennifer. Jen is Officer Lange's sister. He just got married to Shannon, who is my oldest sister."

"So, you all are real close."

"We're trying to be."

That sounded cryptic, but Gwen didn't dare ask for more information. "I'll do my best to stay out of the way."

"No one is going to expect you to do that. As long as you pick up your dishes and don't leave a mess in the bathroom, it should be all good," she added as she parked the car.

"I don't have much to clean up, so that shouldn't be a problem." Looking up at the building, Gwen gaped. It was three stories, made of brick, and was definitely an older place that had been remodeled. There was also a small sign on the bricks near the door that said "Dance With Me."

"What's that?" she asked.

"The bottom floor is my sister's dance studio."

"Wow." She gave Officer Lucky a sideways glance. "So you're a cop and she teaches dance lessons."

"Yep."

"Do you ever dance?"

227

She frowned. "Not until lately." She turned off the engine. "Don't get out until I come around for you."

"I won't." Watching Officer Lucky check her gun, scan the area, and then walk around to Gwen's side, Gwen felt her nerves ramp up again. This was real. For a moment, there, it had been fun to pretend that she and Officer Lucky were friends and that she was going to stay at her house because her friends wanted to get to know her.

But looking up at the building, and seeing the set lines in Officer Lucky's face, Gwen's reality hit her full in the face. She was in trouble and in danger — and putting her baby and these other women in danger too. "Hey, um, Officer Lucky?"

"Yeah?"

"Thank you for everything. I mean, thanks for stepping in and doing so much for me," she continued, practically stumbling over each word. "It means a lot."

"I told you, it was not a problem."

"You might be saying that, but I know that it has been. I'd be in a really bad situation if not for you."

Officer Lucky's expression softened before she shook her head. "Like I said, this might just be a temporary thing. Come on."

She unlocked the door and ushered Gwen inside.

She was immediately surrounded by the sound of classical music from one direction and the faint sounds of laughter above them.

The decorations in the house were surprising, to say the least. The woodwork was dark and there was a large emerald green velvet couch sitting in the middle of the foyer.

Above them, a fancy crystal chandelier twinkled. Underneath it was a staircase that rose up two floors.

"Wow," Gwen said.

"I know. This place takes everyone by surprise the first time they see it," Officer Lucky said with humor in her voice. "It looks a little bit like a haunted house, huh?"

"I was going to say it looks like it came out of the Addams Family."

Officer Lucky smiled. "We hear that a lot." She paused. "So, this is my sister's dance studio." She pressed a hand on the closed door that had a large glass insert in the center of it. "Shannon's teaching a private class right now, or I'd introduce you."

Gwen stepped closer so she could peer inside. A woman who must be Shannon was in a leotard, tights, and toe shoes. She also had on some kind of wrap around black sheer skirt on. Her student looked about

229

fourteen. The girl was staring at her reflection in the mirror as she kept hopping up on one toe and stretching out her other leg.

"Come on," Officer Lucky said. "Let's head up and I'll help you find a place to sleep."

"Yes, ma'am." Gwen picked up her tote bag and backpack again and followed the police officer upstairs.

Officer Lucky paused on the landing of the second floor. "There are two rooms here, but it's mostly storage. They're not secure, so don't go exploring on your own."

"I won't."

"Good. Come on up." Trotting up the stairs, she turned and frowned as Gwen caught up. "I didn't even think. Are you going to be able to handle these stairs?"

"I can do it."

"You're pregnant. Is it too much?"

"No, ma'am." She was in the nicest place she'd ever been in, all to keep her and Junior safe. There was no way she was going to complain. Besides, one of the books they'd given her at the women's center said that exercise was really good for the baby.

The top floor was far more open and modern-looking than the bottom floor. First she noticed a spacious sitting room with a pair of tan couches and two recliners grouped around a coffee table. A decent-sized television was mounted on one wall. Off to the left was a hallway with a bunch of closed doors.

On the right was a smallish kitchen decorated in gray and white with stainless steel appliances. One of the white granite countertops was oversized and had a group of three barstools situated right next to it.

Also in the kitchen stood two women. One had brown hair, one was blonde. Both were looking at her with interest.

And neither was smiling. For the first time, she wondered if Officer Lucky was the nicest of the bunch. If that was the case, she was going to have to really watch herself.

CHAPTER 28

"Life isn't about waiting for the storm
to pass; it's about learning to dance
in the rain."
— VIVIAN GREENE

Until that very moment, Traci never would
have thought she would be a good mother.
She'd known she was a fighter, she'd known
she had a fierce protective streak. Both of
those traits had helped her to be a good cop.

But she'd always thought she was too hard
to be a good mom. Unlike other girls at the
home she was raised in, she'd never felt
strong feelings for the little new arrivals.
While some of her roommates would go out
of their way to hold their hands, even give
them hugs at night when they were scared,
Traci had always kept her distance. She
hadn't been mean or anything — she just
hadn't felt much for them. Well, nothing
beyond irritation that, with their arrival,

everything was going to change again.

But now, standing beside Gwen, who was visibly trying not to tremble as she gaped at Kimber and Jennifer, Traci felt a maternal instinct surface that she'd never believed she possessed. Suddenly, she wanted to shield Gwen from anything bad — even if it was simply a group of women who weren't being especially welcoming.

"Put your stuff down," she muttered before stepping slightly in front of her. "Everyone, Gwen's here." Yes, there might have been a bit of iron in her voice.

Jennifer approached first. "Hi, Gwen. I'm Jennifer. It's nice to meet you."

"Hi." Gwen smiled shyly.

Kimber held out her hand. "I'm one of Traci's sisters," she said. "Shannon's downstairs teaching a class."

Gwen nodded. "We saw her through one of the windows."

"She'll be excited to meet you too. So, welcome."

"Thanks." Gwen paused then blurted, "You don't look much like Officer Lucky."

"That's because we share the same mom but not much else," Kimber said. "Do you have siblings?"

"A brother."

"Where's he at?"

233

Traci groaned. "Kimber, I think question-and-answer time can wait. Don't you?"

"I don't mind," Gwen said. "Um, I don't really know where Billy is. We're not real close. He took off on his own a while back."

"Is he older or younger?"

"Older, but not by much. Only by fourteen months." Gwen shifted from one foot to the other.

Traci rested a hand on Gwen's shoulder. "Hey, did you all figure out where Gwen's going to sleep?" She chuckled lightly. "Where everyone's going to sleep?"

"We did," Jennifer replied. "Dylan and Shannon made themselves a room on the second floor."

"How?" The second-floor rooms were clean but mostly empty. Where would they sleep?

"Dylan ran to a mattress store the minute it opened and bought a mattress. Then, he and a couple of guys loaded it into a truck and carried it upstairs. I went over with Shannon and brought a lamp and a couple of other things from their house."

"Wow. I can't believe you got that done so quickly."

Jennifer winked. "Shannon said that the move was a piece of cake. So, don't you worry about them. They'll be just fine."

"Uh-oh. That makes it sound like someone isn't going to be."

Kimber raised her eyebrows. "That's because you and me are going to be roommates."

"What?"

Jennifer joined in. "Sorry, Trace. I tried to let you have my room, but Kimber and Shannon said I already have the smallest bedroom in the place."

"You do. Your room makes Harry Potter's room under the stairs look like a suite," Traci said.

Kimber looked a little affronted, though Traci knew it was all an act. Kimber was incredibly easy-going, at least when it came to sharing spaces with other women. "Don't worry. I'm traveling again in two weeks. You'll have the whole bedroom to yourself."

"Will there even be any room for me in your bedroom?" Kimber easily had twice as many clothes as she did.

"I moved over some of my clothes into another closet."

"And the bed?"

"We're going to get to share a bed." She raised one eyebrow. "I hope you don't kick."

"Well, I hope you don't snore."

"I feel terrible that I'm causing you all so much trouble," Gwen said. "I bet I could

235

probably sleep on one of those couches."

"No way," Jennifer said. "You need your rest."

"She's right," Kimber said. "Don't worry about us sniping at each other. It's normal."

Turning to look at Gwen, Traci realized that she'd kept her standing on her feet this whole time. Hadn't even offered her a glass of water. "Hey, I'm so sorry. I've been a terrible hostess. Are you thirsty? Hungry?"

"Not really, but I kind of have to pee."

Kimber chuckled. "Traci, I'll go show Gwen where the bathroom is. You go take her things to your room."

"I can help," Jennifer said. "Are your other bags downstairs?"

"No. This is it."

Jennifer blinked. "Oh. All right. Do you need anything else? We've got lots of extra blankets and pillows around here . . ."

"No, I'm fine. I promise, I'll do my best to stay out of everyone's way. I don't need much."

Kimber walked to her side. "Honey, if you've got to be bothered by a crazy ex-boyfriend, you've come to the right place. Between the four of us girls, you're going to have plenty to wear."

Gwen's eyes practically bugged out. "Are you serious?"

"Of course. Now, what size are you normally?" Kimber asked as they walked down the hall.

"She's cute, Traci," Jennifer said as she picked up Gwen's two items.

Thinking about the way Gwen had been looking around at things like she just won the lottery, Traci slowly smiled. "Yeah. I guess she is."

She lowered her voice. "Even though you told me she was just a kid, I was imagining someone far different. I feel kind of bad about that."

"Don't. Asking you all to take her in was a lot to ask. Of course you were imagining the worst." She held up a hand. "And before you start feeling worse, let me tell you that I've seen my fair share of women in crack houses. I've seen what drugs and bad situations can do to people."

"For what it's worth, I think it's really great of you to look out for her."

"I didn't do anything much," Traci protested, but realized that she was talking to the empty room.

Down the hall, she could hear Kimber, Jennifer, and Gwen talking in Traci's room. The two of them were now acting like a welcome wagon, and from the way Gwen was giggling, they had a way with her that

Traci had never managed. The girl was relaxing.

Even though she could probably go down there and grab some of the clothes and cart them to Kimber's room, Traci walked to the refrigerator, searched in the back and uncovered one of her "absolutely necessary" Dr Peppers.

She tried to be reasonably healthy by nature, which meant she tried to keep the cans of sugar and caffeine to a minimum. But sometimes she needed a pick-me-up to get her through the day.

And, given that it was only a little after eleven and she felt like she'd already been on duty for twelve hours, Traci knew this was one of those days. Popping the top, she sipped from the can, practically moaning with happiness.

Buoyed by the pleasure only forbidden food could bring, she opened a cabinet, grabbed a bag of goldfish crackers — parmesan, not cheddar — and sat down at the counter bar and helped herself to a little feast.

"Oh my gosh! Did Gwen not come after all?" Shannon asked the moment she appeared on the landing. "What happened?"

"Not a thing. She's down the hall."

"Oh." Shannon walked to her side. She

238

was still wearing her leotard, tights, and filmy skirt. Her feet were now bare, though — her toes looking as ugly and misshapen as ever, thanks to a lifetime of dancing. "What's she doing?"

"I have a feeling she's currently trying to get a word in edge-wise. Kimber and Jennifer are showing Gwen her new room."

"And you're just sitting here having a snack?"

"Yep."

"Well, I'm going to go down the hall and say hello."

"Good. But get ready, Gwen saw you dancing in your studio. She looked mesmerized."

"Really?"

"Uh-huh. It was sweet. I have a feeling that she's going to have some questions for you."

Shannon brightened. "Great!" She scampered down the hall, greeting Gwen with enough West Virginia hospitality to make Traci smile as she popped another goldfish into her mouth.

It seemed that, in the light of day, her sisters had all warmed to Gwen's presence. Kimber had been right. Gwen had gotten the roommate jackpot. But not for the clothing situation.

For the women who lived there.
Traci couldn't think of any finer women
to be around.

CHAPTER 29

JIVE: *A spicy swing dance set to big-band music in which the man leads. It is a fast and energy-consuming dance.*

Matt looked at the clock above his desk and groaned. It was already a quarter after six, and he'd started the day doing rounds at the hospital at seven that morning. If he wasn't careful, he was going to put in a fourteen-hour day. Not his favorite way to begin the week. At least he only had two more calls to make before he could go back to his apartment and collapse.

Just as he picked up the phone, Hartley poked her head in his doorway. "I'm heading out, Dr. Rossi."

Hartley had once been a nurse, but now was his office manager. She'd decided about five years ago that the stress of the job had taken a toll on her. He'd supported that decision wholeheartedly, though when she'd first taken over the retiring Ellie's position, he'd been a little skeptical. He had a fairly big practice and not every patient was a piece of cake. A couple of them, in particular, needed to be handled with kid gloves.

She'd done an outstanding job, though. He couldn't imagine his practice running half as smoothly without her.

Getting to his feet, he said, "Thanks for everything today. I don't know what the Sullivans would have done without you smoothing the way for them."

She shook her head. "That darn assistant administrator at that hospital! She doesn't listen and is always multi-tasking." She glowered. "Half the time I want to march right over to her office, turn off her computer, and tell her to stop reading messages while I'm talking to her on the phone."

He grinned. "And the other half of the time?"

"I just want to hang up and try not to ever speak to her again."

"If you're this fired up, it really is time for you to call it a day. Do you want me to walk you to your car? The sun's going down."

"Nope. Bradley's working security. He always has a minute to walk with me. It's relatively safe around here."

"Not always, though."

"Don't worry. I'll ask Bradley." She playfully shook a finger at him. "But if you don't get out of here soon, I'm going to send him upstairs to escort you to your car."

"I'm heading out in twenty minutes. I've just got to make two more phone calls."

Her eyes widened. "Shoot. I almost forgot." Stuffing a hand into one of the many pockets on her smock, she pulled out a bright-pink Post-it Note. "You've got three calls to make, doc. Sorry."

With a sense of dread, he glanced at the paper, then slowly smiled. "Traci Lucky called?"

"Yes. Officer Lucky," she said slowly. "She specifically asked for you call her before eight tonight, if at all possible."

If she'd mentioned that specific time, he knew it was about tonight's dance class. He'd completely forgotten about it — mainly because waltzing was the last thing he felt like doing at the moment. Summoning up a smile, he said, "Thanks for passing that on."

Hartley still hesitated. "Dr. Rossi, I hope nothing is going on with that girl."

"Gwen? I hope not." He paused, then figured he'd rather have Hartley stew on his love life than worry about Gwen or a crime or something. "I have a feeling it's personal.

243

Traci's my date to my brother's wedding. And, since we all have to know how to waltz for their reception, we're taking ballroom dance lessons together."

"Get out." She propped a hip against the door frame. "I'd pay money to see you waltz."

"Believe me, you'd regret wasting your money. Traci and I aren't exactly what you'd call *graceful* together."

"I bet you two are real cute."

Now this conversation was going over the line. "And I bet you need to get on your way."

"Yes, sir." She waggled her fingers. "Have a good night."

"Night." As a new thought entered his mind, he said, "Hey, Hart, don't tell everyone about this, okay?"

"The dancing or the dating?" Her eyes were sparkling.

"You know I mean both."

"Fine. But be warned, I'm going to ask you how tonight went."

"I'll prepare myself," he joked. "Night."

Walking back to his desk, he chuckled. Boy, if he didn't have meddling parents to worry about, he had nosey office managers. He wouldn't have it any other way, though. The more he learned about Traci's past —

and Gwen's present — the more he was grateful for being surrounded by people who cared.

Anxious to speak to Traci, he sailed through his two calls, more grateful than ever that he'd long ago learned to make his more challenging calls first. These last two women were usually open to his advice, and tonight's calls were relaying some positive test results for each.

Finally done with work, he grabbed his backpack, walked through the office, checking locked cabinets, doors, and windows, then at last got to his car.

He dialed Traci's number two minutes later.

"Whew. I was starting to worry about you," she said as soon as she picked up.

"Sorry, it was a crazy day. Long. Plus, I only got your message about a half hour ago."

"I hope you didn't have too many emergencies?"

"Nothing too bad. Just a lot of patients." He liked how she asked that. He'd dated women before who never seemed to understand how erratic a doctor's day could be. He hadn't necessarily been shocked, but it had been difficult when one or two of the women refused to understand how he simply wasn't able to answer a phone when he was on call. "What about you? Were you on shift today?"

"I was." Her voice cracked. "I'm sorry, but can we do a raincheck for tonight's lesson?"

"Of course." He was worried about her now. "Traci, do you want to talk about it?"

"Not really." She sniffed. "I'm sorry. It was just a tough one. A lot of red tape, unnecessary meetings and annoying people. All I want to do is sit in front of the TV and drink a beer. Maybe eat some ice cream."

"I know you live with a bunch of girls, but do you want some company?"

"Sure, but I should warn you — I'm planning to watch the Bachelor."

He grimaced. "I didn't know you watched shows like that."

"It's a guilty pleasure. I binge watch it when I've had a bad day." She kind of chuckled, but it sounded throaty and strained. "Nothing makes a girl feel better than to know at least I'm not about to get a rose."

He had no idea what she was talking about. "I'm trying to be a good boyfriend, but I don't think I can hack it."

"That's probably a wise move. You'd be sitting here with at least three women, two of whom are acting slightly hormonal."

He glanced to his right, made a sudden decision, and pulled into the grocery store parking lot. "I'm not up for that, but I can deliver ice cream with the best of them. What kind do you want?"

"Matt, you don't need to bring me ice cream."

"Five women together on the couch? Uh, yeah, I do. I grew up with two sisters." And they would absolutely kill him if they heard him talking about them like this!

"In that case, we'd love some ice cream."

He smiled, especially since he knew what kind to bring. Graeter's ice cream was the Cincinnati cure-all for any bad day. "Any special flavor?"

"Anything will do . . . but maybe chocolate-chocolate chip? Oh, and vanilla too?"

"I can do that. I'll be over soon with a couple of pints."

"Thank you, Matt."

"Anytime." He stopped himself just in time before calling her sweetheart.

Thirty minutes later, he was knocking on the front door of Dance With Me and then getting ushered upstairs by an ebullient Shannon.

247

"You win the prize for one of my most favorite people," she said as she led the way.

"What about your husband?"

"Dylan is working tonight. He gets my prayers, but no prize," she joked.

Walking into the living area, Matt spied Gwen curled up on the couch and Traci wearing flannel pajama bottoms and some kind of police academy T-shirt. Both looked up at him and grinned. Maybe it was the sack he was holding that made them so happy.

"Hey, Gwen," he called out.

"Hi, Dr. Rossi. Thanks for bringing us food."

He smiled, liking that she was looking so at home with the other women. Getting her here hadn't been easy, but it was so worth it.

"Oh, my gosh! You brought us Graeter's," Traci said, with a note of reverence in her voice as she reached for the grocery bag. "You're the best."

"I think Matt's appearance gives new meaning to a doctor making house calls," Shannon joked.

"I hope you enjoy it."

"Are you sure you don't want to stay?" Traci asked.

"Positive. I picked up some food at the

deli while I was at the store. I'm going home to eat dinner and collapse."

Handing off the sack to Shannon, Traci smiled up at him. "I'll walk you down."

He held up a hand. "Have a good night, ladies."

"You, too," Gwen said.

Walking down the stairs with him, Traci smiled up at him. "There's a fairly good chance that those women are going to have those pints cleaned out before I get upstairs."

"I hope not. I brought over five pints."

"Five?"

"I was only going to get three, but then I started thinking three pints didn't sound like enough for five women on the edge."

"You just keep getting better and better."

Her words were teasing, but they made him feel good all the same. When they got to the door, he kissed her lightly on the lips. "Are you busy tomorrow night?"

"Yep. And the next night. Pretty much every night until Hunter is off the streets."

He nodded. "Then give me a call in a day or two, Traci."

A bit of vulnerability snuck into her expression. "All right. Will you be wanting a Gwen update? If so, I can easily text or email you reports on how she's doing."

"Hearing about Gwen is good and well, but that's not why I want to hear from you, Traci."

"Oh?"

"I'm going to want to hear your voice."

"I'll call you soon, then," she said with a smile.

"That's all it took?"

"Not necessarily. You see, I'm going to want to hear your voice, too."

CHAPTER 30

"The one thing that can solve
most of our problems is dancing."
— JAMES BROWN

"I feel like we're looking for a needle in a haystack," Traci said to Dylan as they spent a now-rare afternoon driving around Bridgeport and the surrounding areas. "And, yes, I know I'm beginning to sound a lot like your wife."

Dylan, who was driving, slid his sunglasses back over his eyes. "I didn't say anything, Lucky."

She noticed his lips twitch. Figuring she might as well get the teasing over with, she prodded at bit. "But . . ."

"Okay, fine. If you start craving peas and cornbread, I'll know that you're a Cleveland girl no longer."

She wrinkled her nose. "I have no idea why anyone would want peas and cornbread together."

He grinned. "On second thought, you might get to keep your city girl status a little longer. I was talking about black-eyed peas, not green peas."

"I had no idea there was a thing."

"Sure you did. Remember? Shannon made all of us eat them on New Year's Day."

She thought back as Dylan drove to yet another address where they were hoping to find evidence of Hunter. "She cooked them all day with peppers and bacon. They weren't bad."

He smiled. "They really weren't. And, since my sister made the cornbread, it was actually a decent meal."

"Ha-ha. When you start attempting to cook instead of living off the glory of Jennifer's culinary skills, you can start talking trash."

"I wasn't talking trash about anyone, Lucky."

"And I wasn't either, so don't get all snippy, Lange," she said as he pulled to a stop in front of a pair of rundown houses. "Where the heck are we, anyway?"

"Back in the day, in the late forties or so, a metal company moved to Bridgeport and even built themselves a company town."

"Really?"

"Yep. All the houses were catalog houses. Some, a couple streets over, are real cute. The owners fixed them up and have a lot of pride in them. Others, like these close to the river, have seen better days."

"Better years is more like it." She scanned the notes on her iPad. "It looks like we got a credible witness who hung out with Hunter over here. When . . . ah. Two nights ago."

He turned off the ignition. "It's amazing how our best informants always share information just a little too late."

Getting out of the cruiser, Traci shrugged. "There's a part of me that can't really blame them. Rats who are found out don't live very long."

"Let's hope this one gave us enough to be useful," he said as they walked to the rundown house.

Traci had already checked her weapon, but the grouping of houses made all her senses light up. The five of them hugged the end of a cul-de-sac and each one looked more worn down than the last. A couple of old toys littered one of the yards, old tires and the remains of a lawnmower were scattered over another one. No one was around outside, but it was a little on the chilly side.

However, she did see slight movements in

253

more than one window.

The house they approached had a sagging front porch, was an unfortunate shade of faded mustard yellow, and had some dusty-looking curtains hanging listlessly over the front windows.

"Television's on," Dylan said.

"Maybe someone is home," she joked. Now that they'd been partners for close to a year, they'd developed a rhythm to their calls. They'd begun to enjoy stating the obvious, affectionately making fun of one of the older guys in the precinct who always said the most obvious things like he was giving sage advice.

Dylan rapped on the door. "Hello?" They heard some shuffling but no one came to the door. Dylan knocked harder. "Open up, please. Police."

After a few more wasted seconds Traci heard a deadbolt click and the door opened a couple of inches.

A guy around her age peeked out at them. "What?"

"I'm Officer Lucky, this is Officer Lange. We'd like to speak to you for a few minutes."

Suspicion entered his eyes. "I didn't do anything."

"No one said you did," Dylan replied easily. "Now who are we talking to?"

"Do I have to answer that?"

"Yes," Traci said. "What's your name, sir?"

He blinked like he wasn't sure she was even talking to him. "Smith."

Traci rolled her eyes. "Your last name is Smith, buddy?"

"Yeah. And my first name is Billy, not buddy."

He could try the patience of a saint. Keeping a firm hold on her temper, she said, "Billy Smith, do you want to talk with us out here or inside?"

"I don't want to talk to you at all."

"You don't have a choice, buddy," Dylan said. His voice was still easy but there was a harder edge to it.

When Billy still hesitated, Traci said, "You might get a little more privacy inside."

The man sneered. "Everyone's already seen you two. Plus your car's down there."

So, he'd been watching and wasn't quite as oblivious as he'd been acting. Traci decided to call his bluff. Making a big show of pulling out her pencil and a pad of paper, she said, "All right, fine. Now, maybe you can tell me where you've —"

"Hold on. Come on in." He pulled back the door with a flare of impatience and walked across the room.

Traci and Dylan looked around for a few

255

seconds, then followed him in. It was a smelly mess inside. Cigarette ashes, old mail, empty beer bottles. Fast food wrappers. Dylan walked forward. "You alone?"

"Yeah. I live alone." His eyes darted around the room as if he wasn't sure.

It was obvious the guy was lying, but Traci figured they would have heard someone else by now if Billy had friends hiding in one of the rooms. Guys like him weren't always the stealthiest of people.

Not wanting to sit on the worn, stained couch, Traci leaned against the wall. "So, where were you two nights ago?"

"Here."

"Sure about that?" Dylan asked.

Billy's expression turned more mutinous. "Hell yeah." After a second, he looked confused again. "Why?"

"Because we're looking for someone we heard was here too," Dylan replied. He looked around the room like he was imagining hanging out there on a Saturday night. "This is a pretty big room. You've got a nice television, too. You were seriously hanging out here alone?"

"Yep." Billy nodded.

"Really?" Traci gestured to the bottles on the floor. "You've been drinking all of these by your lonesome?"

256

A line formed between his brows as he looked at the small pile of discarded bottles. "I didn't say that."

"Who was here then?"

Billy crossed his arms over his chest but didn't say a word.

Traci stared at him until he started to fidget. Then she darted a look at her partner.

Dylan stuffed his hands in his pockets. "Billy, I don't care what you've been doing in here. I'm not even interested in you at all. I just need a name. If you give it to me, then we can leave."

"Who are you looking for?"

"If we tell you the name, you need to tell us the truth. Because we're looking for someone specific, Billy," Traci said. "We need him. Need him bad. But, if you lie, the three of us are going to run into some problems."

Traci could practically see Billy processing what she just said. He began to perspire. She guessed it was because she and Dylan were staying silent and he was thinking about the consequences of either lying to the police or ratting out his friends.

After almost five minutes passed, he looked up at her. "I just remembered. There were some people over here two nights ago."

"Was any of them Hunter Benton?" Dylan asked.

Slowly, Billy nodded.

"Is he coming back anytime soon?"

He looked uncomfortable. "Maybe. I don't know."

"If Hunter comes back, you need to call me," Traci said.

"There's no way. I'm not a snitch."

"If you don't call me next time you see him, there's no way we're going to leave you alone," Dylan replied. "We'll be here in your business most every day. Parked in front of your house. Contacting collection agencies. Anyone who can make your life miserable."

"If Hunter finds out I'm telling you guys about his where-abouts, I might as well pack up and move. He's going to be pissed."

"I guess you'll have to make that decision, Billy," Traci said as she handed him her card. "I'm going to give you a week. If we don't hear anything, I'll know that you don't want to play."

Dylan smiled as he stepped out the door. "See you soon, buddy."

Traci gave Billy a mock salute before following her partner. As she walked through the weed-infested yard, she felt slimy, like she needed a hot shower, fast.

Getting in the passenger seat just as Dylan

was starting the vehicle, she said, "What do you think?"

"I think we've got more than we used to. And, I think my money's on him calling you."

"Really?"

"Look how he was living, Lucky. Hunter's not giving him anything much. Billy's going to be on the move soon. Guys like him always break."

"I hope you're right," she said just as their radio beeped.

Connecting to the dispatcher, she started calling out information to Dylan. "Multivehicle accident just off the Bridgeport exit off of I25. Ambulance and firetrucks are en route."

Dylan switched on their sirens and lights and sped off.

Billy, Hunter, and Gwen were temporarily forgotten.

CHAPTER 31

"Ballroom dancing is the art of getting
your feet out of the way faster than your
partner can step on them."

It seemed that the fifth time was the charm.
After learning more about how Officer
Lucky, Shannon, and Kimber had only
recently found each other but were already
so close, Gwen decided to try harder to
reach out to her brother — to find him.

She and Billy had never been all that
close, but she was beginning to wonder if
that distance had less to do with personality
differences as it did with their upbringing.
Their parents had pretty much ruined them
for normal interactions with anyone.

Billy, even though he was barely a year
older, had lit out of their apartment as soon
as he got a decent fake ID. With Billy gone,
her dad had even less reason to want anything to do with Gwen. Her mother? Well,

she had taken to barely subsisting.

It was no surprise that Gwen had clung to Hunter like a vine. He wasn't great, but at least he had wanted her around. She'd needed that.

But now that Hunter had gone south and turned scary, Gwen was starting to wonder if Billy had been more like her than she'd thought. Maybe he, too, had been searching for someone to connect with.

So, she'd started calling him every day and leaving messages. Serious ones. Not-so-serious ones. Promises that she didn't want anything other than to hear his voice. To have a conversation with him.

On the fifth day she called, he picked up.

"What do you want, Gwen?" he rasped.

"Why do you sound like that? Did you just wake up?" She glanced at the clock on the wall. It was two in the afternoon.

"Why are you asking?"

"You sound groggy, like you were asleep."

"Is that all you have to say? 'Cause if it is, you need to stop calling me. I don't need to pick up the phone just to hear you whine."

Wow. He sounded a lot like their father now. Her stomach sank. Reaching out to him had been a stupid idea. "I called to let you know that I left Hunter."

There was a pause, then Billy said, "You

dumped Hunter? Why would you do that?"

His new, far-more-alert tone caught her off guard. "He got really weird, Billy." He'd also been a drug dealer, but she decided to keep that to herself for now. "I realized that if I stayed with him much longer, he was going to hurt me." Or she'd lose the baby. Or she'd die . . . that had been a possibility.

"Where are you now?"

"I'm still in Bridgeport. What about you?"

"Uh, I'm up near Dayton." His voice turned suspicious. "Why do you want to know?"

"No reason. I'm just asking." Practically feeling his impatience with the conversation over the phone, she rushed on. "Billy, I got to thinking. Maybe our problems with relationships don't have as much to do with each other as they do with our parents."

"Our parents sucked, Gwen."

"I know. See, that's what I'm talking about. We have things in common that we weren't even aware of."

She heard the snap of a cigarette lighter and a sharp inhale. "What brought all this on? You just decided to mend our broken family out of the blue?"

Yes, he sounded sarcastic. And yes, he was making her say things that she'd wanted to keep to herself. But remembering some of

262

the advice the counselor at the women's center said, Gwen forged on and found some courage. "Well, I had some trouble with Hunter. After I left him, he didn't want to leave me alone."

"How come?"

Sometimes she forgot that her ex and her brother knew each other. "Well, I left during a police raid. He was selling drugs, Billy. Meth."

"Where did you go?" His voice was sharper now.

"First, I went to the hospital for a week."

"How come so long?"

"I was malnourished and needed to gain some weight."

"You must have looked like crap if they kept you so long."

"Well, um, there's more to it. You see, I'm pregnant."

"You got knocked up?"

For the rest of her life, she was going to really get mad at anyone who said something like that to her. She hated when people acted as if she got pregnant by herself. "Hunter had a part in that, too, Billy."

"Are you still pregnant?"

"Yes."

She could practically hear the wheels spinning in his head. Billy had been such an obvious thinker when they were little. He had the exact opposite of a poker face. "Kind of surprised to hear that, Gwen."

She was surprised he hadn't said exactly what he was thinking — that she should have had an abortion. "I don't know why Hunter even cares. If it was up to him, I'd be hooked on meth and either be a terrible mother or harm the baby so much he'd have a ton of problems."

"He? You're having a boy?"

His voice sounded different again. She thought he sounded even more strained, though she wasn't exactly sure why. Unless this baby news had done what all her phone calls and cajoling had not? She liked that idea. It would be so great if he finally started caring about her. "Yes. And the last sonogram I had showed that he is doing just fine."

"If you're getting a sonogram, you must be somewhere decent. Where you at?"

"I was at a center, but Hunter found me and broke in."

"So, where are you now?" His voice was firm, more direct. "Are you still in Bridgeport?"

"Uh, yes. I'm staying with some friends right now." That was all she wanted to tell him. Something about his tone sounded off.

"You have friends?"

He sounded so incredulous, it pained her. But then she told him the truth. What could it matter anyway? This was the first conversation she and Billy had shared in years. "To be honest, the cop who has been looking out for me invited me to stay with her for a little while. At least until they find him."

"Hey. Hold on a sec." She heard the click of the lighter again. Then, a muffled noise . . . and was that another voice?

When he got back on the line, she said, "Billy, who are you talking to? I mean, I know I don't know any of your friends . . . but are you doing okay? What kind of job are you doing?"

"He's working for me," Hunter said. "Which means he's gonna be real happy when I give him his bonus."

White-hot panic engulfed her as she quickly hung up the phone.

And as, she did so, she realized two more things.

She'd been foolish to hope that her brother cared about her.

And she'd been just as stupid to think Hunter would ever give up so easily.

Looking around the loft, with the sounds

of music floating upstairs from Shannon's
latest class, Gwen wondered what she'd just
done.

CHAPTER 32

"To dance is to be out of yourself.
Larger, more beautiful, more powerful.
This is power, it is glory on earth, and
it is yours for the taking."
— AGNES DE MILLE

Out of everything Traci had gone through
with Gwen, the idea of Gwen watching
Shannon teach her and Matt to waltz made
her the most uncomfortable. So much so,
she'd asked Shannon to keep the lesson
private.

"Our class is going to be fine, Traci,"
Shannon soothed for about the third time.
"I promise, you're making mountains out of
molehills."

Traci loved her newfound sister. She really
did. But honestly, there were times when
she was sure she was going to scream if she
heard one more down-home saying. Gather-
ing her patience, she said, "Shannon, we

don't really know this girl. I don't want her to know so much about my life." Of course, what she really meant was that she didn't want Gwen to see her making a fool of herself.

"It's kind of too late to worry about that, don't you think? You moved Gwen in here with us and pretty much forced us to accept her because she needed people who cared."

"I did that for her safety."

"I know. But, tell me the truth, did you ever think of the logistics of it all?"

"I thought about how it would affect Dylan and my schedule. We cleared it with the lieutenant."

"Traci, I mean, did you think about what she would do all day?"

"Not really." Even though Shannon's door was closed, she lowered her voice. "I guess I just thought Gwen would be napping and hanging out a lot."

"You thought she'd be hanging out alone in her room for hours and hours every day?"

"Well, yes. I mean, that's what she did at the hospital." Of course, now she realized that that expectation was both stupid and selfish. Gwen was eighteen, scared, and lonely. Of course she wasn't going to want to sit all day by herself. It wasn't good for her, either.

"She was sick then, honey." Shannon propped both hands on her hips. "Traci, I'm just going to say it. Expecting her to sit by herself in a room all day long isn't healthy or natural. The girl needs companionship."

"But I don't want to push her on you." What she really didn't want was for Gwen to somehow bother her sisters so much that they'd want to kick Gwen out. And, maybe even get mad at her.

Okay, maybe that was what she was worried most about.

"If Jennifer didn't want Gwen's help in the kitchen, she would say so." She arched a brow. "And, honey, if I didn't want her hanging around the studio, I would've told you so."

"Fine. I hear you."

"If you do, I hope you hear what I'm about to tell you."

"Which is?"

"You are so afraid of getting hurt that you keep everyone at a distance."

Stung, she retorted, "I'm not afraid of getting hurt by Gwen Camp."

"But maybe you're afraid of getting hurt by Matt Rossi?" Before Traci could set her straight, Shannon said, "I don't think there's anything wrong with Gwen knowing you are taking dance lessons with the handsome doctor."

"It's out of convenience, Shannon." Which wasn't true at all.

After giving Traci an "I know what you're saying, and it's ridiculous" look, Shannon shrugged. "Gwen already knows the talented and very convenient Dr. Rossi, so there's no veil of secrecy there. You need to calm down and stop looking for trouble where there ain't none."

Only hearing Shannon's last three words made Traci back-track. Shannon's accent got thicker whenever she was upset or tired. No matter what, she didn't want to be yet another source of distress for her sister. "Fine. Let's go downstairs and dance."

Shannon raised an eyebrow. "You want to dance the waltz looking like that?"

Traci looked down at her tennis shoes, leggings and oversized T-shirt. "What's wrong with this?"

"You're about to be waltzing Strauss. Go put on a skirt."

"You have got to be kidding me."

"I don't kid about Strauss. Give the man respect, Lucky."

"Fine. But if Matt makes fun of me, you

270

get to tell him that you made me wear a dress."

"I'll happily tell him that." She made a shooing motion with her hands. "Get going, girl! Matt will be here any minute."

She pulled open the door. "Next thing you're going to tell me is to put on heels, too."

"I'm so glad you suggest that. Yes, put on heels, Traci," she said sweetly. "Thank you. Thank you very much."

Traci rolled her eyes at her sister's giggles as she walked back upstairs to her new room that she shared with Kimber. Luckily, Kimber was still out of town so she wouldn't be teasing her mercilessly when she borrowed a pair of her pumps.

Just as she reached the entryway, after carefully navigating down two flights of stairs in four-inch heels, the front door opened and Matt strode in. The moment he caught sight of her he drew to a stop.

And gaped.

Heat traipsed across her neck and shoulders — both of which were on display, thanks to the only dress she'd found that was comfortable enough and matched Kimber's gorgeous black patent leather pumps. "Hi," she said.

"Hi." He kept staring as he walked toward her. "You look . . . you look . . ."

"Ridiculous?"

"Fabulous. Absolutely gorgeous."

"Thanks. You look . . ."

He glanced down at his light green scrubs and Crocs. "Like I just got out of surgery?"

"You ran over here, didn't you?"

"I didn't want to be late."

"Shannon would have understood if you had to cancel."

"I wasn't worried about upsetting your sister, Traci. I didn't want to cancel on you."

Making lemons out of lemonade, she smiled. "Actually, I'm really glad to see you dressed like that. Now I can go back upstairs and put on a pair of jeans. I told Shannon that I didn't need to wear a dress and heels, but she was all like 'You must respect Strauss.' "

"Strauss?"

"He's some fancy, dead classical composer. We're going to be waltzing to him tonight."

"Would you do me a favor? Would you keep on that outfit even though we don't exactly match?"

She raised an eyebrow. "Really?"

"You're a pretty woman in jeans or sweats or like I saw you the other night in pajama pants. You're smart, and an incredibly able police officer. But, Traci Lucky, I think you look absolutely gorgeous right now."

She was so touched by his words, she searched for something to say. "It's the makeup . . . and Kimber's shoes."

"It's you. So, do you mind keeping on that dress and heels even though it's all probably not very comfortable?"

"I don't mind at all." Feeling sheepish, she added, "Honestly, it was kind of fun to get dressed up for a change. Plus, Shannon would kill me if I didn't keep this dress on."

"Good." Looking just beyond her, he smiled. "Hey, Mrs. Lange. You're looking lovely tonight as well."

"Thank you, Dr. Rossi," Shannon replied. "Shall we dance?"

He winked at Traci as they entered the studio. She followed him, shaking her head at Shannon's corny saying that somehow always sounded better than it should.

But as soon as Matt spied Gwen sitting in the corner with a stack of papers on her lap, he stopped. "What's going on, Gwen?"

Shannon raised her chin. "Gwen asked if she could help me, so I told her I'd love her help organizing some of my files. It's easiest for her to be in here. You don't mind, do you?"

Matt looked taken aback but smiled after a second. "Not at all."

Noticing that Gwen looked uncomfortable, Traci said, "You had better be careful, Gwen. If you hang out in here too much, Shannon's going to have you dancing before you know it."

Gwen giggled. "I'd look like a moose trying to dance with this belly. I'll stick to filing."

"If we can learn to waltz, you could too," Matt said. "Traci and I aren't exactly the most graceful couple in Bridgeport."

Before Traci could think of anything to say about that, Shannon put on the music.

"Okay, you two. Let's get started. Get into position."

Traci held out her left hand for Matt's right, stepped closer when he circled her waist with his right, and remembered at the very last minute to stand up straight.

"There you go," Matt murmured.

When he smiled at her, she could feel her breath catch.

And just for a second, nothing else mattered in the world. Nothing at all.

CHAPTER 33

"Life is like dancing. If we have a big
floor, many people will dance. Some will
get angry when the rhythm changes.
But life is changing all the time."
— DON MIGUEL RUIZ

Sitting in the corner of the studio, trying to be inconspicuous while she tried to take in every little moment of the lesson, Gwen felt something shift inside her. It was as if, until that moment, she'd only known one way to go, but now she realized that there were other roads it was possible to travel as well.

Though it was a little bit over the top, she felt like she'd been wandering through her life, simply trying to survive, but now she had a path to take. Somehow, some way, she wanted to one day be the woman dancing in this room.

Just hearing the music pour out of the speakers and seeing the graceful way Shannon carried herself made Gwen want to be a little more like that too.

"You doing okay over there, Gwen?" Shannon asked when Dr. Rossi and Officer Lucky were getting a sip of water.

"Hmm? Oh, yes." She held up two sheets of paper. "I'm making progress."

Shannon wore a puzzled expression as she approached. "You've had the sweetest look on your face while you've been watching Matt and Traci."

"I've never seen two people learn to waltz before."

Shannon smiled. "It's not a dance for everyone, I know."

Gwen knew she should leave it at that. If she didn't try to explain herself, then no one would ever have to know how intrigued she was. But another part of her thought that it was time to stop being so safe. "Um, I was actually thinking that it looks fun."

A new warmth entered Shannon's expression. "It is fun." Her smile widened as her husband, Officer Lange, entered the studio. "Right, Dylan?"

He'd walked right over to Dr. Rossi's and Officer Lucky's sides. But his head popped up at Shannon's question. "Is what right, Shan?"

"I was just telling Gwen here that waltz-

276

ing is fun. You've enjoyed it, right?"

"I did. Absolutely."

"Gwen, would you like to dance a little bit tonight too?"

Feeling four sets of eyes on her, three of which looked shocked, Gwen shook her head. "That's okay. Like I said, I'm bound to make a bunch of mistakes since I can hardly see my feet."

"No one minds. You could dance with Dylan."

With her husband, the police officer? This was getting more and more awkward. "Thanks, but I'll pass." She kicked a bare foot out. I'm not dressed for dancing anyway."

"No one cares about that. I dance in black leggings and tank tops half the time." She motioned with her hand. "Come on. Why don't you give it a try?"

Feeling like a cornered rat, Gwen glanced at Officer Lucky.

But instead of looking irritated, she looked amused. "Come on Gwen. Give it a try. Waltzing is better than paperwork, I promise."

Officer Lange chuckled as he stood in the center of the room. "Traci means that in the best way. I promise."

"Okay." She set all the papers she'd been

holding in a neat pile on the floor and got to her feet. Next thing she knew, Shannon was giving her instructions about where to put her hands and Officer Lange's hand was at her waist — or where her waist would have been if she still had one.

Once all four of them were settled, Shannon put the music back on. "Ah, my favorite!" she exclaimed. " 'The Blue Danube Waltz.' "

"Oh, brother," Officer Lange joked. "Now we're going to be hearing this the rest of the night."

"You will if you don't keep your arms steady, Dylan. No noodle arms! Now, yes, one, two-three. One, two-three. Come on Traci. You're not marching in a parade. Be more fluid."

"I'm trying. I have on heels here."

Gwen did giggle as she counted under her breath and moved where Officer Lange guided her.

He looked down at her and smiled. "You're doing a good job."

"I've never waltzed before. Or done anything like this."

"I hadn't either until I met Shannon. But it's actually kind of fun."

"Thank you for being my partner. I mean, I know you are doing this for your wife, but thanks."

"It's not a problem. I agree with Traci. It's better to dance than do paperwork. Especially at seven at night."

Shannon appeared at their side. "There you go, Gwen. Now, I know it's hard because you're barefoot, but try to step more on the ball of your foot." As Gwen adjusted her step, Shannon smiled again. "You're a natural."

Gwen peeked at the mirror and shook her head. She was in black leggings and a top that someone gave her at the women's center. But even more than that, she knew she was only a five-month-pregnant eighteen-year-old in the arms of one of the police officers who was hunting her ex-boyfriend. There was nothing graceful or elegant about her.

But then, as Officer Lange turned her and she laughed, she caught sight of herself again. There was color in her cheeks, she almost looked like she was doing well . . . and her eyes were bright.

She looked happy. That was enough.

Later that night, two hours after the class ended and Gwen went to her room, there was a knock at her door. Assuming it was Officer Lucky, she pulled it open. "Oh. Hi,

Shannon."

"Yes, it's me." Her gaze darted to the bed. "Oh, no. Did I wake you up?"

"No. I was reading." She held up a novel Kimber had let her borrow.

"Oh, good. Can I come in?"

"Of course." She stepped aside.

Shannon smiled at her as she sat down in the small chair next to the desk. "I had an idea and I'm afraid I got so excited about it, that Dylan told me to come up here to talk to you."

She perched on the edge of her bed. "Yes?"

"You know how I've been teaching lessons to that group of senior citizens on Wednesday nights?"

Gwen nodded. About a dozen men and women between the ages of seventy and eighty or so came in for a group lesson. It was a going joke upstairs that they were noisier than Shannon's teenagers in the afternoon.

"Well, I could always use the help. I tell you what — some of those folks just about killed me last time we practiced swing dancing. They don't know their own limits." She chuckled. "Gwen, what would you think about helping me with the class?"

"I don't know how to dance."

280

"I meant what I said today. I think you're a natural. You picked up the steps right away. And even better, it seemed like you enjoyed it."

"I did enjoy it."

"Well?"

"You don't think it's going to be weird?"

"They're all really accepting. Plus, I think they're going to be glad to have someone young in there with us." Her voice quickened. "Now, it wouldn't be all fun and games. They bring snacks and we provide decaf and water. You'd have to help with setting up and cleaning up. And, you'd have to help me with some of my students who need an extra hand but don't want to admit to that."

"I'd be happy to help."

"What do you think about ten dollars an hour?"

"What?"

"You know, to pay you?" Shannon asked patiently.

"You don't have to pay me. I'm living in your house."

"I spoke to Dylan, and he thinks that amount sounded fair. Plus, it is work. And don't say no. It's a two-hour class, so it's just twenty dollars a week."

But it was twenty dollars more than she

was making right now. More than she'd made in months. "If you really think it's okay, I'd love to do that."

"Really?" She got to her feet. "That's, well, that's just fantastic." Before Gwen could brace herself, Shannon hugged her. "This is going to be great. Thank you!" she said as she walked out of the room.

Gwen carefully closed the door and locked it, then got back into bed.

And then she allowed herself to smile too. Something amazing had happened tonight and she hadn't even seen it coming.

CHAPTER 34

"First comes the sweat. Then comes the beauty, if you're very lucky and have said your prayers."
— GEORGE BALANCHINE

They'd worked together. They'd danced together. He'd taken Traci to Sunday dinner and kissed her when he didn't think anyone was looking. But one thing Matt hadn't done was take his new girlfriend on a real date.

It wasn't all his fault. Between his on-call schedule and her nearly twenty-four-hour surveillance of Gwen, neither of them had been able to find more than a couple of free hours. But things were about to change.

He'd decided to invite her over to his house for dinner. He could grill a better-than-average salmon and throw a couple of potatoes in the oven with the best of them. Added to that was some steamed vegetables and a platter of cupcakes from the local bakery, and Matt knew it was as good as he could do without a lot more money and time.

When she entered his kitchen at five o'clock, her eyes widened. "Wow, look at this spread. You've been busy."

"Not that busy with this. I bought the cupcakes at the bakery."

Her eyes warmed. "You weren't baking at all hours of the night?"

"Yeah. I guess that was a given."

She ran a finger along one of the placemats that Bennie had run out to buy for him. "I'm teasing. Everything looks really nice. Wonderful, even." She looked up at him and smiled. "Thank you."

"You're welcome. I was determined to do this up right, even though we're kind of stuck here." Since he was on call and she didn't want to go far, they'd decided to have their date at his house. He pointed to the two pitchers on the countertop. One was filled with iced tea, the other with lemonade. "Want an Arnold Palmer?"

"Absolutely."

After he handed her a glass, she sipped it appreciatively. "This is great."

"I wish I could have given you a glass of wine, but this will do."

"It's perfect. Now, what I can't help with?"

"Nothing. The potatoes are already in the oven and the vegetables are in a bowl. I just have to put them in the steamer." He checked his watch. "The salmon won't take long. Want to sit outside for a few minutes before I turn on the grill?"

"Sure."

She followed him outside. As he pulled out a chair for her, Matt realized he was a little nervous. He wanted everything to go well with Traci. Even though they knew a lot about each other, they didn't know everything.

He still wasn't clear on some of the most basic things about her.

"I feel like we've done everything backward," he said. "I know how you react in a crisis, but I don't know if you even like fish. Do you like salmon? I realize now that I should have asked earlier."

"I like it fine. I'm not a picky eater." She took another sip of her drink before setting it down. "I've, um, thought the same thing about you from time to time. I know that you're a caring doctor and a dutiful son, but I don't know where you went to college or how you decided to become an obstetrician."

"I went to Ohio State for my undergrad,

285

Nashville for medical school, and did my residency out in Kentucky."

"Why out there?"

"It sounded exotic, I guess. I knew I wanted to practice in southern Ohio if I could. I realized that between growing up and all that schooling, I really hadn't seen anything. I was able to choose between Milwaukee and Phoenix." He smiled. "The warm weather won."

"I haven't been anywhere. Not really."

"You worked up in Cleveland."

She nodded. "I did. And me and two girlfriends went to Florida for a vacation after we graduated the academy. But other than that, I've only been around the state."

"Do you ever want to travel?"

Biting her bottom lip, she nodded. "You know how I grew up. I never had big dreams of seeing the world. My dreams centered around having my own address. But now that I have Kimber in my life, I'm a little jealous. She goes everywhere. All over the world with her modeling career."

"I remember you saying that she was going to Mexico or something for a photo shoot."

"That's just the tip of the iceberg. She's done runway shoes in Italy and France." She shook her head. "Isn't that something?"

"Maybe she'll take you with her one day."

"No way."

"Why not?"

"Me hanging out with a bunch of models? It will be like junior high again and I'll start analyzing every flaw I have. No thank you."

"Do you really think you have flaws?"

"Ah, yes. But it isn't that I do or not. It's normal comparison." She raised a finger, shaking it like a schoolteacher. "And don't say that's a female trait. I work around lots of men. They're always competing."

"I can't deny that." His voice warmed. "I still think you'd have fun with her." He grinned. "Maybe you could go as her security guard or something."

She brightened right up. "Maybe so. Though, Shannon, Kimber, Jennifer, and I were talking and we've been thinking we should just plan a girls' trip together. You know what they say . . . if it's not on the calendar, it will never happen."

He was charmed. Completely charmed, and he hadn't seen that coming with a woman like Traci. Impressed, yes. Amused? Absolutely. But now that they were talking about nothing, just life, he was beginning to realize that she was all girl underneath all those hard layers.

Wariness entered her eyes. "What did I say?"

"Hmm? Oh, nothing." He laughed. "That's not true. I was just thinking that you've got a lot of homespun sayings for a city girl from Cleveland."

"Oh, my gosh. I know! I've picked every one of them up from Shannon. She's the queen of clichéd sayings and Southern comfort."

"Don't be upset by that. I think it's cute. Charming, really."

"I never thought of myself that way but I'll take it. Desiree, my house mom, always said there was more to me than I realized. Maybe she was right."

Her house mom. "Do you talk about your childhood much?"

"I just was talking about it."

He shook his head. He wanted to know more about her. He wanted to hear what she'd liked and what she hated. Specifics. "No, I mean, dinners, the other kids. What living in the group home was like? Do you tell many people about that?"

"I never tell people about that." Her voice was cool.

And there went the layers right up, like a roll of Saran Wrap had just tightly concealed every part of her that was out for anyone to see. He mentally cursed himself. He was usually a little smoother.

"Okay. You know what? I think it's past time for me to get that fish on the grill."

"Do you want some help?"

"I got it. You sip your tea. I'll be right back." Walking into the kitchen, he retrieved the cedar planks that he'd prepared earlier and placed them on a big baking tray.

When he came back out, Traci was sitting exactly like he'd left her. "These don't take long. Only about ten minutes."

"Sounds good."

He could feel the tension rise up in her as she silently watched him place the planks on his grill. He stood for a few seconds, pretending to watch the fish cook, but what he was really doing was wondering how he was going to get her back to herself. No, get them back to where they'd been — before he'd decided to play Dr. Phil with her life.

When he turned around, she looked him in the eye. "I'm sorry."

"Nothing to be sorry about." He meant that, too. She'd already shared a lot with him.

"I've gotten pretty good at going over the basics. You know, relaying information like it happened to someone else. I guess I have a lot to learn when it comes to sharing my feelings."

Getting up to check on the fish, he said, "I shouldn't have pushed. I want to get to know you better, but that doesn't mean I couldn't have stuck to some easier information." He turned to face her. "Like, why didn't I just ask you what your favorite color was? Why did I have to start with the tough stuff?"

"Red," she said as she walked to his side. "My favorite color is red."

He pulled her into his arms and kissed the top of her head. "Red is my favorite too."

CHAPTER 35

"You live as long as you dance."
— RUDOLF NUREYEV

Dr. Matt Rossi could really kiss. Standing in his entryway, practically glued to every inch of him, Traci pulled away at long last. She inhaled deeply, because somewhere in the midst of all those kisses, she'd forgotten to breathe. "I better go," she whispered.

"I know. We both need to get some sleep," he murmured as he curved his palms around her cheeks and leaned down for another kiss.

And she let him. Because, well, it was nice, she would rather make out with him than do just about anything else. And because once she left his house and headed back she was going to have to return to her real life.

But finally, after another five minutes went by, she stepped back with a laugh. "No more!" she teased. "If we go much further,

291

I'm not going to want to leave."

"If we go much further, I'm going to want you to stay."

Oh boy. That was definitely what they did not need to be doing. For a number of reasons. She smiled. "Thank you for dinner. The salmon was delicious. The cupcakes were even better."

"Shoot." He turned to the kitchen and picked up the pastry box filled with no less than twenty cupcakes inside. "I almost let you leave without them."

She smiled up at him. "My roommates will be very grateful. And don't worry, if they think you made them, I won't tell a soul."

He laughed. "I appreciate that. I'd hate it if you ruined my baking credentials." Walking to the door, he said, "I'll walk you out."

"I am a cop, you know. People pay me to keep them safe."

"Then don't pay me a thing to look after you," he said as he closed the door behind them and walked her out.

And . . . there it was again. He was spouting those phrases that she didn't think real men ever said. After clicking on her key fob, she held out her hands. "I'll take these now. Thank you again."

He handed them off then stepped back.

"Text me when you get home?"

"I will. Good night, Matt."

"Night."

He stayed where he was until she started her car and backed out his drive. Then waved to her as she went on her way. And what had she done? She'd waved to him right back.

Because she'd wanted to. Because she'd wanted to be that silly, giddy girl that she'd never been. Just for a while.

And just like that, their awkward conversation came back to her. She knew what she was going to have to do.

At the next stoplight, she pulled out her phone, scanned through her list of contacts, and then clicked on Jan's name. As it rang, she realized she was both hoping and fearing that Jan would pick up.

"Traci? Everything all right, girl?"

And, that was Jan for you. She started every conversation like they were in the middle of it. She wasn't good at small talk.

"Hi to you too."

"Whatever. Answer me. Are you okay?"

Traci could practically see Jan. No doubt she was wearing an old pair of faded jeans and a button-down that had probably seen too many washings. Her feet would be encased in Birkenstocks and her toenails

293

would be painted something bright. "I was just calling to see how you were."

"At nine on a Friday night? Traci Lucky, don't you start messing with me."

"Yet, you didn't say how you were," Traci fired back.

"Fine. I'm good. Nothing much to report."

"Do you have any kids in the house?"

"Three right now."

"Just three?"

"Two are permanent residents. They're nice girls who've been through hell and back. I've decided to be more selective of who I put around them."

"Do you have your toenails painted?"

"Are my — Traci, what is going on with you? And yes, ma'am, they are. I'm rocking alligator green and have rhinestones attached to my big toes."

"I'm sorry I'm missing that."

"If you finally start talking to me, I might snap you a picture when we hang up. Now, talk to me."

"Okay. Um, hold on a sec." She parked on the street, rolled her windows down a few inches, and then turned off her engine. And texted Matt to let him know that she got home safe. "Sorry, I had to text someone."

"In the middle of my call?"

"It was to the guy I'm dating. He likes to know when I made it home safe."

Jan chuckled. "You've got yourself a keeper?"

"He's a keeper, no doubt about that. But I don't know if I have him."

"Why not?"

Her voice had lowered. Softened. Traci knew it was Jan's way of coaxing information from a rock.

And it had worked with her every time. "His name is Matt and he's a doctor, Jan. And obstetrician-gynecologist. He's gorgeous and Italian and he made me dinner tonight. And bought cupcakes for me and all my roommates."

"How'd you meet him?"

"Through work. I was bringing in this girl named Gwen . . . she's pregnant. She's another story. Anyway, he was the doctor on call."

"And you two connected just like that?"

"Kind of. We've been taking small steps. And have kind of done things out of order. I've already met his whole family, but tonight was our first real date."

"Traci, why did you call?"

"He asked me to talk about my past. And not just that I was given up, never adopted,

295

moved to a group home spiel."

"Which is the truth but also a complete lie."

Ouch. "It's not a lie. But you're right." She drew a breath, then added, "He asked me if I ever talk about specifics. How I felt. What it was like. What I was like."

"Did you tell him the truth then?"

She nodded. "I told him never."

"And?"

"And he was disappointed in me. I apologized, then he apologized and said he shouldn't have pushed."

"Maybe he was right. He shouldn't have pushed you for information."

"But Jan, I know I need to tell him. I mean, how can I have a real relationship with someone if I keep a whole section of my life as off limits?"

"Say it, Traci. Say what you're thinking of."

"Fine. How can I share that I was in some really terrible foster homes and got beaten and abused in them?"

"And that you almost died when you were five."

She ran a finger along the scar on her side — the scar she'd told a former boyfriend that she'd gotten in a knife attack while on the job. "And that I almost died when the family's real son decided to try to kill me, so I'd go away."

"There. You said it."

"I hate saying it." Her voice was shaking now. "And don't you dare tell me that it would get easier with telling because I don't like thinking about it. I really don't want to think about it out loud."

"I understand."

"I don't want to tell the best guy I've ever met that I've got issues either."

"You don't have issues. You were a little girl and people hurt you." Jan's voice was harsh. "You can take credit for a lot of things, but you don't need to take credit for that, Miss Lucky."

That name bolted her out of the spiral she'd been falling into. She shook her head. She hated how it didn't take much, even after all this time, to still remember how helpless she'd felt in some of those foster homes.

"Jan, do I have to tell Matt about my past?"

"You called to tell me that you did."

"But I haven't even told Shannon and Kimber."

"Do you want to tell them?"

"You know I don't. But even worse than that, I don't want them feeling guilty for

297

something that wasn't their fault."

Jan sighed. "Traci, I don't have the right answer for you. I really don't. I've had my share of kids in this house, and I've tended to more than one who was in a lot worse shape than you when you got here. Every time, I said a prayer for them. Prayed that one day they would be just fine and have a life to be proud of."

"Your prayers worked for me."

She laughed. "They did. In spite of your mulishness, you have a real nice life to be proud of. You're not the only one who's done okay, either."

"You raised a lot of decent people." Which was a compliment. "You did a lot of good, Jan."

"What I want to tell you, Traci Lucky, is that I never tried to teach you how to talk about your bad. I never told you to forget it. You can't undo a life."

Traci nibbled her bottom lip, trying to locate the advice in Jan's words. "I still don't know what to do. Do I keep it all inside? Can I still love if I don't share it? What about Matt? What about Shannon and Kimber?"

"Have mercy, Traci. You are wearing me out."

"All you have to do is —"

"Tell you what to do? No thank you. I order around plenty of teenagers, I have no desire to start ordering around grown women."

She looked toward her house and saw that Shannon was standing in the doorway watching her. "I think I have to go soon. Shannon's standing at the door."

"What's special about that?"

"You know. She's waiting on me."

"So you've got yourself some love and family right there, don't you?" She chuckled again. "Looks like you've got your answer."

"What? But —"

"I'm going to go make myself some hot tea. I suggest you do the same, sweet Traci. After, you know, you assure that girl in the doorway that you're just fine. Night, doll."

She hung up before Traci could say a word. Staring at the phone, she clicked END and wondered what she was supposed to do now.

Then she noticed that Shannon wasn't standing alone. Next to her was Kimber. Right behind, Jennifer and Gwen peered over her sisters' shoulders.

And she realized that her heart was already full. It turned out she'd been wrong.

A person could absolutely find love even if they didn't share all their ugliness.

She was living proof of that.

Opening the door, she slowly got out and walked to the passenger side to retrieve the box Matt had passed to her.

"Traci! What are you doing?" Kimber asked.

She looked down at the box with the bakery's logo emblazoned in bright orange across the lid. Matt was going to have to offer her cupcakes that didn't tattle on him if he wanted her sisters to think he could bake. "Getting out a bakery box. Matt got all of us cupcakes from Pizzazz."

"Pizzazz Cupcakes? I love him," Shannon said really loudly.

Traci grabbed her purse and walked toward them. She knew one day she was going to tell Shannon that she wasn't the only one who felt that way.

CHAPTER 36

"Dancing — however you do it, even if it's
in your living room — is a great workout."
— CIARA

Gwen had now been living above the dance
studio on Plum Street for three weeks. Even
though she was living in a police officer's
room, getting bigger by the minute, and
basically hiding from a crazy ex-boyfriend,
she'd never been happier. For the first time
in her life, she didn't wake up stressed or
mad at the world. Instead, she was feeling
useful and cheerful.

It was all because of the women who had
essentially adopted her. Jennifer asked for
her help every day in the kitchen and
praised Gwen whenever she was able to do
a new task well. Kimber brought home
books from the library and bookstore for
her and often invited her to sit in the living
room and read.

But her favorite part of every day was her time with Shannon in the dance studio. Shannon loved to dance and loved to teach other people how to dance.

And to Gwen's surprise, she enjoyed the lessons, too, even though she was inexperienced, not very flexible, and pregnant. Shannon didn't seem to care about any of that, though. She just kept bringing Gwen water, vanilla milkshakes, and her smiles. After a little fifteen-or-twenty-minute lesson, Shannon would make Gwen sit down and rest for a bit.

Usually, Gwen would only do so reluctantly. She loved her little dances sessions with Shannon.

Unless they were tap dancing. *That,* she was discovering, was far harder than it looked.

"That's right, Gwen," Shannon said. "Step, hop, step, ball-change." She demonstrated the simple-looking tap move twice, each slight movement of her foot making a clear, distinct tap.

Staring down at her feet, Gwen repeated the steps, then frowned as it all came out as a clunky mess. "Argh. Let me do it again," she said before Shannon could correct her. "Step, hop, hop, shuffle." She froze. "Wait, I just messed it all up, didn't I?"

Looking amused, Shannon nodded. "Yep, but it's not a problem. We just need to break the combination into small sections." She lifted her right foot. "Ready?"

She took a steadying breath and nodded. "Ready as I'll ever be."

"Hey, will you do me a favor?" When Gwen met her eyes in the mirror, Shannon continued. "Instead of looking down at your feet, look at the two of us in the mirror. It helps. I promise."

"All right." Taking a deep breath, she looked in the mirror and said out loud the steps with Shannon. After two tries, Shannon clapped.

"Good for you! Well done."

Gwen laughed. "Not hardly. But, it was better."

"Are you liking tap any better yet?" Shannon asked as they sat down next to her little desk.

"A little," Gwen said after taking a sip of water. "It's frustrating because it looks easier than it is."

"I agree. People always act like those high kicks are the hardest things the Rockettes do. I've always believed it was all the other perfectly done movements."

Gwen started to nod, then said, "Don't get mad, but who are the Rockettes?"

"Oh, Gwen. Are you in for a treat! I'll find a video of them on YouTube. You're going to love them."

"Hey, Shannon?"

"Hmm?"

"Traci told me that you used to dance in competitions."

"She's right. I did."

"What happened?"

"I got hurt." She pursed her lips. "And, to tell you the truth, I had to face the facts that while I was good, I was never going to be one of the best."

"That had to be tough."

"Oh, I don't know. To be honest, I get more enjoyment teaching classes here than I did competing. I guess everything works out for a reason."

Gwen figured that was true, but she wasn't sure why everything was working out the way it was for her. Looking up at the clock, she said, "Our old people are going to be here in an hour."

"That would be senior citizens, Miss Camp," Shannon said. "So, are you ready to waltz tonight?"

Gwen smiled. Last week, she'd been partners with a seventy-five-year-old man who fancied himself a Fred Astaire. She could hardly keep up with him. "As ready as I'll ever be."

Bending down, Shannon unbuckled the straps on her tap shoes. "We better go get ready . . . if you feel up to it?"

"Of course."

Setting her tap shoes neatly in a cubby in the corner of the room, Shannon winked. "I'll see you back here in about forty minutes. And don't worry, Jennifer or Dylan is going to help me bring down coffee, water, and cookies," she added before sailing out of the room.

Gwen propped one of her feet on Shannon's empty chair and unlaced a shoe, then did the same with her other foot. Just as she was walking to the cubby to put her tap shoes away, Officer Lucky appeared at the door.

"Gwen. Good. You're here."

Gwen's stomach sank as she turned to face her. "What happened?"

"Hunter turned up. Dylan got word that he's laying low over in Newport."

"Newport? That's in Kentucky."

Officer Lucky nodded as she took the chair that Shannon had just vacated and gestured for Gwen to sit down as well. "I didn't give him much credit, but crossing state lines was pretty smart. We've got our contacts there helping out, but it's going to be harder to pick him up."

"But he can just cross any of the bridges and get back to Ohio. He can even walk on the pedestrian bridge across the Ohio River."

"You're right. This is one of those times that following the law makes things harder than they should be."

Though it wasn't good news, Gwen couldn't help but think that things weren't all that different either. She was still hiding out from Hunter.

Unless . . .

"Officer Lucky, are you telling me this because you want me out of here? Do you want me to leave?"

Her eyes widened. "Leave? No," she said firmly. "Gwen, I wasn't thinking that at all."

"Are you sure? Because you look like there's something else you want to tell me."

"There is. We've already filed a restraining order, but Dylan heard that Hunter might send someone else to find you."

"Rick."

Officer Lucky pulled out her phone and started typing notes. "I know you told me about this guy, but tell me about him again."

"He's Hunter's friend. I know him. My girlfriend was dating him when she introduced me to Hunter. He's dangerous too."

306

Watching Officer Lucky write more notes, she said, "I don't understand why they care about me, Officer Lucky. I know he doesn't love me. I know he doesn't want this baby."

"I couldn't tell you the answer for sure. Sometimes people act like little kids. They want what they can't have. Sometimes they transfer blame. They see their situation as wrong and instead of taking responsibility for themselves they pick someone else to be the cause."

"It doesn't make sense."

"These guys aren't known for making sense, Gwen."

"I guess not. So, what should I do?"

"Well, first off, I think you're going to need to come to West Virginia with all of us."

"For Shannon's party?"

"Uh-huh. Gwen, I was going to ask Ellen if you could stay at the women's center for two nights but I don't think that's a good idea."

"But we've talked about me staying here by myself with just some of your cop friends stopping by."

"I never thought that was a particularly good option," Officer Lange said. "Now it's a definite no-go. Plus, I think Kimber and Jennifer would really like your company.

Don't worry. Going to West Virginia will be fun."

Based on the way Traci Lucky was looking — which was like she'd rather be eating a bowl of tofu, Gwen was fairly sure this trip wasn't going to be fun at all.

But at least she'd be safe.

"I heard that you've been doing a few small errands with Jennifer and Kimber," Traci said.

"Yes. But I haven't been doing much. Just going to the grocery store and the library."

"I need you to stop that. Stay inside."

The anxiety about her situation jumped up a notch. "Do I have to stay hidden? I'm supposed to help Shannon with her class tonight."

Officer Lucky looked like she wanted to say no, but her expression softened. "You really like helping Shannon, don't you?"

"Yes. It makes me feel like I'm not useless."

"You aren't useless. Not by a long shot." Staring at Gwen again, Officer Lucky seemed to come to a decision. "Fine. You can help out. But I'm going to be hanging out in the lobby, just in case something weird happens."

"Weird in the middle of a senior citizens'

308

ballroom dance class?"

"I know it sounds like a long shot, but if I've learned anything, it's that weird things happen when you least expect it. I'm determined to expect everything."

"I will too, then."

Officer Lucky stood up. "You best get dolled up then." She winked. "Someone told me that you've got quite a smitten dancing partner."

She laughed. "He's patient, that's what he is. Last week I stepped on his toes twice. Mr. Holt is a sweetie, though."

"I'm thinking you are too, Miss Camp," she said as they walked to the stairs.

Walking up the stairs, Gwen swallowed hard. Officer Lucky didn't seem to look down on her anymore.

In fact, it was almost like they were friends.

CHAPTER 37

CHA-CHA: *This flirtatious dance can be thought of as a slower mamba. Much hip movement will be involved.*

"All told, this car trip hasn't been so bad," Traci said as she guided her Subaru Forester back onto the highway after they'd taken a brief stop for lunch at a fast-food restaurant. "At least we're all together."

"Well, we're kind of all together." Pointing to the sedan behind them, Kimber said, "Our girl Shannon's not here."

"Which is a good thing, I promise," Jennifer said. "Her parents keep calling, then mine do. I, personally, needed a little space."

"Amen to that," Kimber said. "Your parents were texting you like crazy while we ate."

"I think they're as excited as Mr. and Mrs. Murphy are about this shindig." Jennifer chuckled. "Plus, our four parents are having a great time together. Next thing you know, they'll all be planning vacations together."

"At least they won't be calling you so much," Kimber teased. "Even with all the excitement, I can't deny that I like this trip much better than the last one we were on. I'm telling you what, Traci. Last time I was a nervous wreck."

Thinking of just how hard it had been to first meet Kimber, who was beautiful, polished, and extremely well-traveled while she had been none of those things made her wince. "Me too."

"Really? You sure didn't act nervous at all. I thought you had to be one of the most confident women I'd ever met."

"I'm good at hiding things like that."

"How come you both were so nervous?" Jennifer asked. She was sitting in the back seat next to Gwen. "I know your general history, but I thought you two would have reacted differently."

"I can't speak for Shannon, but half of me was excited and the other half was scared to death," Traci said. "I was so worried that they weren't going to accept me."

"I felt the same," Kimber said. "We'd never met face-to-face before, you know?" She held out her arm. "Then there's my skin color. Obviously, I'm biracial. Most

311

people don't think anything about it, but every once in a while, I meet someone who isn't so accepting. I had this little fear that as soon as my sisters actually saw me I'd discover that they weren't okay with having a sister of color."

"Shannon and I are not racist," Traci said.

"No, you aren't. But I didn't really know that. Right?"

"Did you all meet in Bridgeport?"

"Oh, no. Kimber flew down to Cleveland from New York City and spent the night with me. Then we loaded up my little SUV here and headed down to Bridgeport."

Peeking into the rearview mirror to see Gwen's face, she added, "We spent the first few hours trying to get to know each other without sharing too much."

"I never thought about what your first meeting must have been like," Jennifer said.

"What was weird was that we were all so different, but every once in a while one of us would do some mannerism that was faintly like the other's."

"Like what?" Gwen asked.

"Like Kimber and I kind of raise our eyebrows in the same way, one higher than the other, when we hear something we aren't sure makes sense."

"Or, Traci, Shannon, and I all relax by

putting on pajamas and watching old reality shows. Not everyone likes that."

"I never asked, what was Shannon like when you first met her?"

"Oh boy. Nervous, excited."

"Mother-like," Kimber said with a chuckle. "She was the most sheltered out of all of us, yet she was trying to protect us. It was beyond sweet."

Traci nodded. "It really was. She's a hugger and says things like 'I love you' the way other people might say 'good morning.' I'd never been around that much love before. I had no idea how to react."

"But it just goes to show you that our taking that leap of faith and doing something that was scary was the right thing to do," Kimber said. "I learned that I needed these women in my life. As a matter of fact, I couldn't imagine going back up to New York and living on my own in some crappy apartment with other models again. I needed a home."

Traci glanced up at Gwen again and was happy to see that she was looking reflective. She really hoped that there was something in their story that had struck a chord with her.

It really was possible to start over again at any age, and to be accepted and to accept

313

other people even when they were different. It certainly made for a richer life.

Mrs. Murphy ran out to greet them like Traci and Kimber were her own daughters. "Traci! Kimber! I'm so glad to see you. Welcome."

"Thank you, Mrs. Murphy," Kimber said as she walked right into the lady's hug.

"Traci, come here, dear. You're not getting out of my hugs, either."

"Yes, ma'am." Dutifully she hugged Shannon's mom and then reached over and shook Mr. Murphy's hand.

After she hugged Jennifer with the same exuberance, Mrs. Murphy smiled at Gwen. "Hi, dear. Let me guess. You're Gwen."

Gwen was looking up at them with wide eyes. "Yes?"

"I'm so glad you're here, dear."

"Thanks?"

Traci walked to Gwen's side to give her a little support. "They hug a lot, but they don't bite."

"Not unless you're acting up or something," Mrs. Murphy said.

"I won't be doing that, Mrs. Murphy," Gwen promised, her expression solemn.

"Oh, honey. We're teasing. And you don't have to call me that. You're welcome to call

314

me Deanna."

"Thank you."

Her eyes softened. "Whew. I meant to warn y'all that it's hot as blazes around here already. I bet you're ready to get into some cooler air. Come on."

Traci grabbed her bag and Gwen's too. "I've got this," she said quietly. "Let's walk slowly. Deanna will be talking nonstop to Kimber and Jennifer anyway."

Gwen raised her eyebrows. "Shannon's mother is really friendly."

"She sure is."

"Do you ever call her Deanna?"

"Nope."

"Why not?"

"I don't know. I just can't. She's such a mom, plus I really respect her. Her and me being on a first name basis feels odd. But you can if you want. She won't mind."

"Does Kimber call her by her first name?"

"I don't think so. It's hard to explain, but even though Mrs. Murphy is Shannon's mom and not ours, there's a part of Kimber and me who kind of think of her as ours, too." She pursed her lips, trying to come up with a better way to describe it. "I guess she's kind of like our surrogate mom."

Gwen frowned. "Oh."

"I know it doesn't quite make sense, it's

just how we feel. You can call her by her first name if you'd like, I promise it's fine."

"She's kind of fancy too. Did you notice her pearls?"

"I did. But she's not a judgy sort of person. I promise, you'll enjoy being here."

Gwen looked up at her. "I'm sorry you had to bring me along. I bet you feel like you've got a piece of baggage constantly tied to your wrist."

Traci shook her head. "What? Are you kidding? It wouldn't be the same without you."

And as they walked in, sharing smiles about the huge welcome spread in the kitchen, the scented candles, and the pristine rooms that looked like Mrs. Murphy had slaved over them for days, Traci realized she hadn't been lying. She really was so glad Gwen was there. If she'd been back at home, it would have felt like she'd been missing a limb.

It seemed that Gwen was an essential part of her life now.

CHAPTER 38

"Dancing and running shake up
the chemistry of happiness."
— MASON COOLEY

It didn't happen very often, but sometimes Gwen's baby decided that it didn't want to sleep at night, and instead took up kick boxing.

After getting kicked in the ribs pretty hard, Gwen was wide awake. She sat in her double bed on one end of their gigantic bedroom, shifting uncomfortably, trying not to wake Traci, who was fast asleep in her own double bed on the other side of the room.

Eventually, both a need for the bathroom and a craving for milk got her to her feet.

Smiling at the fleece robe and matching slippers that Kimber had bought her "just because," Gwen slipped them on, carefully

317

shut the door behind her, and headed downstairs.

Mrs. Murphy had told them several times that they should feel comfortable in the house, eat anything in the refrigerator or in the pantry, and make themselves at home. Shannon had even pulled Gwen aside and said that her mom meant it sincerely too.

So, after using the pretty little pink powder room, Gwen walked into the kitchen. The lights under the cabinets were on, so she didn't have to turn on an overhead light. Soon, she was pouring herself a glass of milk and eating a slice of cake at the kitchen table.

Two bites in, Gwen was already thinking about seconds while telling herself that having two slices of cake was a bad idea. But boy, was it good. Shannon might not be able to cook worth a darn but her mom sure could!

She'd just about cleaned her plate when Mrs. Murphy shuffled in wearing fuzzy pink slippers. Gwen froze midbite.

"Oh! Hi, Gwen. I thought I heard someone in here, so I thought I'd investigate."

"I'm sorry. I didn't mean to wake you."

"You didn't wake me." She sighed. "It's my age, I'm afraid. I used to sleep through anything, now I'm up half the night. What

318

about you?"

Gwen patted her tummy. "This little guy decided to start kicking my ribs. I thought milk might settle him down."

Mrs. Murphy's eyes widened. "I couldn't have any children, my husband and I weren't blessed, so I can't commiserate. It sounds exciting, though."

"I guess it is."

"Does he kick you often?"

"Not really. Honestly, Dr. Rossi said that I seem to be having an easy pregnancy, all things considered."

Mrs. Murphy eyed Gwen's snack, then walked over to the refrigerator, poured a glass of milk, and then went back with a plate, fork, and the whole cake. "You have an excuse and I don't. But I can't resist."

"It's really good. I love the fudge icing."

"A lot of people would rather have fudge icing with chocolate cake, but my favorite is with yellow cake." She took a bite. "Yes, it turned out just fine, didn't it?"

Gwen smiled. "Yes, ma'am."

"Would you like a tiny bit more?"

"I shouldn't."

"But?"

"But, okay."

Shannon's mother laughed as she sliced another piece. "There you go, dear. You're

319

eating for two, after all."

After Gwen accepted a second piece of cake, Mrs. Murphy said, "So, Shannon's told me a little bit about what's happened to you. I'm so sorry, honey."

Those words hit her hard. Lots of people had asked how she was doing, but they'd also had many pointed questions. No one had simply offered their sympathy. "Thank you."

They sat in silence for a few minutes, simply eating the gooey dessert and sipping milk.

Then Mrs. Murphy stood up. "I don't know about you, but I think I'm going to be able to fall back asleep now." She covered her mouth with a yawn. "Want to give it a try?"

"Yes." She walked her plate to the sink.

"Oh, don't worry about washing it, honey. We'll do that in the morning. Go get some rest."

"Mrs. Murphy? I mean . . . Deanna?"

The lady turned around immediately. "Yes, dear?"

"Thanks for coming down and sitting with me."

Her brown eyes softened. "It was my pleasure, honey. I'm glad you were here."

After making yet another trip to pee,

Gwen went back upstairs and crept into her bed.

"Gwen?" Traci asked drowsily. She opened one eye. "Hey, were you up?"

"Yeah, but I'm fine now."

"Need anything?"

"No. Go back to sleep." She'd just had a good dose of homemade cake, milk, and a mother's love. Right at that moment, she didn't think she needed anything else at all.

"How are you holding up, partner?" Dylan asked about two hours into the party.

Traci was sitting under a large white umbrella on the Murphys' back patio, simply enjoying the twinkling white lights, scented candles, and the string quartet that the Murphys had hired for the party. Gwen had gone inside to their room for a few minutes and Kimber was currently chatting with almost everyone in the room. A couple of the guests had recognized her from the pages of fashion magazines and were star-struck. It had been awesome to see.

Looking up at Dylan, she gestured for him to sit down in one of the empty chairs nearby. "Better than I expected, if you want to know the truth. I didn't think standing around, sipping expensive wine, and eating good food was my thing, but it seems I was wrong."

The laugh lines around his eyes deepened with his smile. "I see you've been watching Kimber too."

"Yep. Isn't it something? Fashion was never my thing, so I didn't really think anything about Kimber being on magazine covers. Other than it was awesome and she deserved the success because she's beautiful and cool." She shrugged. "I guess I always think of her in old clothes and no makeup."

He nodded. "And either hardly eating. Or, eating almost as much as I do."

She laughed. "Tonight, seeing her all glammed up and those girls gazing at her in wonder, I kind of can't believe that I never thought about her success all that much."

"Shannon said the same thing, although of course, she was worried about all the men trying to hit on her." Chuckling, he lowered his voice. "I think she's half-hoping that you or me will fend off all the admirers if they get to be too much."

"I'd be happy to, if Kimber needed it. But she doesn't." Recalling how she'd watched Kimber neatly sidestep a man who was getting a little handsy, Traci said, "I think she can handle this crowd without a problem."

"I told Shannon the same thing."

Traci looked around. "Where is your bride, by the way?"

"Catching up with a couple of her girlfriends from high school. I was with them for a bit, but I could only take so much squealing."

"Since I don't squeal, you're safe with me, buddy."

When a waiter walked by, Dylan snagged two bottles of beer. "Want one? I know you're liking that Merlot, but this is still my speed."

She held out her hand. "Cheers."

"I know Gwen went upstairs. Is she coming back down?"

"I think so, but I'm not sure. She's a young thing and she's eight months pregnant. I told her that if she wanted to stay in her room the rest of the night, she could. Whatever she wanted."

"Good. Shannon was worried she was going to be bored."

"I don't think she was. She's just getting big, you know?"

Jennifer joined them with a laugh. "I just got beaten at pool downstairs."

"Who have you been playing pool with?"

"Mr. Murphy and his buddies. When they asked if I'd like to play, I said yes."

"Uh-oh. When did they learn you were a

fledgling pool shark?"

"Only after I almost beat them all." Looking slightly annoyed, she said, "They upped their game after that."

"I'm glad you came," Dylan said.

"I am too. Of course I wanted to be here for you and Shannon, but to be honest, things at home have been tense."

Traci looked at her intently as Kimber sat down to join them. "What's been going on? Are you having some panic attacks again?"

"Oh, no. Nothing like that. It's more about Gwen. I keep being afraid that someone was going to break in and snatch her before I could stop them."

Dylan lowered his voice. "Jen, honey, I told you we would make sure she was protected. You too."

"I know. And I believe you would. But things happen."

"I've worried about that a time or two as well," Kimber said.

Dylan exchanged a glance with Traci. She knew what he was thinking, because she was thinking the same thing.

"Do you want me to try to move Gwen someplace else?" Traci asked. "I know I pushed for her to be with us, but I hadn't thought she'd be with us so long. Honestly,

I thought she'd be with us a week at the most."

"What? Of course I don't want you to kick her out," Jennifer said.

"I wouldn't kick her out. I'd find her —"

"No."

"Are you sure? Because it never occurred to me that you would be worrying like that. I should have realized it, though."

Kimber shook her head. "If I'm going to be real honest here, I wasn't all that excited about her moving in. She's a young thing and she's got a heap of problems, none of which are going to go away easily, not even when she has a baby or her ex-boyfriend is behind bars. But . . . I like her. I like her a lot."

"And she's ended up being a huge help. She pitches in the kitchen all the time."

"Shannon says she's amazing with her senior citizens."

"I've watched her with them. I think some of them want to adopt her," Traci said.

"That ain't gonna happen," Kimber said. "That girl is ours."

Jennifer nodded. "We're keeping her. It's decided."

"What is?" Shannon asked as she joined them.

"That I'm keeping you forever," Dylan

said as he pulled her closer to his side.

"Oh, no. Here we go again," Jennifer griped.

"Don't worry, I'm going to get him off your hands for a moment. The quartet is about to play a waltz. Will you dance with me, Dylan?"

"I will, as long as you let me lead this time."

They all grinned as Shannon and Dylan walked over to the dance floor, the music started playing, and they began to waltz.

Traci watched, feeling content. The music was pretty, the atmosphere magical, she was with some of their favorite people in the world. Yes. She could get used to this indeed.

CHAPTER 39

"A star danced, and under that
I was born."
— WILLIAM SHAKESPEARE

Both Matt and Gwen had acted like Traci had a screw loose when she'd suggested that Gwen get her monthly check up at the house. Well, Gwen had looked appalled and said that was weird and Matt had firmly reminded her that he was a doctor and Gwen was his patient.

He'd also reminded her that Gwen was now eight months pregnant and, while out of the danger zone, was firmly in the perimeters of low risk.

"You seem to forget the state she'd been in when you brought her to the hospital, Traci. She was undernourished and under the influence. Both her body and the baby are going to be dealing with the effects of that for some time."

She'd taken his warning to heart — and had also felt both embarrassed that she'd begun to take Gwen's pregnancy for granted, and frustrated because she was worried sick about the girl. As hard as she'd tried not to be, Traci cared about her. A lot.

"Okay, but I'm just telling you that this ex-boyfriend of hers is a danger."

"If she's in that much danger, why don't you have her someplace more secure?"

And . . . that was something that she and Dylan had talked about more than once. Bridgeport wasn't a big city and it didn't have a big city budget. They also didn't have a lot of safe houses in the area, just waiting to be used.

Furthermore, since Gwen and her baby were currently in good health, Traci was unable to move her to the hospital.

She'd explained all that to Matt. He'd said he understood, but she wondered if he was thinking she wasn't doing enough.

She was still thinking all of this around midnight while she was sitting in their kitchen and eating a peanut butter and jelly sandwich with a tall glass of milk. She'd tried to fall asleep an hour before but had been haunted by all her doubts and insecurities.

Afraid to wake up Kimber, who had just

328

gotten back from her latest modeling job looking exhausted, Traci had slipped out of the room. Of course, sitting in the kitchen late at night meant eating late-night food. As far as she was concerned, one couldn't do one thing without the other.

"Hey," Kimber said as she walked in.

"Hey back. Sorry, did I wake you?"

"Yeah, but that's okay." She smiled as she pushed back a chunk of her hair from her forehead. "As soon as I realized you were in the kitchen, I started thinking that food sounded good."

"I still have out peanut butter and jelly if you want that."

"Hmm. I'm not sure. Let me see what Jennifer's got in here."

Watching Kimber stand in front of the open refrigerator, Traci had to smile. Sometimes it caught Traci by surprise that Kimber looked so "normal" when she was home with them. She wore baggy gray sweatpants, a stretched-out T-shirt, an unzipped fleece hoody, and her feet were bare. With no makeup and her hair in a messy topknot, Traci figured she looked like just a pretty coed who was taller than most women.

Finally electing to have cereal, Kimber pulled out the gallon of milk from the fridge then started rooting around in the cabinets.

"Yes! Corn flakes!"

Traci laughed. "You are hysterical. Most people would only get that excited about Lucky Charms or Captain Crunch."

"When you limit carbs and sugar like I do half the time, Corn Flakes are nirvana."

After pouring herself a heaping bowl — and turning on the kettle for peppermint tea — Kimber sat down beside her. "Why can't you sleep?"

"Gwen."

"Is she giving you trouble? I really like her."

"I like her too." After glancing toward the hallway, she continued. "Maybe that's the problem. She's supposed to be my job, not . . . not whatever she is."

"Your friend?" Kimber raised her eyebrows.

"Fine. My friend." Hating how that sounded, she said, "It's not that I don't want to be her friend, I just don't know how to handle her as my friend. It's easier to be a cop when emotions aren't getting in the way."

After shoveling in another spoonful of cereal, Kimber spoke. "Traci, no offense, but that's what life is, right? If you care, you get involved."

She made it sound so easy, but it really

wasn't. "What if something happens?"

"Like what?"

Like Gwen gets snatched from this building and Kimber, Shannon, and Jennifer get hurt in the process. "A lot of things can go wrong," she murmured just as Jennifer walked in. "Ugh. I'm sorry we woke you."

"I was having trouble sleeping anyway." Jennifer looked at their snacks and shook her head in mock dismay. "Don't you two know that only cookies and milk taste good after midnight?" She reached up on her tiptoes and pulled out a box of oatmeal cookies.

"I didn't know we had those," Kimber said. "How come I didn't know we had a stash of cookies?"

"I guess you didn't look hard enough," Jennifer said as she got a glass and filled it with milk. She joined them at the table. "Yum."

"Look at you, girl," Traci said. "Do you always wear stuff like that to bed?"

"What?" Jennifer looked down at her pink silky nightgown and the floor length robe.

"Nothing. Only that it's really pretty."

"I like pretty things." Gazing at Traci, she blinked. "You were wearing that same outfit all evening. Have you not been to bed yet?"

"Nope."

331

"She's worried about Gwen," Kimber supplied.

Jennifer sobered. "I know. I am too. But, she'll be okay."

"I need to make sure of it."

"You're not a guardian angel, Traci. You're just a cop. You can only do the best that you can, right?"

"It doesn't work like that." At least, it didn't for her.

"I like Gwen. I even like her being here and I kind of don't want her to leave. But, that said, even though she's a victim, she's also lived through some pretty tough situations. I don't think she's as fragile as you're making her out to be."

"She's not all that street-smart and tough, Jennifer. She's just a kid."

"Who is?" Shannon asked as she joined them.

"Gwen," Kimber replied. "And what are you doing up? You should be downstairs with your hunky husband."

"My husband is snoring. And, it turns out that our bedroom is right below the kitchen. I heard y'all walking around. Hanging out with y'all sounded like more fun than listening to Dylan snore." Looking at all their dishes on the table, she brightened right up. "Oh, we're eating!"

Jennifer grinned. "You say that like you've just found a secret prize or something."

"Eating after midnight with no guilt? That is a prize."

She opened the freezer and pulled out a pint of ice cream. It was the last of the pints that Matt had brought over. "I do love me some chocolate–chocolate chip ice cream." After pulling out a spoon, she sat in the last chair.

"You're going to eat right out of the carton?" Jennifer asked.

Shannon tilted the carton, showing it was only half filled. "I'm saving dish soap, Jen."

Traci smiled at her sister. She was the oldest in the room and also the most petite. "Look at you. Are those new pajamas?"

Shannon was wearing a knit short set with one of Dylan's open button downs over it. "Yes." She smiled. "I bought a lot of cute nightclothes for our honeymoon."

Kimber sighed. "I never wanted to be married until I see how blissfully happy you two are."

"I am happy," Shannon said. "And Dylan is so perfect."

Jennifer held up a hand. "Before you share any gooey details, let's all remember that Dylan is my big brother."

"And my partner," Traci said. "I'm glad

333

he's happily married to you, but I don't want to know too much."

"Oh, don't worry. I'm not going to start kissing and telling. Too much." After scooping up another bite of chocolate ice cream, she said, "So, was this get-together planned and I just happened to miss it?"

"It was not planned," Kimber said. "But Traci started it."

Traci shrugged. "I couldn't sleep."

"Because you're worried about Gwen," Shannon said.

"Yep." She was glad she didn't have to go through her reasons again. "I would rather be sleeping, but this is kind of fun."

"I agree," Jennifer said. "One day, when we're all married and living on our own, I'm going to miss these days."

Just as Traci was about to say that probably wasn't going to happen for a while, she spied Gwen lurking outside the entryway to the kitchen. "Gwen, come on in. We'll pull up a chair for you."

Kimber hopped up. "Come take mine. I'm done eating. Do you want some corn flakes?"

"No, thanks."

Looking at her with concern, Traci stood up as well. "Hey, you look kind of pale. Did we wake you up?"

"I'm sure we did," Kimber said. "I'm sorry, sweetie. That was rude."

"No, it's okay. I've been up for a little while," Gwen replied. "Um, I've been in the bathroom. I think I'm sick."

Immediately the four of them surrounded her. "What's wrong?" Traci asked. "And come sit down. Is it the baby?"

"I don't know. I feel dizzy and I've got a really bad headache."

Jennifer placed her hand on Gwen's forehead. "You don't feel feverish. Maybe it's a cold or something?"

"Maybe. But I don't know. I've never had a migraine but this sure feels like one." She held up her hands. "And I think my hands and feet are swollen. I don't know what's wrong with me. I really don't feel good." Tears filled her eyes. "I'm scared about the baby."

Traci headed for her room. "I'm going to call Matt."

"Oh, don't wake up Dr. Rossi!" Gwen said. "He needs his sleep."

"You might as well wake him up," Dylan said from the stairs. "The rest of us are."

Traci sent her partner a look of thanks as she strode down the hall to her room. She was just thinking the same exact thing.

335

CHAPTER 40

"Why waltz with a guy for ten rounds
if you can knock him out in one?"
— ROCKY MARCIANO

After double-checking that Gwen was resting and comfortable in her room, Matt walked out to the waiting room. Traci, her sisters, Dylan, and his sister Jennifer were all there. Each of them had a cup of bad hospital coffee in their hands.

"One of you should have gone out for some decent coffee," he said as he greeted them.

"None of us wanted to leave," Traci said. "Besides, I've had my share of bad coffee. As bad cups go, this isn't the worst. How is she?"

"Yes, can we go see her?" Jennifer asked.

"I admitted Gwen," he announced. When they all started talking at once, he held up a hand. "I just checked on her and she's resting. I'd like you all to wait until morning to pay her a visit."

"She's that bad?" Shannon asked. "Oh my gosh, Matt. Have I been making her do too much?"

"I don't think it was you, though I am going to recommend bedrest. We need to get her blood pressure under control."

"When should I come back in the morning?" Traci asked.

If they were alone, Matt would have pulled her into his arms and told her that he was worried about her too. She took too much on her slim shoulders. Traci didn't need to fix everyone and everything all by herself. "After eleven," he said.

"That late?"

"She needs rest, and then she'll need to get some more tests in the morning. Probably a sonogram too. If you're here, all you're going to be doing is sitting in this room again."

"What if she thinks we've all forgotten her?"

"She already knows that every one of you was here tonight. I'll take the blame for keeping you away until tomorrow. Go on, now."

"What about you?" Kimber asked. "Are you going to get some rest?"

"I will. Don't worry about me." He was going to sleep in one of the rooms reserved for doctors on call. All he needed was three or four hours and he'd be fine.

Dylan stood up. "You heard the doctor, ladies. Let's get some rest."

Traci turned to them. "Give me a minute?"

"We'll pull the car up and wait for you by the door," Dylan said.

As soon as they walked out, Matt took her hand and pulled her through the stainless double doors to a quiet meeting room. He flicked on a light, shut the door, and then pulled her into his arms.

"I miss you," he said, running his hands down her back. He liked feeling the indention of her spine. Liked how she felt — muscle and soft skin and solid enough to hold on to.

"I miss you too. I can't wait until things are calmer for us."

"Will they ever be?" He couldn't help but reflect that the chaos wasn't a result of either of their schedules — instead it was brought on by a need to help a girl who desperately needed someone to care about her.

But, wasn't that the nature of their jobs? His schedule was always going to be determined by his patients' needs. Traci's was going to be a result of whatever case she was working on.

She frowned. "Maybe. I don't know." Lowering her voice, she said, "Maybe one day, even if our schedules are crazy, we'll still be able to carve out time together."

"That is something that we'll be able to count on." He kissed her lightly on the lips. Then kissed her again, more deeply, but then pulled back sheepishly. "We need to stop."

"We do, 'cause they're all waiting for me, and it's the middle of the night."

Dropping his hands, he walked to the door. "I'll call you tomorrow."

She smiled at him. "I know you will, which makes me happy. Don't walk me out, doctor. I can get there by myself. Get some rest."

Matt let her leave, but stayed in the room for a minute before heading down the hall to the dorm-like cubicles that personnel used when needed.

Kicking off his shoes, he pulled the curtain on the cubicle, grimaced at the flat pillow that he'd somehow forgotten the beds always had, then finally closed his eyes. Willing his body to relax, he thought about Gwen, his rounds scheduled for the morning, and finally the way Traci had sounded both when she'd woken him out of a deep sleep and after he'd held her in his arms tonight. Two different sides of her that he found equally fascinating.

He fell asleep wondering what other secrets he'd discover about her in the future.

Four hours later, Dr. Rossi was dressed in scrubs, his lab coat, and was sitting next to Gwen's bed. He'd just told her the news. It was official, she had preeclampsia and was going need to stay in bed or on the couch for the foreseeable future. Probably until she delivered, but he wasn't quite ready to break the news to her yet.

"I'm scared, Dr. Rossi."

"I know. But we're going to keep you here for another two days. I won't sign the release for you to go home until we're both sure you're stable." He'd also pulled a little weight. Technically, she could have probably gone home, but she'd already been through too much. Plus, everyone knew it was safer for her to stay at the hospital.

"I'm scared about my health, but about the baby too."

He pointed to the monitor attached to her stomach and then to the monitor next to them, where they could both see the baby's heartbeat. "Your baby boy is doing okay. Try not to take everything on your shoulders."

Though her eyes looked haunted, she nodded. "All right."

He paused. He didn't want to speak out of turn, but he also realized it was foolish to ignore what they were both thinking. "Gwen, Officer Lucky isn't going to let you down. She's going to keep you safe."

"I know. Thank you."

Walking out of the room, he realized that she didn't believe him. Actually, she looked both older and more stressed than she had in weeks.

He was starting to feel like something bad was about to happen.

CHAPTER 41

"In my dreams I am not crippled.
In my dreams, I dance."
— LOUISE BROOKS

"Guess what? You have company here to see you," Marissa said brightly at ten the following morning.

Gwen had been listlessly watching some Home and Garden TV episode, thinking that all these house hunters were the neediest people on the planet when her favorite nurse popped her head in.

Reaching for the remote, she pushed the button to raise her in a sitting position. "Really? Who?"

Marissa beamed. "Your brother Billy and your cousin Dan are here. Isn't that a nice surprise? Have a good visit," she added as she stepped to one side.

Pulse racing, Gwen inhaled, ready to yell for help — just as her brother and Hunter walked in. They hardly looked like themselves. Hunter was wearing jeans and a long sleeved T-shirt that covered all his tattoos. He'd pulled his long hair into some kind of man bun and he'd shaved.

Billy, who she hadn't seen in years, looked much like she remembered him, except older, more muscular, and a whole lot meaner. He also had on a long-sleeved shirt, even though it was June and hot outside. His blond hair was almost shaved.

"Hi, Sis," Billy said, ignoring her yelp as he walked straight over to her and hugged her hard enough to hurt. "I'm so glad we were able to see you."

"Yeah," Hunter said as he walked to her other side. "We've been worried sick."

Just as she was about to push the emergency button that was next to the bed, Hunter placed the sharp tip of his switch blade on her wrist. Anyone who walked by or peeked in would think that he was holding her hand.

She and Hunter both knew better.

Marissa had been typing something on her phone, but now looked over at Gwen. "Do you need anything before I head down the hall?"

"We'll take care of her just fine, ma'am,"

Hunter said. "We've got a whole lot to catch up on."

Just before walking out, Marissa gazed at her again. "Gwen? Are you okay? You look like you might be in pain."

She felt the knife's point pierce her skin. "I'm fine," she said. "I'm just surprised to see my family. That's all."

"Oh, good. Well, enjoy your visit," Marissa said before closing the door.

The moment it was closed, Hunter's voice turned cold. "Damn, you've gotten big, girl."

She didn't know what to do except keep them talking. It was a long shot, but she could hope that either Dr. Rossi would hear about her visitors or that somehow Officer Lucky's daily visit would occur while they were here.

"I can't believe you found me," she said.

"It wasn't hard," Hunter said. "I've known where you were for some time. But you knew that."

"How come you've been hanging out with the cops, Gwen?" Billy asked.

"I've been under their protection."

"Until when? The baby comes? Then what's going to happen?"

She didn't know. She'd been too afraid to think that far. But there was no way she was going to share that. "That is none of your business."

"You're carrying my baby, so it is."

"It's *my* baby. If I was still with you either I or it — or both of us — would have died by now."

"You don't know what you're talking about."

"I know enough. I know you scared a lot of people at the women's center."

"That's on you. You shouldn't have run."

"We're over." Yes, her voice wasn't exactly steady, but she realized that even though she was scared, she wasn't the same person she used to be. She was much stronger now.

Hunter's light blue eyes turned deadly. "We're not over until I say we are."

"I don't agree. My baby and I are doing better without you. I'm not going back."

Her brother narrowed his eyes. "Listen to you. You're acting like you've got a say in this. You don't, Gwen."

"As soon as the hospital personnel realize that you lied about who you are, the police are going to come. You're violating the restraining order."

"They're not going to do much. Get dressed. We're leaving."

"I can't leave. I'm sick."

Billy frowned. "Yeah right. You look fine to me."

Any hopes that her brother had gotten smarter or had developed a conscience flew right out the window. "I'm in here for a reason. I have preeclampsia."

Hunter's eyes narrowed. "What's that?"

"It means I have high blood pressure. If I don't stay in bed and rest, it could hurt the baby."

He laughed darkly. "Maybe you don't need me after all. Sounds like you're hurting that baby all on your own. Get up, girl."

She lifted up her hand. "I'm attached to these IVs."

Looking as cold and calculated as she'd ever seen him, he calmly leaned over and pulled the tube from her hand.

She cried from the sudden, sharp pain, just as the monitor started to send out an alarm.

Billy stared at the door. "Turn that off, girl."

"No," she said, just as Hunter pulled at her. The patch that was monitoring the baby's heartbeat ripped off, sending off another alarm. "Stop!" she cried.

Someone tried to open the door. Billy slammed it shut and leaned into it.

"They're going to call for help. I bet the

police are already on the way."

Hunter's sharp blade sliced her skin. "Don't fight me, Gwen. Get up and dressed or get hurt."

She realized then that she had a choice. She could either be at Hunter's mercy or she could fight. There wasn't another choice. There was no way was she going back to the life she'd had with him. No way was she going to ever believe that she didn't deserve anything better.

So, she didn't go quietly. She didn't give up. She stood firm and she screamed at the top of her lungs: "Help me!"

Hunter growled and grabbed her roughly. Just as his knife sliced into the soft patch of skin under her clavicle, the door burst open.

A security guard, an orderly, and two nurses ran in. Everyone started yelling at Billy and Hunter.

Hunter held her arm and yanked her. "I'm taking her."

She stumbled, now aware of her own blood dripping down her chest and pain coursing through her abdomen.

"She's bleeding bad, sir. We need to help her."

"No, I need to take her with me. She's —"

The room started to go black just as she

thought she heard Officer Lucky's voice in the hall.

But as she fell to the ground, Gwen decided that she'd probably just imagined that.

After all this time, it seemed like she was finally going to get what she deserved.

CHAPTER 42

"The dance is a poem of which
each movement is a word."
— MATA HARI

They'd taken Hunter Benton and Billy Camp into custody. Dylan had called for assistance, and soon they'd had enough cops and help to transport both men to the station and begin processing them.

Traci had done what she could to help, but she was flustered. Actually, she was too rattled to do much except try to wash the blood off her skin and clothes. One of the nurses who had helped calm Marissa down had eventually handed Traci scrubs and pointed her to a shower.

She hadn't wanted to take the time to either change or shower, not until the woman had pointed out what a danger she was with so much blood on her in a public place.

Now she was sitting in a private waiting room while Gwen was in surgery.

No, while Gwen and Matt were in surgery. Gwen's knife wounds hadn't been life-threatening, but the premature labor pains together with her dangerously high blood pressure had been.

Traci had been forced to stand off to one side feeling completely helpless as more nurses and doctors scrambled into the operating room. That had been over an hour ago.

Now, everything felt suspiciously silent. She kept retracing everything that had happened over the last two months. She'd been one of the most decorated cops in Cleveland. She'd prided herself on being street smart and all business in a crisis.

But neither of those qualities had been apparent of late.

What if she lost this girl before she ever even had a chance to really live? What if both the baby and Gwen died? Traci didn't know how she was going to be able to live with herself if that happened. She'd promised her that she'd keep her safe and that she'd stop Hunter from ever seeing her again.

She might have failed on both parts.

As the clock ticked on, Traci stared at the

closed door leading to the operating rooms. She felt more alone than ever before. Too alone to call her sisters and tell them about Gwen. Too alone to do anything but sit and wait and worry. She had no idea what to do next.

"Traci?" Shannon rushed in. "Oh my word! Dylan told me about Gwen," she said, reaching for her and giving her a hug. Just as Traci lifted her arms to hug her back, Shannon continued. "So, where is she?"

"Surgery."

Pulling away, her eyes widened. "Goodness, look at you! Are you okay? What happened?"

"I . . . I don't know," she murmured.

"What are you talking about?"

"She means that you need to give her a minute, Shannon," Kimber said as she walked in, moving more slowly than their eldest sister. After giving Traci a gentle hug, she gave Shannon a steady look. "You're pounding Traci here with questions and not even giving her a minute to breathe."

"I'm giving her time. Okay, I guess I'm not," Shannon said with a wince. "I'm sorry, Traci. Do you want to sit down?"

"Hmm? Oh. I will in a minute. Thanks." Unable to help herself, she looked toward the stainless-steel doors again, but Jennifer

351

and her boyfriend Jack were blocking the way. "Hey, you two."

"Traci," Jack murmured.

"Jack was helping me make a meal delivery when we heard the news," Jennifer explained. "We came right over as soon as we heard. How's Gwen?"

"We don't know," Kimber answered.

"She's in surgery," Traci said again.

"Oh, honey, come on. Let's all go sit down."

"I'm okay. I think I'll go walk down the hall . . ."

"Nope." Kimber clasped her hand. "You need to sit down and relax for a minute, super-cop. You know Gwen's in good hands."

The teasing phrase jarred her out of her daze. "I'm far from a super-cop right now." She not only had failed Gwen, she wasn't even at the station booking Hunter and Billy.

Shannon shook her head. "I'm not sure what you are thinking, but I heard how wonderful you were. Dylan said that you grabbed hold of that ex-boyfriend of Gwen's, pulled his arm back and had him against the wall in less than a minute."

Jack whistled low. "No way. Good for you, Traci."

"It wasn't quite like that. Dylan got Billy and everyone else was trying to help Gwen." She closed her eyes. All that blood. She didn't know if she'd ever not see it in her dreams.

"Traci, I know you're worried about Gwen. We all are. I love that little thing," Kimber said. "But what is going on with you?"

"I know I should have been there for her. I told her I would and I completely failed." She helplessly gestured toward the steel doors that had remained stubbornly closed. "Matt's in there with her. Probably a couple of surgeons too. And what looked like a dozen nurses."

"And it's silent."

"Yeah. I'm so afraid she died." There, she said it.

"Don't think that way," Jennifer said. "I can't speak for what Gwen's been going through, but you know my story. I was attacked by three men. Though it took me a long time to recover, I never would have made it through without Dylan reminding me of how much I had to look forward to. You need to be positive, Traci. Gwen is going to need to be able to lean on you."

Traci stared at her in surprise. "Jennifer, I've always admired you and considered you to be a survivor, but you are so much more than I realized. You're a pretty amazing person."

Jennifer smiled. "Honey, that's what I've been trying to get you to see. We all are." She gestured around the table. "You, me, Shannon, Kimber, and yes, even Gwen. Maybe even Gwen most of all."

Looking toward the doors again, she saw they were open and Matt was walking toward them. He wasn't smiling and his expression was intense.

On shaky legs, she stood up and walked into the hallway. She felt the presence of her sisters walking alongside her, giving her support.

"Matt?"

"Hey, Trace." He nodded. "Ladies."

"How's is Gwen?" she asked.

"Well, I'd say she's going to have her hands full."

"Wait, she's alive?"

His expression grew concerned. "Oh, Traci. Have you really been out here thinking the worst? Honey, yes, she's alive." He grinned. "She's alive, bandaged up, and currently holding a very tiny baby boy."

"Oh. My. Word. She had the baby?" Kimber asked, awe in her voice.

"We didn't have much of a choice. He's

354

right at five pounds and we're going to double-check his lungs, so he might have to be in NICU for a couple of hours, just to make sure everything's good, but the pediatrician says he's a fighter."

Traci reached for his hands. "You did it! Matt, you saved Gwen and delivered her baby."

He kissed her brow. "No, you saved Gwen. And Gwen, our very own little fighter, delivered her baby boy. I just helped her along."

CHAPTER 43

"What we want from modern dance
is courage and audacity."
— TWYLA THARP

Five Days Later
"You know, Bridge is kind of growing on me," Officer Lucky said from her chair next to Gwen's bed.

Gwen, who'd just gotten dressed for the first time in real clothes since her surgery, sat down on the edge of the mattress and looked at her baby fondly. "What do you mean? The baby or the name?"

"Ha-ha. I meant the name, but maybe both?" She cuddled the baby closer to her.

"He likes you a lot. You do a better job feeding him than I do." For a number of reasons, Gwen hadn't been allowed to nurse Bridge, and she was secretly thankful for that. He was so small, she was constantly worried about doing something wrong. But

Traci and her sisters never seemed as nervous around the baby as she did. Officer Lucky — Traci — was especially attached to Bridge and seemed content to hold him for hours.

That was the reason she'd talked to Melanie, the social worker, and Ellen so long over the last couple of days. Though both cautioned her not to make any major decisions, Gwen was feeling pretty good about the plan she'd come up with.

Now she just had to find a way to talk to Traci about it.

Traci finally looked up from Bridge's sleeping face. "So, are you ready to get out of here?"

"I am. More than ready. Although, I'm pretty nervous about taking Bridge out of the hospital."

"You have to keep positive, remember? The nurses said that he's now a pretty sturdy little guy. He made it back up to five whole pounds, and he's eating well. There's a lot of good things to be proud about."

"I know. It's just that sometimes he cries and I feel like I don't know what to do."

"That's why you're coming home with us, right?" Traci asked as she cuddled the baby again. "You won't be alone."

Gwen supposed this was as good an opening as she could hope for. "Traci, can I talk to you about something?"

"Of course." Her brow wrinkled. "Wait, is there something wrong with Bridge or you?"

"No, but it is about me and Bridge . . ." She took a breath. "You see, I've been talking to Melanie. She's the social worker, you know."

"I know."

"Well, um, I was telling her about how I feel like such a kid, and Bridge is so little . . ." Her voice drifted off. She knew she wasn't doing a good job of setting this up.

Traci shifted to face her. "What are you saying?"

"I'm saying that I . . ." She cleared her throat. "Traci, I'd like you to consider being Bridge's foster mother."

"What?"

"I'm not going to leave you or Bridge or anything. But I, well, I just don't know if I'm ready to be a mother." She lifted her chin. "I mean a good mother. A mother to be proud of. But you would be great." When Traci continued to stare at her, hardly moving a muscle, Gwen talked faster. "Melanie said there are some legal things we have to take care of, but legally you would be Bridge's foster mother."

"His foster mother."

"Yes. Then, um, maybe even one day, if you wanted . . . you could be his adopted mother. I would still be here. You know, be around, but I could get myself together. Finish high school. Maybe even help Shannon with more classes. Take classes. Help Jennifer with her business, 'cause she's getting really busy now." Feeling like she was talking in circles, Gwen finished up. "You know, I'm hoping I could actually be something besides what I am now."

Traci pursed her lips. "I don't know what to say."

Gwen felt like crying. Shoot, she knew she wasn't going to be able to ask Traci right. Holding out her arms, she said, "It's okay. I'll take him. Sorry I asked."

"No, no."

"Sorry?"

"I meant, Gwen, I'm honored that you've asked me to do this. So honored I'm speechless, and we know that doesn't happen very often."

"Wait . . . you're not mad at me?"

"Am I mad that you've asked me to help you raise your beautiful baby?" She shook her head. "No, honey. I'm not mad."

Carefully holding the baby, Traci stood up and sat next to Gwen. "I want to think about it and talk to Matt and my sisters.

359

It's a lifelong commitment, right?"

"Right."

"But more importantly, this is something I want *you* to feel at peace with. I don't want you to wake up in a month and wish that you'd never asked me to do this. Do you understand?"

"Yes."

"How about we go home and play it by ear for the next thirty days. I'll help with Bridge as much as I can, and you think about being his mom."

"And if I don't change my mind and you still want him?"

"I would love to be Bridge's mother, Gwen. I would love it. But listen to me," she added, as she held out a hand to her. "I want to be someone for you too."

"Like my mom?"

"Now, I'm a little young to have an eighteen-year-old. But maybe I could be your big sister?"

Hope flared in her heart. "Are you sure you want another sister?"

"I seem to be collecting them left and right, and if it's taught me anything, it's that I always have room in my heart for one more sister."

"Thank you."

"No thanks are needed," Traci replied,

sounding hoarse. "We're in this together, right?"

Gwen nodded. "Yes, ma'am. All three of us are."

Marissa lightly rapped on the door. "Are you ready to get out of here, Gwen?"

"More than ready."

"Okay. I'll bring over the final paperwork and a wheelchair and we'll get you out of here and home."

Gwen smiled brightly. All of it sounded good. Every bit of it.

CHAPTER 44

"Promise me we'll always be this free,
dancing for eternity, underneath a
galaxy of stars."
— CHRISTY ANN MARTINE

It was late, and Traci and Matt were sitting on the couch in Dance With Me's entryway. Traci knew it was an odd place to have a private conversation, but in this building, privacy was at a premium.

Matt had come over for supper and all of them — Kimber, Gwen, Bridge, Shannon and Dylan, and Jennifer and Jack — had eaten together. Jennifer had made chicken and vegetable shish kabobs with baked potatoes. Gwen had helped her make a fruit trifle. It had all been wonderful.

Matt had seemed as relaxed as the rest of them, and had even taken a turn holding Bridge when they were all cleaning up after dinner. Traci had loved seeing how comfortable Matt was with the new baby.

"Trace, I'm happy to sit here with you all night, but you did tell me that you had something you wanted to talk to me about."

"I did. I was just sitting here wondering how to get started."

"You know the answer. Just start."

"Okay. Yesterday at the hospital, Gwen asked me to consider being Bridge's foster and maybe even real mother."

"Real mother?"

"Like I would adopt him."

"She wants to give him up?"

"Technically, yes. I think she realizes that she's not ready. Gwen wants to get healthy and get herself together. Finish high school, learn a trade. She doesn't have family, Matt. She's essentially alone in the world."

"But I thought she was going to stay here for a while?"

"Yes, that's still the plan. So, she would be the boy's birth mother, but for all intents and purposes, I would be Bridge's mom. He would be my son." Her voice wavered as she tried to retain her composure. But it was hard — every time she thought about truly being Bridge's mom, she got chills.

"What did you say?" Matt was watching her carefully, which was making her nervous. Was he upset about the things she had

363

told him?

Was it going to be a deal breaker for him? Maybe he didn't ever want kids, or at least never anyone else's kids.

That would be hard to hear. Her heart would also break, since she now knew she was in love with him and wanted Matt Rossi in her life for a very long time.

But there was something about Gwen's predicament that spoke to her heart as well. She wasn't going to be able to turn this baby, or Gwen's suggestion away.

She honestly felt like there was a reason she'd met Gwen. She was the right person to help this lost girl and Bridge. But just as importantly, she'd needed Gwen to help heal her soul. She'd needed to learn to forgive her mother and father and to stop being so angry and hurt about her childhood. No, it wasn't ideal — it had been very far from that — but Gwen had helped Traci remember that she wasn't the only child who'd had a challenging upbringing. Not by a long shot.

Swallowing hard, she looked into Matt's eyes. "We're going to wait a bit to make sure Gwen doesn't change her mind, but I already know how I feel. I want to be Bridge's mom, Matt. I already love him so much."

She could practically feel the tension in the air.

Then, to her surprise, he smiled. "I'm glad."

"You're glad? That's it?"

He laughed. "What did you want me to say?"

"I don't know. That I needed to think things through better. Maybe that I was being naive and I didn't know what I was promising." She looked at the ground. "Maybe that me being single and a cop didn't make me the best candidate for single parenting."

"Traci." He cupped his palm around her cheek. It felt both like he was holding her close and offering her solace. "You're a lot of things, but naive sure isn't one of them. Plus, you know Gwen and Bridge. Of course you are going into this situation with your eyes wide open." He smiled softly. "And, as for the other thing? The part about you being a single mom? That's not technically true."

"Because?"

"Because you're going to be living with Kimber, Jennifer, and Gwen, so you're going to have a lot of support."

Feeling a little disappointed, though he didn't lie, Traci nodded. "You're right."

His expression warmed further. "Then there's the fact that you've got me and my family." He took a breath, shaking his head slightly. "No, I mean you and Bridge will have me and my family."

"We will?"

"You know how much I like you, don't you?"

"Yes?" And yes, that was a question. Because she wasn't a hundred percent where they stood together.

He linked his fingers with hers. "Hmm. I don't think you do know." He wrinkled his brow. "Have I never said?"

"Not in so many words." Not that she had either.

"Traci, from the moment I first saw you in that emergency room, fighting for a girl who it looked like everyone else in the world had given up on, I knew you were someone special. Then, after I got to know you more, I started seeing you as Traci Lucky. Not just a cop. Not just a champion of girls in need. Someone pretty incredible."

"That is very sweet." And yes, she was probably sounding very lame.

He chuckled. "Is it? I think it's the truth. But, just so you know, what really made me realize that I was falling for you was the first time we waltzed."

"Matt, I stepped on your toes!"

"You did. And I gripped your waist too hard, like I was afraid you were going to run off. But, before I knew it, we were dancing." His voice softened. "We were listening to Shannon's crazy ballroom tapes and moving in sync and all I could think about was how lucky I was to have you in that moment. And how glad I was that you'd already said yes to going to Anthony's wedding with me, because then we would have to keep taking lessons together. I would get to see you again."

No one had ever spoken to her that way. Everything he was saying was sweet and wonderful and made her feel like she wasn't as flawed or as damaged as she'd always feared she'd been.

Those words also gave her the courage to reveal more of her heart.

"I'm falling in love with you, Matt." Inwardly, she winced. Here Matt had just listed a half-dozen beautiful reasons why he liked her — and all she could come up with was seven words. "Sorry. I mean —"

"Don't say sorry. Just tell me again."

"I'm falling in love with you, Matt."

"I'm falling in love with you, too, Traci."

She smiled at him then. She was no poet, and was sadly lacking in the expressing

herself department. But Dr. Matteo Rossi
liked her anyway.

No, he loved her anyway.

CHAPTER 45

"I'm going to dance in all the galaxies."
— ELIZABETH KUBLER-ROSS

"Have you ever heard of so many people going to so much fuss over a wedding?" Traci asked as she tried on dresses for Anthony's wedding and reception.

All of her roommates were sitting in the living room and making Traci go back and forth from her room as she tried on each outfit. So far, she'd had to go back there, put on a new dress, a pair of her new "dancing" pumps, and then walk out to the peanut gallery to hear everyone's opinions four times.

And boy did everyone have a lot of those!

"Ah, yes, I actually *have* heard of a lot of people going to a lot of trouble," Shannon said. "Don't you remember my wedding?"

"It didn't feel like it was this big."

"That's because it wasn't. Plus, my mother

did everything, and you just had to wear the bridesmaids' dress I assigned to you."

"I still think I could have made that dress work for this wedding." She certainly wanted to. It was a two-hundred-dollar dark-pink dress that was just sitting in the back of her closet. "Should I go try it on?"

"No," Jennifer, Shannon, and Kimber said in unison.

"But —"

"No offense, Shannon, but that dress says 'bridesmaid' all over it," Jennifer said.

"As in *all* over it," Kimber agreed. "You are not wearing it out on a date."

"Wow, guys," Shannon said, sounding hurt. "All of you told me you liked them."

"We did like them," Kimber said. "But I'm just saying that we liked being your bridesmaids more, so we would have said we liked anything you picked out."

"So, none of you want to wear your dresses again?"

"I do," said Traci.

Gwen, who was bottle-feeding Bridge on the couch, frowned at Traci. "No offense, Traci, but I don't think dark pink is your color. You're not really much of a pink kind of woman."

"I can't argue with that. Fine, I'll go change into one more dress. But it's the silvery blue one."

"That's my favorite," Kimber said. Standing up, she said, "Come here and I'll unzip you. You're in this one pretty good."

Traci stood while Kimber unzipped her. "I can't believe you do this all the time."

"Do what? Wear clothes?"

"Ha-ha. Kimber, you know what I'm talking about. This is so hard, putting on things and having a bunch of people analyze it."

"It's not like this, honey. It's ten times worse. First of all, I'm practically naked under the clothes, because no one wants any lines to show. Next, half the designers are always gonna say that the fit or the cut or the design or something is perfect and that *I'm* the problem."

"You could make a potato sack look good," Jennifer said.

"Thank you, but we know that's not true." She smiled. "It's fine, though. I mean, it's given me a good living." She shooed Traci out.

Back in the bedroom, Traci stepped out of that dress and finally put on the last one. It was a vintage-style gray-blue-satin strapless number that was fitted in the bodice and flared out to mid-calf. She felt exposed in it, but she couldn't help feeling pretty in the thing too.

After slipping on her shoes, she stepped in front of the mirror and gaped. It was extremely flattering. The cut made her athletic figure almost look delicate, and the color didn't clash with her fair skin and dark hair. It actually made both stand out.

This was the dress. Even if all the girls said it was all wrong, she knew she was going to wear it.

Having made up her mind, she walked out to model again. "I'm just telling you all right now that I like this one. I like it a lot." She stopped in front of them and did a little twirl. "I can even move in it, too. See?"

When she turned back around, she realized all of them were staring at her.

"Now what's wrong?" she asked.

Kimber spoke up first. "Not a darn thing. You are going to make Matt stop in his tracks."

"Really?"

Kimber smiled at her. "Really."

"She's right, Trace," Shannon said. "You look beautiful and you're even going to look beautiful waltzing in it."

"It's *way* better than your pink bridesmaid dress." Jennifer winked. "No offense, Shannon."

"You guys, stop," Shannon said.

Traci looked at Gwen. "Well? You might

372

as well chime in, doll. What do you think?"

"You don't look anything like Officer Lucky in that dress," she said.

Traci smiled at her softly. "I'll take that as the best compliment." Glancing at her watch, she said, "And, I'll be right back in sweats to take Bridge. You need to get ready for your tutor."

"Okay," Gwen said with a smile.

Twenty minutes later, Traci was dressed in comfortable sweats, Shannon had gone home, Jennifer was in her room and Gwen was in Traci's old room with her tutor.

Traci was sitting with Kimber in the living room. She had a cup of hot tea by her side, and little Bridge asleep in her arms.

So much had happened in the last two months, she still sometimes couldn't believe it. After she and Gwen had their talk, Traci had contacted Melanie and a judge she'd become on pretty good terms with. They were still in the middle of the process, but for now, Gwen was still technically Bridge's mom and Traci was being approved for foster parenting.

Everyone assured her it was all just a formality. Traci was an upstanding member of the community, had a big support system and a lot of people in her corner.

Gwen was also in complete support of giving up her formal rights, which was also helping to move the process along.

At first Traci was worried that she wouldn't do well as Bridge's new mommy, or that it might be awkward between her and Gwen, but the opposite was becoming true.

Gwen seemed so relieved to just be a teenager again. She was happy to have her side jobs with Jennifer and Shannon, but she was also happy to be enrolled on her online schooling too. She hadn't even balked when Traci suggested getting a tutor for her. If anything, Gwen seemed grateful to have someone looking out for her.

And as for Bridge? Well, he was simply wonderful. Traci had moved down to the room that Shannon and Dylan had used on the second floor. Bridge's cradle was down there with her, and she was spending lots of sleepless nights as a new mom.

When she was on a rare night shift, the other women and Gwen took a turn. And the other night, Matt came over to help out with nighttime feedings so she could get some sleep as well.

It wasn't perfect, but it felt pretty perfect for her.

Now, sitting with Kimber, Bridge in her

arms, Traci couldn't believe how far she'd come.

"You're happy, aren't you?" Kimber asked.

"I am. Happier than I'd ever thought I'd have a right to be."

Noticing something in her eyes, she said, "What about you? Are you happy?"

Kimber shrugged. "I don't know."

"How come?"

"I think I want to be done modeling. I think it's time."

Though Traci was secretly glad for Kimber, she was also surprised. Kimber made a really good living and was so in demand that she had to turn down jobs. She'd once told Traci that if she worked another two years, she'd be set for life. Or at least for a really long time.

"What are you going to do instead?"

"I don't know. Eat." She smiled. "Honestly, the dieting isn't the worst part. It's all of it. Traveling. Dealing with people I don't want to deal with. Feeling scared all the time that everything I've worked for is going to evaporate before I can do anything about it."

"I'm sorry. I guess I've been so focused on myself, I haven't asked you enough about your life. That wasn't fair."

Kimber blinked, then smiled as she

reached out to run a finger down Bridge's cheek. "Life isn't fair, Traci. We're living proof of that. But, every once in a while? Everything turns out just fine."

Feeling a lump in her throat as she took a moment to appreciate that she was sitting in a building owned by one sister, sipping tea with another sister, mentoring a girl who was so grateful for everything, and becoming the mother of a small miracle, Traci knew Kimber was absolutely right.

CHAPTER 46

"To be fond of dancing was a certain step towards falling in love."
— JANE AUSTIN

"I didn't expect you two to be the entertainment for the evening," Anthony said to Matt during the middle of the reception.

"We're hardly that," Matt replied. But damn if he and Traci weren't pretty close to resembling Fred Astaire and Ginger Rogers. Not only had they danced three waltzes together, they'd actually enjoyed dancing them.

His brother raised his eyebrows. "You're working on it."

"Are you ticked at me for doing what you asked me to do?"

"No. Hell no." He grinned. "I just didn't know you had it in you."

"I would agree with you there."

And that was pretty true for everything

that had happened over the last three months. He'd not only helped a girl, but had fallen in love with a cop, and there was a very good chance he was going to be a father to an adorable baby boy in the very near future.

"I just wanted to say I think it's great," Anthony said. "I know we've always been close, but I probably haven't told you enough that I'm proud of you."

"I haven't done that either. Marie's great, Anthony. I hope you two will have many happy years together."

"Tony, come on!" his bride said. "We have to go say hello to Mr. and Mrs. Arnold before they leave."

"I've gotta go," he said. "See you later."

"I'll see you after the honeymoon. Have fun."

Matt smiled at his brother's retreating form, glad they'd had a few minutes to talk. He was also glad that the reception was winding down and people were beginning to leave. He, for one, couldn't wait to be alone with his girlfriend.

"There you are!" Traci called as she walked toward him. "I've been looking for you everywhere."

"Sorry. I was spending a couple of minutes with Anthony." He scanned her face. "Is everything all right? Last time I checked, you were sitting with Vanny in the corner laughing."

"Oh, I'm fine. Vanny and I always have a lot to talk about."

He didn't need a sixth sense to know that he was probably their favorite topic. Pushing that aside, he reached for her hand. "So, are you ready to get out of here? We could go somewhere private."

But instead of nodding, she shook her head. "Matt Rossi, you're crazy if you think your mother is going to let you sneak out of here early. I came to find you because the band is about to play the Blue Danube Waltz."

"And?" It was kind of fun to play dumb.

"And, that's our song." She tugged on his hand and started pulling him through the French doors that led out to the balcony where they'd been standing.

For a second, he considered teasing her about their "song." After all, who else in their mid and late twenties would feel in tune with a waltz from the eighteen hundreds?

But, noticing how the grayish blue satin chiffon shimmered in the candlelight of the ballroom, he kept his mouth shut. The truth was that he loved waltzing with her, especially to this song that brought back so many memories.

They stepped onto the dance floor just as the ten-piece orchestra began the first lilting notes of violin.

Looking into her eyes, he said, "May I have this dance, Miss Lucky?"

Instead of teasing him, she lifted her right hand to his shoulder and slipped her left into his own. Just the way that they first attempted to dance but felt so clumsy. "Yes, Dr. Rossi. But this time I'll only dance with you on one condition."

"What's that?" He brushed his lips against her temple.

"This time, you take the lead."

He couldn't help it. As they waltzed with the rest of the couples, practically stepping and twirling as one, he raised up his head and laughed.

Leading Traci around the dance floor, knowing that in just a few hours he was going to get on one knee and propose marriage?

It was an incredible feeling.

Few things had ever felt so good.

The End

ACKNOWLEDGMENTS

As always, I'm so grateful for the number of people who have helped me organize a bunch of ideas and thoughts into a real story. I don't know what I'd do without so many helping hands!

First, as always, I owe a big thanks to my husband, Tom. We go on lots of long walks together, and at least half of them are spent plotting my books. He always helps me turn my convoluted plots into smooth-flowing story lines.

I am also indebted to several other people who helped so much with all the details in this novel. Once again, Officer Alex Napier's patient explanations helped with my "cop questions." Though I obviously took a few liberties, he was instrumental in helping me create a tough police officer with plenty of vulnerabilities. My new friend and neighbor, Tiffany, spent a whole afternoon talking to me about nursing duties in a hospital and navigating a young woman through a high-risk pregnancy. She gave me an even greater appreciation for everyone who works in the medical field.

Once again, Yvette, ballroom dancer extraordinaire, patiently guided me through several dances. She also answered lots and lots of questions about teaching folks ballroom dancing.

Thank you to Lynne who read this whole manuscript, even though she didn't have a lot of time and, as usual, provided lots of "fixes" so I could turn in a book I was proud of to my editor.

I am so grateful to the whole team at Blackstone Audio and Publishing for working so hard to make this book shine. Everyone goes above and beyond to make my books the best they can be. I'm especially grateful to my editor, Ember Hood, for both her insight and her cheers. She makes me excited to turn in a book!

Finally, this letter wouldn't be complete without thanking my Bridgeport Book Club readers and the many people who have embraced these books. I have always wanted to write novels about imperfect people who truly care about their families, friends, community, and faith. Thank you for accepting them into your lives. I'm so very grateful.

ABOUT THE AUTHOR

Shelley Shepard Gray is the *New York Times* and *USA Today* bestselling author of numerous romantic fiction series and mystery novels, including the Seasons of Sugarcreek series, the Sisters of the Heart series, the Families of Honor series, and others. She is a recipient of *RT Book Reviews* Reviewers' Choice Award.

The employees of Thorndike Press hope you have enjoyed this Large Print book. All our Thorndike, Wheeler, and Kennebec Large Print titles are designed for easy reading, and all our books are made to last. Other Thorndike Press Large Print books are available at your library, through selected bookstores, or directly from us.

For information about titles, please call:
  (800) 223-1244

or visit our website at:
  gale.com/thorndike

To share your comments, please write:
  Publisher
  Thorndike Press
  10 Water St., Suite 310
  Waterville, ME 04901